Anarchy

CURSE OF FATE
BOOK FIVE

SAMANTHA BARRETT

To my Dream Team,
Thank you to all my amazing dreamers. Your love
and support means everything to me.
Anarchy is for you.

Prologue

RAYA

"Lucian, we have to hurry, or we're gonna get caught!" Nerves wrack my body. Something doesn't feel right. This is too easy: a potion this strong should be guarded all hours of the day, not just sitting here in the open. Lucian turns to me, and I can see the strain on his face. He knows something isn't right, either, but we need this potion to help my mom.

"Ray, I don't think this is right." We're standing in the middle of an empty vault. I mean, this huge-ass room is empty except for a small round table with a glowing green potion bottle sitting on top of it. This place isn't even warded. We were able to portal straight in, and my hope began to dwindle.

Lucian's violet eyes soften, and he moves toward me and rests his hands on top of my shoulders. I stare up at my cousin. His full lips try to smile reassuringly, but he fails. He lifts one of his hands from my shoulder and runs it through his silver and black hair. He just cut it, and I must say it looks good—shaved on the sides and a bit longer on top. "I don't think this is going to work out, Ray."

My shoulders droop, and I drop my gaze to the floor. This was supposed to be it; if I don't get this fucking cure, I don't know what I am going to do. I know my cousin is loyal as fuck to my mom, and he wouldn't dare go behind her back if it wasn't in her best interest. I used to think their relationship was so odd but now...I'm just used to it, I guess. Lucian begins to click his fingers in front of my face.

"What?" I snap.

"You totally zoned out on me; I said we need to get out of here. Something is so off with this place, and if the witch or warlock who made the moonstones just left this sitting here, then I'm guessing that's because it's cursed—" A loud bang on the other side of the thick vault door has us scrambling apart.

"Open a portal now!" Lucian whisper-shouts at me, and I turn and quickly raise my hands.

"*Portaly openinga faylinga!*" Huh? What the hell is happening! I turn to Lucian and see that he is staring at me like I'm thick.

"I can't open a freaking portal, Luce." Lucian huffs and then tries to open a portal of his own...nothing.

"What the fuck, Ray? Whoever owns this vault let us in but won't let us out. I think this room is spelled!" Fuck, we don't have time to dwell; the vault door starts making a whirling sound and then the locks start to unclick. Lucian turns to me and cups my face between his hands. The look on his face has me standing up taller and gulping. "When the door opens, I'll fight them off while you run–"

"No, I won't leave you, Lucian!"

"Shut up, Ray, I'll be right behind you."

"What if you're not, Lucian?" His eyes soften, and he releases a long exhale.

"Ray, you are the princess and heir to the throne of Farrarie. You need to get out of here and stay safe." I start to shake my head.

"I won't go home without you!" A look of unease crosses Lucian's face, but he knows what I say is true.

"Go to Melakai Cane. He lives not far from here. Tell him who you are, but do not tell him why you are here. Lie to him, but be convincing about it, Ray. Kai is not someone you want to cross. Dad, Uncle Jax, and your father never hunted him down for a reason. His club is in Breckenridge. It's called Salut." I don't get a chance to answer or question my cousin. The vault door opens, and then all hell breaks loose..

CHAPTER 1

Malakai

I kept my word. I left my brothers behind after Dom and So-So tied the knot. I was beyond elated that So-So finally got her happily ever after; she bloody well deserved it. I still kept tabs on my brothers and the girls, but I can't go back. It's been twenty years since I have seen any of them.

I missed Jax and Aurora having their first baby, and I missed Ryan and Nico having theirs. Dom and Soph even welcomed twins into the world. I missed it all. But that is the way it had to be. After Mya's vision I couldn't chance it.

I have always been the quiet one in the group; I only speak when I need to or have something to say. I don't like mindless chit-chat. It annoys me.

I made a home for myself here in Colorado. I now own a few nightclubs throughout the States, and I'm doing well. I still keep up with my *king* duties, but I leave a lot of the day-to-day stuff to Eric, my second in charge. I don't want to go back to Wonder Lake, or to Farrarie those places hold too many dark memories for me.

It's been good being here on my own. I'm slowly starting to accept the fact that I am never going to be a fae again, and it is making my daily life easier. I even admit I am starting to like being a vampire. It has its perks.

"Boss, we got a problem." Cam's voice on the two-way radio pulls me from my thoughts. I pick up and answer him.

"What is it?"

"I think you need to come down for this one, boss."

Shit, this can't be good. "On my way." I push back from my desk and stand, buttoning my suit jacket as I stride out of my office and down the stairs that lead to the club below. As soon as the door opens at the bottom, the heavy bass of the music assaults my ears. The dance floor is a writhing mass of bodies but I pay them no mind and move toward the security room behind the bar. I feel like Moses—everyone moves out of my way. They may be human, but even they can sense they are in the presence of a predator. I push the door open and move down the dimly lit hallway and enter through the door at the end without knocking.

My eyes land on Cam and David, my two heads of security. I move toward them and then notice someone in the back, sitting on a single metal chair, is the most beautiful woman I have ever seen in my life. She has long brown hair that is loose, the ends resting on the tops of her thighs. Full set of lips that look like they have been stung by a bee, and her eyes are so piercing green they look like they're glowing. She has the cutest button nose with a stud in the left side of it, high cheekbones, and a body that you would die to have wrapped around you. She's wearing a plain black crop top that is stretched tight across her ample chest, dark wash denim jeans that look like a second skin, and her outfit is completed with a pair of black Chuck Taylors.

"You gonna keep checking me out or are you gonna let me go?" Her voice is like a song, and I find myself wanting to get closer to her and scent her. I manage to stop myself at the last second and turn to face my guys.

"What did she do?"

"She's underage, sir, and when we asked for I.D., she put up a fight and broke Damien's nose." I spin back to face the girl and narrow my eyes at her when I see her trying to conceal her smile.

"He shouldn't have grabbed me. Then I wouldn't have head-butted him," the girl snaps. "Can I go now? I need to find somebody." For some unknown reason, anger flares inside me at the possibility that she is meeting another man here.

"Who are you looking for?" I growl.

"Geez, calm down, Godzilla, I'm looking for a guy named Kai." Huh? She is looking for me?

"Why are you looking for Kai?" I ask, and her eyes harden and her face scrunches up. She looks so fucking adorable when she scrunches her nose like that. She drops her gaze from mine, and what she has to say next surprises the fuck out of me.

"Because, my mom and dad are pissed as fuck at me. Mom said I need to find him and he would be able to teach me some manners or some shit." I reel back, slightly shocked. Who in their right fucking mind would send this beautiful creature to a monster like me?

"Who are your parents?" I ask, and she lifts her gaze and locks her eyes onto mine.

"Ryan and Nico Stone, king and queen of Farrarie." I stumble back, shocked. Of course the only woman to stir any feelings inside me since my dreams with Ryan is her own fucking daughter! God, no, I can't do this; she can't stay here with me.

"No, get up now! We're taking you back." She doesn't move an inch, just looks at me like I'm stupid.

"Not gonna happen, Zilla. My mom closed the portals.

Judging by the look on your face, I'm guessing you're Kai, anyway you're stuck with me for a month. My dad will come for me when the month is up."

"Your father would never trust me with his daughter!" She stands and moves toward me, not stopping until my chest is against her. She runs her hands up the lapels of my suit jacket and then yanks so I'm now looking down at her.

"He doesn't know I'm here with you, only Mom does. I was pissed about her sending me here, but now that I've met you and seen what you look like? Not even gonna lie, you're fucking hot, and I think I can find ways for us to pass the time together, if you get what I mean."

Jesus Christ help me, this woman is going to fucking ruin me, and her father will no doubt kill me seven times over when he finds out where she is. I need to figure out a way to get her home and away from me—fast. She is stirring feelings inside me I haven't felt in decades, and I have only just met her. If she doesn't go home soon, I fear I will rob her of her innocence and keep her.

Malakai

Sorrow and grief is so deeply ingrained in my bones that I have forgotten what happiness feels like. I don't remember the last time I have actually smiled or laughed. Well, that is until two weeks ago, when a hurricane of a woman came barreling into my life and left me no choice but to come out of my dark shell. I have lived in the shadows for most of my life. I hate being front and center. But whenever Raya Stone looks at me, I feel like a spotlight is on me. I tried to send her home, back to her parents, but when we got to one of the portals, it was locked. She just laughed and gave me an I told ya so look. I had been keeping my distance from her. She was like a vortex that kept sucking me in every time I was near her.

I set her up in one of the apartments I owned in downtown Colorado and gave her a job at my club. She is only nineteen, so technically she shouldn't even be inside my establishment, but something tells me that if I denied her, she would find a way inside anyway. So far she hasn't caused too much trouble, and I learned pretty quickly she can hold her own. A patron got handsy with her on her second night working here, and before I could get to her, she had him on his ass. Raya is fearless...and reckless. I have no idea what trouble she has gotten herself into or why in the fucking world would her parents send her to me, since I haven't seen them in twenty years.

"Boss, we got a problem downstairs." Groaning, I pick up the radio off my desk and answer Cam.

"What has she done now?" For the past two weeks every time Cam or David has called me about trouble in the club, Raya always manages to be a part of it.

"Uh...it's not her per se. Some guy is here and demanding that he speak to you about her."

"Cam, start making sense now, or I'm gonna lose my fucking cool." I hear him take a deep breath before he speaks again.

"This guy claims to know you and know Raya. He said he needs to talk to you now."

"Coming." I push back from my desk and check the video monitors before leaving my office, just to make sure Raya is okay. I see her behind bar one, wearing another tight pair of jeans, the club shirt with the logo on it, and her long hair tied up in a ponytail. Just the sight of her has me feeling things I shouldn't be feeling.

After making my way downstairs and through the club, I head toward the front but turn left before the entrance and exit out the side door. Standing out in the alley are Cam and David. I see a man standing behind them with his back to us, and I cock a brow at David in question. He looks to Cam before turning back to me and shrugging his shoulders. Something is going on here, and I don't fucking like it one bit!

"You have five seconds to get to the point," I growl out at the stranger, and he spins around and looks me dead in the eyes. I suck in a sharp breath at the person standing in front of me.

"Uncle Kai, we need your help. Raya is in danger." The air deflates out of my body at Lucian's words. The kid hasn't aged a day since I last saw him. Well, he has filled out more, that's for sure, and he's cut his hair, but his eyes are still the same, violet with a silver ring around the pupil. The little pup looks good. I must say I am glad to see him, even if he does come bearing bad news.

"You know him, boss?" I don't take my eyes off Lucian as I nod. Cam and David don't know much about my life, and I like it that way. They work for me, I pay them, and that's as far as our relationship goes. I don't need friends.

"Why is she in trouble, Lucian?" Lucian's shoulders droop, and I take a good long look at him and notice how tired he appears. What the fuck is going on and why is he here and not Ryan or Nico? She is their daughter, after all.

"Maybe we could go inside and talk? It's a long story, Uncle Kai." Lucian moves toward me.

"Why did they send her to me?" Lucian stops and looks me in the eyes, remorse present in his gaze.

"They didn't. I was the one who sent her here to you." I reel back in shock. Raya told me Ryan sent her here.

"Why?"

"Because Raya and I got into some trouble, and I need to make sure she is safe."

I'm starting to get annoyed now with all these half-truths. "Get to the point, Lucian," I snap.

"It's a really long story, and I'm not the one who should tell you—"

"Tell him, Lucian." I spin around to see Raya standing in

the doorway. I narrow my eyes at her. She has an uncanny ability to turn up at the right places at the right times.

"Hello to you, cousin." Raya doesn't lift her gaze from mine or even acknowledge that her cousin just spoke.

"I fucked up, and I need your help."

CHAPTER 3
Raya

Kai led us upstairs to his office. Luce and I are currently sitting in front of his desk in the single seats while he sits behind his huge desk, with his fingers steepled together. I know my head should be focused on the situation, but all I can think about is Kai fucking me on this desk and making me come so hard I see stars and scream his—

"Ray!" I shake my head and turn to face my cousin and smile sheepishly. Lucian sighs and narrows his eyes to slits. "This is serious, Ray, you need to focus!" I turn to glare back at my asshole of a cousin.

"Really? So where the fuck have you been for two weeks, huh?" Lucian slumps slightly and darts his gaze to Kai before focusing back on me. I get it; he doesn't want to say too much in front of Kai.

"You either talk some truth—both of you—or I pull it out of you." I look to Kai and find he is serious. I turn back to Luce.

"He can't really do that, can he?" Luce flinches and then nods his head.

"He wasn't the head of Randall's enforcers for nothing, cousin. I told you not to piss him off."

"I am done with you babbling, start talking!" Melakai roars. I don't take well to being bossed around, so I do what I do best and annoy the shit out of people by pushing their buttons. I stand and move around the desk, gripping the handles on either side of Kai's chair and push until there is enough room for me to slip in front of him and plant my ass on the desk. Then I lean forward and grip the handles again so I can pull him forward so he is now sitting between my legs. I ignore my cousin's odd noise of laughter combined with alarm.

Kai sits there still as stone, no emotion displayed across his handsome face. His eyes give nothing away as he sits there and stares at me like I'm some kind of side show act.

"Is there something you want to tell me, cuz?" Lucian asks. Me being me, I don't filter my response, and if I'm honest, I only answer Lucian because I'm trying to get a reaction out of Kai.

"Just trying to fuck my boss, but he doesn't seem keen." Lucian chokes on his own spit and then begins to cough up a lung while I sit here with my gaze still locked on Kai. I have pretty much thrown myself at this guy, and not once has he shown any interest in me. It's driving me fucking mad. To be honest, I am kind of used to getting what I want. What can I say? I'm a daddy's girl.

"You do know who he is, right?" I search Kai's gaze, hoping to find the answer to Lucian's question in his eyes, but yet again I come up blank. I honestly don't give a fuck who Lucian thinks Kai is; his opinion is irrelevant to me. I don't judge people on what others say. I form my own opinion. From what I have learned about Kai in the past two weeks is that the guy has no idea how to have fun or even let loose. Sitting here between my legs, he still shows no emotion. I'm not vain or anything, but I know I'm not ugly, and this guy is acting like I'm not even here.

"Enough. You're here, Raya, because you're in deep shit."

"You have no idea what I'm into, Kai." I see a flicker of emotion cross his eyes before he quickly masks it.

"You being here with your mother's sidekick gives me enough of an idea."

"What is it you think you know?" Kai narrows his eyes at me, and for the first time tonight I get a read on his emotions— anger.

"That you are reckless, and the two of you have landed in deep shit because you are both stupid. Ever since you showed up on my doorstep—" I shove Kai back with a foot and as he rolls backward, I jump to my feet. He springs out of the chair, seething. We both stand there glaring at each other.

"You do not get to tell me what the fuck I can and can't do! You are not my father!" I shout.

"Well thank fuck for that! If you were mine, I would have locked your ass up long ago and thrown away the goddamn key!" My hand itches to slap him. Kai must sense it, as he flicks his gaze to my hand and then back to my face.

"Go on, do it. Make it good, though, *mon espoir*, because unlike your father, I will punish you!" I have no idea what the hell *mon espoir* means, but it sounds hot coming from Kai's mouth. I also know I should be scared or even intimidated by him and how close he is to me, but I'm not. I can't explain it, but I just know deep down inside of me that Kai would no sooner hurt me than he would hurt himself.

"Ewww!" I jerk slightly at the gagging sound; I forgot Lucian was in the room for a second there. Kai lifts his gaze from mine to look at my cousin.

"What?" Kai growls out.

"Dude, I'm a wolf, and I can scent her fucking arousal from here! Not fucking cool, Ray. I could have gone my whole life without scenting that, fuck you very much." Kai darts his gaze back to mine, and for a split-second his mask falters and I see lust in his eyes before he quickly shields himself from me again. I'm not embarrassed in the slightest. I have nothing to be ashamed about. I told Kai from the first time I met him in the basement that I thought he was hot.

"You and I will never happen. I will help you with whatever problem you face, and then you will return to your parents." Hurt, anger, and annoyance war inside me. How can he be so callous and so cruel? "Don't look at me like that. There is a reason why I choose to live alone and have isolated myself for so many years."

Not wanting his fucking pity, I school my features and square my shoulders as I answer him. "Good riddance. I can't fucking wait to get back home and see Wyatt, anyway." As I turn to storm out of the office, I see anger flash across his face at the mention of Wyatt before he quickly masks his emotions once again. I don't look at my cousin as I make my way to the door, but just as I pass the threshold, Kai's words have me stumbling to a stop.

"Pack your shit after your shift. Cam will be there to pick you up." I turn slowly and make sure I have the filthiest look on my face as I stare at the giant vamp.

"Why?" I grind out through clenched teeth.

"Because you are staying with me until we figure some shit out."

Raya doesn't answer me; instead, she stomps down the stairs like the spoiled brat she is. That woman stirs the beast inside of me, and twice tonight I nearly let him out to play with her. She is going to push every one of my fucking buttons, and I'm not sure whether I am thrilled or pissed about it. It's so strange to feel something other than self-loathing and sorrow. Raya makes me feel...alive.

"Sooooooo, you and my cousin huh?" I turn to Lucian and pin him with a "don't fuck with me" look. But because he is the spawn of Dominic Silver, he has no idea when to take a fucking clue and shut his mouth. "Dude, do I need to spell it out for you?"

"Go home, Lucian," is my only reply before I make my way out of my office and down the corridor to the door at the end. I enter and head straight toward the fridge, searching through the shelves until I find a bag of O negative. I haven't drunk from a vein in years. Drinking from a blood bag helps me hate myself, and what I am, less. I opened these clubs across the States so I could build up a resistance to the temptation that humans bring, with their sweet scent.

I have never wanted to drain a supe before. Well, until two weeks ago, when I met Raya. I want nothing more than to sink my fangs into her neck and guzzle her blood. I rip the tip off the bag and drink. The blood coats my tongue and then slides down my throat, and I close my eyes and relish the taste. I know as soon as this bag is empty, I will go back to hating myself and what I am.

"You know, she won't give up; she is as stubborn as her father." Fucking hell, I thought Lucian had left, but I guess not. Finishing off the bag of blood, I lift the lid to the bin and chuck the pouch in. I turn to Lucian and scowl at the little shit.

"Don't look at me like that. I'm your only friend; everyone else is pissed at you." Pain hits me in the chest, but I make sure to keep my face blank. I won't let him know how much his words affect me.

"I don't need any allies; I work better on my own." I move to brush past him, but his words stop me.

"They all miss you; they searched for you, for years. Dad found you and tried so many times to approach you and mend the bridges he burned, but he was scared that you would push him away. Nico even tried, but Smurf stopped him. She said you were finally free of them and coming to you would just suck you back into the life you wanted so badly to escape." I meet Lucian's gaze and make sure that he can see the seriousness in my eyes.

"Go home, Lucian. I won't tell you again. I will deal with this situation and then you can come back and take Raya. I don't want to know why her parents haven't come for her. The less I know, the better."

Shock crosses Lucian's face. "H-how did you know I was lying?"

"Because I know Nico, and I know he would have had some way to track his daughter. There is no way the king of the fae would let his daughter—his world—come to me. So, whatever you and Raya have gotten yourselves into, I suggest you hurry up and fix it before Ryan and Nico come after you as well." Lucian starts to rub the back of his neck and avoids looking me in the eye.

"So, here's the thing. I can't actually go home."

"Why?" Lucian finally meets my gaze, and I see fear and uncertainty in his gaze. What the hell have these two gotten themselves into?

"I don't have access to my fae or witch side, and I believe Raya can't access her magic either." Fuck, this is more complicated than I thought. I brush past Lucian, and as I'm about to descend the stairs, I call back over my shoulder.

"Get a ride to my place with Raya. You will stay with me too, until we sort this shit."

I turn the faucets off and step out of the shower. I rub the towel roughly over my head before wrapping it around my waist and heading out of the bathroom to my walk-in closet. As I round the corner and enter my closet, sitting there on the ottoman is none other than Raya Stone. She is leaning back on her elbows with a shit-eating grin on her face, her eyes traveling up and down my body shamelessly. She darts her tongue out and moistens her lips. Fuck, this girl is like an addict's worst nightmare. She is stirring things inside of me that I haven't felt in over twenty years.

I can't let her inside my head; she's already playing my body like a piper. I am constantly rocking a hard on whenever she is around. She and I can never be, I would bring her nothing but pain and sorrow. I'm the guy you confide in and who will protect you, but I'm not the guy you spend the rest of your life with.

"Penny for your thoughts, Zilla?" I huff at her stupid nickname for me and march past her to pull a pair of sweats from my drawers and a black shirt from its hanger.

"No boxers?"

"Don't like the restriction and easier when you need to fuck in a hurry." I don't know why I even entertain her or answer, but I seem to lose all control over my mouth when she is around.

Her gasp follows me to the bathroom. As soon as I shut the door behind me, guilt and shame starts to war inside me. Why the fuck did I just say that? Get your head out of your ass, Melakai! She is your best friend's daughter, and she also happens to be the daughter of the woman whose dreams you invaded and fucked!

After changing and berating myself some more, I finally emerge from my room and follow the sound of voices to the kitchen. As I round the corner, I see Raya bent over, her ass in the air and her head in my stainless fridge. I never use the kitchen; I have no need to. All the appliances are brand new, shit–I don't even know how to work any of them.

"There is no freaking food in here! How does he get a body like that if he doesn't eat?" I fight the grin that wants to spread across my face at her words. Lucian is sitting on a stool at the island. I decide to let them carry on and perch up against the wall.

"Dude, he's a vampire. He doesn't need food, duh." Raya

stands up and slams the fridge door. She spins around then pins Lucian with a death glare.

"I know that dippy, but he demanded that we stay with him and didn't think to, like, you know...have some real food here for us?" Her comment both pisses me off and fills me with shame. I've worked hard on not letting others' opinions bother me, but hearing Raya complain about my thoughtlessness pisses me off. I enter the kitchen and both of their gazes snap to me. I scowl down at the beautiful brunette, but she doesn't cower or shy away. She loves to push me and challenge me at every turn.

"It wasn't exactly my plan to have guests, but your circumstances and lack of honesty gave me no choice." Remorse shines in her eyes at my words. She reaches and clasps my hand in hers.

"Kai, that isn't what I meant. I'm sorry if I offended you; I know you don't eat food like us. I'm a bitch when I'm hungry; I guess I get that from my mom's side." Lucian chuckles and so do I, remembering Ryan's hangry fits all too well.

My laughter cuts off the moment I realize I'm doing it. Feeling slightly awkward and out of place, I snatch my hand back and pull a stack of takeaway menus out of a nearby drawer. I toss them on the island, along with my black card, and tell them to order whatever they want.

Lucian sucks in a breath. "Dude! Seriously? You're gonna let us go crazy on your credit card?" I pin Lucian with a don't-even-fucking-think-about-it look. But before I can answer, Raya speaks.

"Thanks, Kai, I swear we will only order food. I mean, it is the least you can do, since my tight-ass boss doesn't actually pay me!" I turn and head back toward my room with a smile on my face. I will make sure that Raya has a bank account opened in the morning with a hefty deposit.

CHAPTER 5
Raya

Lucian and I order our body weight in Chinese food and absolutely pig out. I love chicken fried rice and chicken chow mein. Mom loves it too, when her and dad visit Uncle Jax she gets her fill of human food. In my realm, we don't have these kinds of pleasures. We have food, obviously, but it tastes bland compared to what humans eat, and we sure as shit don't have fast food places.

I pack away our leftovers and put them in the empty fridge. The only other items in there are Kai's blood bags. I have noticed since arriving here that Kai is very private and doesn't let his emotions show, I have never seen him drink blood and I don't think it's because he isn't hungry, I think it's because he is embarrassed about it.

My mom and dad never really told me a whole lot about him. They just said he used to be a fae and that he and dad grew up together. I guess having the hots for one of your father's best friends, or ex best friend, isn't exactly ideal, but look at the world we live in now. Nothing is ethical, and the lines between right and wrong are always blurred. I feel a connection to Kai. I don't know what it is, but I'm so drawn to him.

I have never chased a guy before, not even Wyatt. Don't get me wrong—Wyatt is an amazing guy, and he is so kind and generous, but he is also so...vanilla. I want a man that will challenge me, who will put me in my place and take charge. Wyatt always asks me what I want to do, where I'd like to go. I want someone like Kai, who tells me to get my ass to work, pack my shit and move in with him. With Kai there is no doubt in my mind that he is an alpha male and craves control.

"Ray, I think we need to tell him." Lucian's ominous voice pulls me from my thoughts. I close the fridge door and turn to face him, noticing he has cleared our plates, washed them, and even wiped the island clean. I know Luce is right, but I also need to have a chat with my cousin. I signal for him to follow me and lead him toward the sunken living room. Crisp white leather sofas form a U shape around the fireplace, and hanging above that is a large, flat-screen TV. I never pictured Kai's house to be so...clean, almost sterile looking. There are no personal touches, no photos on the walls, no plants or ornaments. It's just the essentials, and that's it. I take a seat on one of the sofas and Lucian sits at the other end facing me. I tuck my legs under me and pin him with a spit-it-out look, but he doesn't get the hint!

"Why do I have no access to my magic, Luce? And why did it take you two weeks to come for me?" Lucian's face takes on a serious look, his shoulders tense and hands clenched into fists.

"Ever since we entered that vault, I can't access my magic either. I only have access to my wolf, so whoever owned that vault must have had it warded or spelled."

"If it was warded, how the hell did we get in?" Luce lets out a long sigh and drops his gaze to his lap.

"I think it was a one-way trap, it was spelled to let us in but not let us leave." The penny finally drops for me.

"So this whole time we thought that potion was fake and to easy—"

Lucian cuts me off.

"I think that potion was the real deal, cousin, and we just blew our only chance."

Fuck! This can't be happening. I know my parents will be worried and searching for me, but without my magic or Lucian's, they won't be able to track me down. Which in hindsight is probably a good thing, since I am kind of living with my dad's best friend, who he hasn't spoken to in years.

"I am so sorry, Ray. I promise we will find another way." I jump to my feet and begin to pace. So many thoughts are running through my head. Did I just fuck up the only chance I had of saving my mom? I should have listened to my dad and waited for them to form a plan, but I got sick of them waiting around and doing nothing! When dad finds out what I have done, and that Lucian and I have lost our magic somehow, he is going to lose his shit!

"We need to figure something out, Luce; dad is going to fucking kill me!" Lucian looks at me and narrows his gaze.

"Bullshit. You're his daughter, he'll give you a slap on the wrist, Me, on the other hand, he is going to fucking kill for going along and supporting your stupid as fuck plan!" I wheel around and pin my oldest cousin with a look that should set his ass on fire.

"You little shit! It was your fucking plan! I said we should wait for Avery and Kailyn to come with us, but no. You couldn't fucking wait, and now we're here with no fucking magic and no goddam cure!" I am vibrating with fucking rage, how dare he!

"I wasn't going to involve my brother and sister in this! My dad is a fucking psycho and would skin me alive! I'm sorry, Ray. I honestly thought we could pull this off. I swear I researched everything to do with that vault. Once I escaped the vault, I had to shift and run for fucking miles! I have never scented so much dark magic in my life, Ray—those three guys that were chasing me are powerful." I can hear the undertone of fear in Lucian's voice, and I have never heard him speak like this before. Lucian and my mom are two of the most powerful supernaturals in the world, so for him to be worried about three guys is not something to take lightly.

"You must be referring to the master's brothers." Lucian and I both turn toward the hallway and see Kai leaning against the wall with his huge arms crossed over his chest. His black shirt is pulled tight across his chest and straining against his biceps. His blond hair is slicked back, and his gray-blue eyes are drilling holes into me. I let my gaze run down his body. I have only ever seen Kai in a suit, so to see him dressed so casually makes him seem more...obtainable. Don't get it twisted Kai is a fucking snack in a suit, but in sweats and a tee he looks so boy next door. This guy has no idea how fucking beautiful he truly is. He's well over six foot and built like a linebacker. His eyes are so captivating and draw you in, his hair is the perfect length to run your fingers through, and those lips... They're so juicy and full you just want to suck on them. Kai is like the bad boy version of Chris Hemsworth.

"The who brothers?" Lucian's question pulls me from my eye-fucking. Kai tears his gaze from me and focuses on my cousin.

"Before we get into this, I'd like to know how you both managed to get near them." Lucian and I look at each other. I can tell from the look in Lucian's eyes that he wants to tell Kai the truth, but I'm not sure we can fully trust him, so instead I ask.

"How do we know you're not working with them, and how do we know we can trust you?" Kai's expression morphs into anger, and this is the first time I have seen his emotions so unguarded. Kai storms toward me but Lucian steps in front of him to block his path.

Kai doesn't miss a beat. He looks at Lucian and says, "You really need to sleep for a minute, don't you?" As if he was a puppet, Lucian nods his head, moves toward the couch, and drops down, and falls asleep. I snap my gaze back to Kai and look up at him, mouth hanging open.

"What the fuck did you just do to my cousin?" Kai is like a blur; one minute there is five feet between us, then in the next second I feel a hand around my throat and we're across the room with my back against the wall. He's plastered to my front like a second skin. He moves back an inch, and there's only enough space for me to crane my head back to look up at him. The grip he has on my throat doesn't restrict my airway, but its firm enough to let me know he could snap my fucking neck if he wanted.

As soon as I lock my gaze onto his, I try to turn my head, but he tightens his hold on my throat, so I have no choice but to look him in the eye. He is angry, and I think I have pushed Godzilla too far this time.

"You know nothing, little girl!" So much anger and venom coat his tone, and in this moment, Kai is every bit the predator and he has the means to hurt me. "I did everything that has ever been asked of me, at the cost of my own life and my own culture! I have never been unfaithful to your father. I always did what needed to be done and in exchange for my loyalty, your father and Uncle Dom fucked me over."

I'm stunned. So, Kai left because of my dad and Uncle Dom? What the hell did those two do?

"Zilla, I'm gonna need you to loosen that grip you got on me." Kai doesn't answer or remove his hand, he just stands there glaring down at me. I try to reason with him.

"I'm sorry, I shouldn't have said that, but the secret Luce and I hold is one that we can't share. I need to know I can trust you, Kai." The anger in his eyes starts to dwindle, and the grip on my throat loosens a tiny bit, but it's enough for me to relax slightly and know he isn't going to kill me.

"I brought you into my home, I let you work at my club. I never asked you any questions as to why the hell you are here, even though I knew you were lying to me from the start." Shock ripples throughout my body.

"H-how did you know?" A small devious smirk graces his beautiful, luscious lips. This isn't the time to be wondering what those lips would feel like against my own but fuck it. Whenever Kai is near, I lose all train of thought, nothing exists in that moment except him.

"Because there is no way in fucking hell that Nicholas Stone would ever let his baby girl near me. Also, no matter how much of a little shit you were, I know your mother. She would never lock the portals on her daughter. I think it's time you start telling me the whole truth. They may not be able to track your magic, but Dom sure as fuck can track Lucian's wolf, so it's only a matter of time before they get here."

CHAPTER 6

Malakai

I see the moment my words register—her eyes double in size. She starts to nibble on her bottom lip, and my eyes zero in on the movement. She looks so torn between trusting me and defying me. I need her to trust me. The Masters brothers are not to be trifled with. I have known about them for a decade now but have never had a run-in with them. I keep to my side of the tracks and they to theirs, so to speak. We have never needed to cross paths. They are rogue fae. I have no idea how they have flown under Nico's radar for so long, but I won't be the one to snitch them out.

"I need you to help me get the potion that is locked in their vault." I furrow my brows. What the hell is so special about this bloody potion they keep going on about?

"What's the potion for?" She sighs and darts her gaze around the room. I tighten my hold on her neck slightly in warning. "You know I can pull the truth from you, right?" She snaps her piercing green eyes back to mine, and I see so much defiance in her eyes. I love that she doesn't fear me and won't cower.

"Oh, Zilla, I dare you to try, tough guy. I may have lost my magic for the time being, but trust me, I will still fight you every step of the way." I lean down toward her and whisper in her ear. My lips brush her lobe, and I feel her shiver.

"What makes you think I won't love the challenge?" I pull back so we're now eye to eye. Her gaze searches my face. She catches me completely by surprise when she snakes out her arms, wraps them around my neck, and pulls me to her. Her lips touch mine, and sparks fly. I stand there, stunned, and she takes full advantage of my lapse of reason and begins to move her lips against mine.

Her tongue begins to prod my mouth, and I give in to temptation. I open my mouth and grant her entry, but a moment later I seize control. I pull her arms away from around my neck and pin each of them above her head as I explore her delectable mouth with my tongue. She tastes like peaches, sweet and heady. She lets out a small moan, and that's all it takes for the moment to shatter. I pull away from her and blur to the other side of the room, panting. She stands in the same spot, staring at me like she has no idea what just happened.

"What the fuck—why did you stop?" I can hear the hurt lacing her tone.

"Because you and I can never be, Raya. You are the heir to a world that no longer exists for me, and I'm not a good guy. I don't do champagne and roses. I live on my own for a reason. I will help you with the brothers, but after that you need to leave and never come back."

After leaving Raya in the living room with a sleeping Lucian last night, I went to bed. Waking up this morning, I feel sluggish and lazy. I slept like shit, and it was all thanks to that stupid kiss!

It played on my mind all night like a movie. I could feel her lips against mine, and I could taste her on my tongue. Arrrgggghhhh! I need to get my head out of the clouds and go for a run.

I change quickly and grab a bag of blood and drain it before I leave my house. Lucian is still asleep on the couch, a blanket covering him. I didn't hear any other sounds, and at this hour of the morning, I expect Raya to still be sleeping. Well, luck isn't on my side. No sooner do I open the front door and step out , I spot Raya stretching by the willow tree in the front yard. I groan and pull the door closed behind me.

She snaps her gaze over to me, and I'm surprised at the look of shock on her face. "What are you doing up this early?"

I make my way over to her before I answer. She's wearing yoga pants and a thin white shirt that lets me see through to the pink sports bra she has on. She has her long brown hair tied up in a messy bun, and her face is clear of any makeup. A random question flies out of my mouth.

"How do you have makeup and changes of clothes?" If I shocked her with my question, she doesn't show it. She continues stretching her legs out as she answers me.

"I may have never lived in this world, but that doesn't mean my mom didn't prepare me for it. She has accounts here, and I withdrew some money to buy what I needed until I can get home." That was...smart. "Now are you gonna answer my question?"

"I'm up at five every morning. I like to run." She looks up at me like I'm some strange alien, that look has me shuffling from foot to foot. "What?" I snap.

"I've just never met anyone who loves to run like I do. Everyone thinks I'm crazy as shit." A chuckle rips out of me before I can stop, and her eyes widen to the size of plates. I don't stop, though. It feels good to laugh. Her next question has my laughter dying in my throat. "Wanna run with me?" And like the idiot I am, I nod my head and take her to my favorite trail.

An hour and a half later, we stumble up the front porch steps. I will admit I am in good shape, but fucking hell, Raya can sure as shit keep up. I didn't expect her to actually be able to keep pace with me. I don't run at vamp speed on my morning runs, but still. We're both panting and sweating, and she reaches down and grabs the bottom of her shirt and proceeds to peel it off her body! I'm standing right here–right here—and she thinks it's okay to do that? She wraps the shirt around her neck and just stands there in yoga pants and a sports bra, her ample chest trying to burst from the fucking bra. I try to avoid looking at them, but then I notice that she has a tattoo on her ribs. This girl is a fucking rebel!

"Like what you see, Godzilla?" Her question has my gaze snapping back to her eyes, and I try to play it off.

"What does the tattoo say?" She cocks her head to the side, confused, and I point to the tat and then it finally registers what I'm saying. She lifts her hand and starts to trace the writing under her breast.

"It says, *It is better to have loved and lost than to have never loved at all.*" The fuck is that supposed to mean? "I have more, if you want to see?"

"How many bloody tattoos do you have?" She narrows her eyes at me.

"Oh please, don't stand there and lecture me. I know you have ink of your own."

"How do you know that?" She prowls toward me like a

lioness and then when she is touching distance, she lifts her pointer finger and begins to trail it down my torso.

"When you came out of the shower in your towel, I saw them. Plus, when I planted my ass on your desk the other night, I saw your planner and saw you had an appointment booked in for a tat next week." The sneaky little brat snooped at my schedule!

"Butting your nose in where it doesn't belong will get you in shit." My words don't deter her in the slightest. She continues to trail her finger down my abs, and then when she reaches the waistband of my basketball shorts, I suck in a sharp breath of air. She pulls the elastic back then leans her head forward slightly and peeks inside my pants.

I refuse to give her the satisfaction of pulling away, but she gasps and quickly lets the elastic go. It slaps against me and has me glaring down at her. A blush begins to coat her cheeks, and I can't pass the opportunity up.

"Like what you see?" She groans and then proceeds to stomp her way into the house. I'll admit I watched her ass sway side to side the whole way to the door. Just before she enters the house she turns back and pops her hip out.

"Like what you see, Zilla?"

Little shit, she got me there.

 Raya

I've been staying at Kai's for two days now. We haven't really spoken to each other since our run. Lucian is staying in one of the other guest rooms, and he and Kai have been working on a way to contact the brothers. These guys are harder to find than Luce and I originally thought; it's like they're ghosts. Tonight's my night off work, but Kai and Luce don't want me staying home alone while they work at the club, so I had no choice but to go with them. I decided to be a pest and visited one of the local boutiques and bought the most scandalous dress I could find. I'll admit I only did this to piss Kai off; I want to get a rise out of him or some form of reaction. He has been giving me the fucking cold shoulder ever since our kiss—he won't even make eye contact. He hired a chef for Lucian and me and even got someone to get groceries for us.

"Girl, it's your night off, why are you sitting here at the bar with us instead of out there dancing the night away?" I shake myself from my thoughts and look to Candy. I can't tell her the truth, that no one has caught my eye since I arrived here and met the infamous Melakai Cane. The guy is as cold as an iceberg and yet I can't get him out of my head. It's becoming my life goal to draw any form of emotion from the man. Out of nowhere, a thought hits me.

"You know what, Candy, I think you're right. Give me two shots of tequila." The bonus about working at Salut is that staff don't have to pay for their drinks. Candy pours me two shots and then hands me the limes and salt. No one knows how old I actually am except for the boss, Cam, David, and Lucian, so Candy doesn't bat an eye as I down the shots. I thank her as I jump off my stool and make my way toward the dance floor. Jennifer, one of the other bartenders, waves at me, and I make my way over to her and she hugs me hello. I can barely hear over the song playing. I have to admit, this artist Jamaica Moana's songs are quickly becoming my favorites. The song playing now has me wanting to sway my hips. He raps about stealing a fur coat, and the double meaning is everything in this song. Jen and I begin to sway our hips and shout the lyrics out. The dance floor is packed. The club is closed on Monday and Tuesday, but every other day it is always filled to the brim. My favorite bit is coming up, so I wink at Jen and shout it out.

"I mean that's cool, boo, I like dick too!" Jen and I burst out laughing, but the laughter dies in my throat when I feel two arms wrap around my waist. I look at Jen and see her grinning from ear to ear. I swing my head to the side to peer over my shoulder and see an average-looking guy with an athletic build. He smiles a cocky smile. He has muddy brown eyes and military-styled brown hair. I know I sound shallow as fuck, judging him by his looks, but come on, entitled much? Just because he sees two women dancing together and looking fine as fuck, he thinks he has the right to come over here and wrap his arms around me.

I'm about to push him away when out of the corner of my eye I see a streak of silver and just know it's Lucian. I have a feeling that he has emerged from Kai's office because they have seen me and Handsy here together. Maybe I'll just let this play out and see if I can get Godzilla to show me his cards. The song changes to "Jerry Springer" by Troy Lanez and T-Pain. I fucking love this song!

I grip the guy's hands and pull him closer so I can feel him plastered on my back. He starts to gyrate his hips, and I can feel his semi through his jeans. It takes everything inside me not to gag and push him away, but I need to see this through. I begin to sway my hips and rub against him. He grabs my waist and pulls me even closer before he begins to run his hands up my sides. He's moving slowly, giving me every opportunity to slap his hands away, but I don't. I need to see if my hunch is right.

CHAPTER 8

Malakai

I have been watching her all night from the cameras in my office. How could I not with that fucking scrap of material she's wearing? It should be a fucking crime to wear something like that out in public, it barely covers her fucking pussy! The red dress has no back and starts just above her ass and ends just below the crease of her cheeks. The front is no better; it's only held up by a small knot around her neck and the front has a slit down the middle all the way down to her belly button. The two sides of the material just cover her tits and how they're staying in place I have no fucking idea. Her long brown hair is down and straight, and she has minimal makeup on, which only show-cases her natural beauty. I have been in a mood since the three of us drove to the club. It pisses me off to no end, watching everyone turn and stare at her.

I manage to get some work done, and I have been trying fucking hard to focus on finding these fucking Masters brothers, but I can't concentrate! I keep turning to check the cameras. I was doing okay until I watched her down a couple shots and then make her way to the dance floor. I was okay with that, because she was dancing with Jen, but then I see some little shit touch her, and my restraint breaks. I storm out of my office with Lucian hot on my heels, and hearing his laughter behind me just increases my rage. Once we make it to the bar, Lucian props himself on a stool and just sits there. I spot her grinding her ass against the dead man's dick and turn to Lucian.

"Are you gonna do something or not?" I can see the laughter in his eyes, and I briefly consider compelling him to do something embarrassing.

"Nah, that's all you, man. I know not to fuck with my cousin, plus I think that bothers you more than me." He cocks his brow at me, fucking little shit. I spin around and spot the fucker moving his hands up her sides, and that's the final straw. I take off toward them before I can stop myself. Like fuck will he be getting a handful of those tits! She leans her head back against him and closes her eyes. The crowd parts for me, so I don't need to worry about pushing fuckers out the way. As I near Raya, Jen spots me, and her eyes go wide. The look on my face must worry her because she stops dancing and darts her eyes back and forth between me and Raya. Just before the fucker reaches her tits, I clamp my hand around his throat. His panic-filled eyes snap to mine.

"You will leave and not come back. She repulses you and means nothing to you!" The guy nods his head and releases her immediately. Raya's angry green eyes glare up at me.

"What the hell did you do that for?" I grip her arm and yank her in front of me so her back is against my chest, with my arm around her middle, holding her tight against me. I hear her gasp, and I smile. I start to move my hips against her ass; I know she can feel how fucking hard I am. She lifts her arm until it wraps around the back of my neck and starts to grind her ass against my dick. I bend down so she can hear me and let my lips brush against her ear as I ask.

"Is this what you wanted?" I thrust my hips forward and

hear a moan escape her. "You wanted me to come down here and make a scene?" She nods her head, her bashfulness a breath of fresh air after the display moments earlier. "Now what, little girl?"

She drops her arm from my neck and pushes my arm away. I let her go reluctantly but am surprised when she spins around and wraps both her arms around my neck. I quickly drop my hands to her ass so I can cover it. This dress is so fucking short!

"I knew you were an ass man." I look down at her and narrow my eyes.

"I don't have a choice right now; if I move my hands every guy in here will get a view."

"And that bothers you?" We both rock our hips in rhythm with each other. Holding her this close to me feels right. Do I let her in, or do I keep pushing her away because of who she is?

"Raya, I am a jealous man, and I don't fucking share, ever." Her brows furrow in confusion. "If this is a game to you then you win—" She cuts me off, smashing her lips against mine, and this time I don't hesitate. I let this kiss tell her what I'm feeling. She moans into my mouth, and that sound has me groaning. I pull back, panting, and her lips are swollen and her eyes are glassy as she looks up at me.

"This won't last, Raya." I need her to understand that. I can't give her happily ever after, I can only give her here and now.

"Then give me all of you now, while you can." Her reply shocks me for a moment, and she takes advantage of my surprise, dropping her hands from my neck and pulling my hands from her ass. She quickly straightens her dress then clasps my hand in hers and pulls me behind her. We're about to pass the bar when she stops, and I realize then that I had forgotten Lucian was sitting there and saw everything that just happened.

Before I can get lost in my own thoughts and spiral, her voice pulls me out of it.

"I know you wanna bang Candy, and she likes you too, so stay there tonight." Lucian chuckles at her, then motions between the two of us.

"Two months of watching the twins and I keep your secret."

"A month, and I won't tell Uncle Dom that it was you that left the clippers out for Kailyn to shave his hair." Lucian scowls at Raya.

"Deal—and you never mention that again, or I tell Smurf and Nico you banged your dad's best friend." Now I growl at the little shit, but before I can say anything, Raya pulls me away but stops just before we're out of earshot.

"Just for that threat, I think we might start in your room!" She doesn't wait for Lucian to answer before she drags me toward the exit of Salut. I'm too stunned at her shamelessness to even comment, so I just follow her lead.

The car ride back to my house is tense, and I'm starting to second-guess my decision. I haven't been with a woman for over two decades. I don't sleep around, and I'm not the type to find 'em, feel 'em, fuck 'em and forget 'em. I have to feel some type of feeling toward the person. I like Raya, but I'm worried about the fallout this thing between us will cause. I can't seem to concentrate on anything aside from her since she arrived. A small part of me is hoping that if I taste her then I'll get over this infatuation I have toward her. Deep down, I know having sex with her will only complicate things. I pull into the driveway and turn the ignition off, and we both sit there silently, just staring out the windshield. The nervous energy in the car is suffocating.

"You know you can back out, right?" I inhale twice before turning to look at her, and I'm shocked to find she is staring directly at me. I reach over and cup her cheek, relishing her warmth.

"This won't work, Raya—"

"How about we head inside and just...talk, then see how things go?" I'm speechless. She has been trying for weeks to get my attention, and now that she has it she just wants to...talk?

"Come on, Godzilla, let's go in." My hand drops to the seat as she gets out of the car. I sit there a second longer, reeling at the twists and turns of the evening, before I follow her into the house.

I shut the front door behind me and go to the kitchen, thinking that is where she will be, but as I round the corner, the kitchen is empty.

"Raya?" I call out.

"In here, Zilla." I groan at the nickname she has given me and follow the sound of her voice. Her bedroom door is open, so I walk in and marvel at the space. I haven't been in this room since I gave the designer my approval. I never noticed before, but now it sticks out like a sore thumb—the room is so bare. The walls are white, there is a white faux fur rug at the end of the bed, a dresser, and a queen bed in the middle. What does draw my attention, though, are Raya's clothes scattered all over the room, and her makeup and hair stuff on top of the dresser. She walks out of the en suite, pulling me from staring at her mess. She's changed out of her dress and is now in a sweater that falls off one shoulder and pair of sweats that look very fucking familiar.

"Are those mine?" I ask with suspicion. She pulls her

sweater up and shows me how she has rolled the waistband of the sweats several times so they will fit her.

"Yeah, I didn't think you would mind since you have like ten pairs." I cock my head to the side, shocked. Has she no boundaries?

"You went through my drawers?" She doesn't even seem fazed.

"Nah, I saw you grab a pair of sweats the other day from your second drawer, so I figured that's where you kept all of your pairs." I scrub a hand down my face, exasperated. This woman has no fucking boundaries and just helps herself to anything.

"Are you mad?" I shake my head and turn on my heel and leave. I can hear her following me. I go straight to my room and head for my closet. I want out of this fucking suit and into something comfortable. Raya jumps on my king bed and crawls up till she is resting on the pillows. She just stares at me, shaking her head I enter the wardrobe and change. I take longer than needed because honestly, I need a moment to gather my thoughts.

"You can't hide in there forever, you know?"

Sighing, I pull my shirt on and leave the closet. Raya is still propped against the pillows. My breath hitches. Seeing her in my bed and in my sweats has me imagining a life where she and I could be something. I could come home each day and find her here in my house, waiting for me, loving me! I quickly push those thoughts out of my head. I can't give Raya what she wants. I can't be what she needs, plus she doesn't even know my history yet.

"Soooooo." I exhale loudly and make my way over to sit on the end of the bed, and she narrows her eyes at the space I left between us.

Why the hell is he acting so cold?

We pretty much humped on the dance floor at his club and now he won't even look at me for longer than two seconds. His mood swings are giving me whiplash. This guy is more complicated than a pregnant woman!

"Raya, you don't want to be with someone like me—"Anger flares inside me. How dare he assume to know what I should or shouldn't want?

"You don't get to do that! You can't tell me what I want!" He jumps to his feet and starts to pace the space at the end of his bed, gripping his hair and pulling it. He stops pacing after a minute and turns to face me, anger in his eyes.

"You have no fucking idea who I am, what I have done! You shouldn't even be here!" I climb off the bed, humiliated and hurt. I have done nothing but make my intentions clear to him. I have never misled him. I walk over and stop when I am two feet in front of him and look into his beautiful gray-blue eyes.

"I don't care about your past or what you have done, Melakai. I never cared. All I wanted was for you to see me—not my mom, not my dad, but me. You're the one who is lying to yourself, not me."

"How the hell am I lying? I have never lied to you." I can hear the anger in his voice, which only fuels my own.

"I know you're attracted to me, but you won't let go long enough to see if this will work. You are a coward. And yes, you are right, I shouldn't be here, so come tomorrow morning I will leave." I move around him so I can go to my room, but his arm snaps out like a snake and hauls me back in front of him. I can see from the look in his eyes that his resolve is dwindling. He's about to lose control, and I'm not sure if I want to push the beast this time.

"If you knew the truth, you wouldn't want me. There is a reason why your father never told you much about me. I'm not the good guy in this story, Raya." He releases my arm and brings his hand up to cup my cheek. I nuzzle into his huge hand and hold his gaze.

"I never meant to hurt you, you were never supposed to find me." My brows furrow in confusion. What the hell does he mean? Before I can answer, the front door slams open, and Kai spins toward his bedroom door and places himself in front of me to protect me. I swoon a little then peek around him and watch as Lucian and Cam come barreling into Kai's room. Lucian's gaze darts from Kai to me when I step out from behind him.

"Boss, we got a situation." Even I can hear the urgency in Cam's voice, and Kai automatically tenses and straightens to his full height.

"What is it?" Cam doesn't answer, Lucian does.

"Well, we don't need to find the brothers."

"What? Why?" I ask my cousin.

"Because they found us." I turn to look up at Kai and find that his gaze is locked onto my cousin.

"How?" Kai grits out.

"One of them dropped a note off to Candy after you both left. They want us to meet them tomorrow." How the fuck did they know we were looking for them? I don't get a chance to answer my cousin, because Cam decides to drop another fucking bomb on us.

"Thomas also called. Six high-level supes just crossed the border." Kai starts cursing loudly and begins to pace the room again. I look to Lucian for an explanation, but he shrugs his shoulders and looks just as confused as me. I turn around and step into Kai's pathway, placing my hand on his chest. My touch seems to get him to snap out of his muttering and pacing. Kai's reaction has me worried. I'm not sure what six supes crossing a border means. I'm more worried about the meeting with the brothers and how the hell they knew we were looking for them!

"What's got you so wound up Zilla?" I see apprehension cross his gaze before he quickly masks it.

"I think we're lucky nothing transpired here tonight." Shocked and slightly embarrassed, I drop my hand from his chest. He reaches out and grips my chin between his thumb and forefinger to lift my head so I'll meet his gaze, and the guilt there is evident. "When the six of them get here, you will be thankful, Raya, trust me." His somber tone sets me on edge.

"Why are you worried about six supernaturals, Kai? You're the king of the vampires," I whisper.

"That's a title I am only now starting to come to terms with. I'm not worried about me, Espoir. I'm worried about the chaos the six will bring for you!"

"Who are the six, Kai?" Kai darts his gaze to Lucian and then back to me, sadness fills his gaze, and he moves his hand so he is now cupping my cheek. He strokes my face with his thumb, and I melt into his touch. When he answers Lucian's question, I understand why he is so on edge.

"The six supes arriving here are both sets of your parents

and Jackson and Aurora. They have come for you two." I gasp, and I hear Lucian suck in a loud breath.

"How did they find us?"

Kai smiles sadly down at me.

"Dom would have tracked his son. They would know if he wasn't in Alaska he would have come to me for help. My brothers have known for years where I live, so it wouldn't be hard to piece it together."

"How long before they get here?" Lucian asks, but it's Cam that answers.

"I would say we have fifteen minutes. I have ordered all the guards to reroute here and form a perimeter around the grounds." Kai moves his gaze from me to Cam.

"The guards won't stop them. Let them through when they get here."

"I have the gates locked, sir."

"They won't use the gates, Cam, they will portal. No one is to touch them. Ryan and Nico will lay waste to anyone who tries to stop them from coming for their daughter." Oh my God! It finally registers for me: my mom shouldn't be here; she should be at home resting. What the hell have I done?

Lucian, Raya, and I wait in the lounge for my brothers and the girls to arrive. Cam, David, and Kyle are stationed inside the house, as they refused to leave me unguarded. I appreciate their loyalty, but I don't deserve it. I have been a shit king to them. I left Eric in charge of all the day-to-day runnings. If there is anything that needs my attention, he lets me know and I deal with it.

I can see from Raya's hunched shoulders and how she keeps chewing her thumbnail that she is nervous. Lucian looks like he is waiting to get a beating, and no doubt he will get one for the shit he and Raya pulled. I'm not nervous to see my brothers, but I am nervous for Raya to find out the truth about me. Will she still look at me the same? Voices over Cam and David's radios pull my attention.

"Portal opening on the east side, Cam. Orders?" Cam looks at me, and I nod my head in approval.

"All units stand down. I repeat, all units stand down! Let them through to the house. The king wants them unharmed."

"Roger that."

Raya jumps up from her seat on the couch and comes to sit next to me. She shocks me when she reaches over and claps my hand in hers. I look her in the eyes and see so much uncertainty in her gaze. She uses her other hand to cup my cheek.

"Whatever happens, I don't regret what nearly happened between us tonight." I smile sadly at her. When she learns the truth, she will feel differently. I don't get a chance to reply before she leans forward and places a kiss on my lips that has me wanting more.

"The fuck is going on here?" Raya and I jerk apart, and she jumps to her feet. I do the same, but I make sure that I am in front of her, shielding her from their view. Seeing my three brothers and the girls sends a wave of longing over me. Nico still wears a permanent frown, and his violet eyes are shooting daggers at me. His jet black hair is a mess, and rings circle the bottom of his eyes. He looks like he hasn't slept in days.

"Answer me now!"

Raya moves out from behind me, and I quickly snap my arm out to stop her from moving any closer to her father. Nico doesn't miss my move and lets his purple magic cover his hands. He moves toward me but is stopped when Ryan pulls his arm back. I turn my gaze to her, and the feeling of heartbreak I used to have whenever I saw her is no longer there. Her long brown hair, the same color as Raya's, is piled on top of her head. Her strange green eyes with a yellow ring around the pupils look sad and tired. I let my gaze travel over her and notice she has lost weight. She looks so frail and...sick.

"Dad, I can explain!" Raya is trying to plead with her father, but his gaze is still locked on me. He just caught me kissing his daughter— he is not going to let that go in a hurry.

"Then explain, Raya, because I'm two seconds away from losing my shit!" he snaps. I growl low in my throat and see Cam and David move closer. Dom snaps his gaze to either side of them and lets out a growl of his own. His eyes have changed from their normal violet color to the color of his wolf–gray. He's grown out his silver hair now, and it's long enough to tuck behind his ears. He still looks like he works out daily, vain bastard.

"Take another step and I blast the pair of you fuckers, feel me?" Cam and David look at me, and I nod my head for them to fall back. My gaze is snagged when I watch Sophia move toward Lucian and embrace her son in a hug. She cut her beautiful long black hair, and it sits just below her shoulders. Her violet eyes shine with love as she looks at her son. So-So looks good; she looks happy. I have waited years to see that look on her.

"Everyone calm down." I turn my gaze to Jax. He has always been the level-headed one out of the four of us guys. Nothing at all has changed with him—his brown hair is still the same and cut the same. His chocolate brown eyes hold more wisdom, though he still hasn't aged, thanks to being a shifter. Aurora clutches his arm, her blonde, almost white hair is tied in a ponytail. Her blue eyes hold so much sadness in them— why?

"How the fuck can I calm down when I just saw him kissing my daughter?" Nico grinds out through clenched teeth. His gaze snaps to Lucian, who now has his mother tucked into his side with his arm around her shoulders. "You need to start explaining, boy!"

"Don't fucking talk to my son like that, dick," Dom growls at Nico.

"Everyone stop!" All eyes turn to Raya, who takes a deep breath and squares her shoulders. "It was my idea, not Lucian's. This was all my fault. Dad, please don't blame Kai." My heart softens at her trying to defend me, but I won't let her take the blame for something I could have stopped.

"It's fine, mon espoir, I can take it." Nico groans and throws his hands into the air.

"Another nickname for someone that doesn't belong to you!" I snap my gaze to him and glare at the broody fucker. He doesn't get to come back after twenty fucking years and start this shit again.

"Enough!" Ryan's voice cuts off my angry reply. She releases Nico's arm and moves toward us. Nico tries to stop her, but she smacks his hand away. She steps down the two steps into the sunken living room and quickly hugs Lucian. Then she turns to Raya and me, stopping in front of me. Her eyes begin to mist as she looks up at me, and guilt slams into my chest.

"I've missed you, Kai." Those four words deflate me immediately. I drop the arm that blocks Raya from moving and hang my head. "Kai?"

I lift my gaze slowly back to Ryan and see her smiling up at me. She opens her arms wide, and all I can do is stare. She sighs then closes the gap between us and wraps her arms around my waist. I stand there stunned for a moment before returning her embrace.

I don't miss the growl that comes from Nico, and I subtly turn my head and smirk at him. A few moments pass and Ryan pulls back, wiping tears from her eyes. She smiles sadly at me before turning to face her daughter. They embrace each other and both of them shed a few tears before pulling apart.

Ryan cups her daughter's face between her hands and asks, "What have you done Raya?" Raya pulls out of her mother's hold and looks to Lucian. He gives her an encouraging smile and nods his head.

"Wait, before we get into this, I need to do something." Everyone looks to Dom as he approaches me, and I tense in preparation. I can't tell from the look in his eyes if he wants to hit me or hug me. He stops a step away from me, and his gaze travels down my body then back up to my eyes. I stand there quietly and let him get his fill. No one makes a sound as Dom and I stand here in our staring contest.

"Twenty years and you're still as ugly as the last time I saw you." A broad grin stretches across Dom's face as he wraps me in a hug, and I don't even hesitate. I wrap my arms around my brother and relish this moment.

Dom and I stand here wrapped in a bro hug and only pull apart when Jax steps in to switch with Dom. Aurora and Sophia are next. Eventually a loud throat clearing has us all looking to Nico, who still hasn't moved. I release a long sigh, ready to get this shit over with, but Raya moves to stand at the bottom of the steps and looks up to her father. Nico still won't pull his death glare from me to acknowledge her.

"Dad?" Nico still won't look at Raya, so I step between Dom and Aurora and move to stand next to Raya. Nico narrows his eyes to slits when I stand beside his daughter.

"Will you at least look at me?" The pleading tone in Raya's voice finally gets Nico to look at her, and I see Raya flinch slightly at the anger in her father's gaze and that pisses me off.

"Don't take it out on her." His gaze jumps back to me immediately, and his hands begin to glow again.

"You don't get to tell me how to deal with my daughter!" he roars. "She is mine, not yours!" My restraint snaps, and so many years of built up anger and tension between us finally spills over.

"You don't fucking own her! She can make her own choices. Say what you really want to say, Nicholas!" Nico stands there glaring down at me with his mouth sealed shut. He knows he has pushed me too far; I'm not ready to let this go. "You have had a fucking problem with me since Ryan first came to Alaska over twenty years ago." That gets a reaction out of him, and he storms down the two steps to stand in front of me. Raya snaps her gaze between me and her father, worry lines marrying her beautiful face. Nico moves forward until we are nearly nose to nose. I'm a few inches taller than him and he has always hated it, so I make a point of looking down at him. He pulls his lip back in a snarl and looks at me like I am shit beneath his shoe.

"You ruined us when you decided to fuck my wife!"

CHAPTER 11

What the fuck?

My eyes dart to my mom, who looks horrified and shocked at my dad's outburst. I look at Kai and see so much shame and guilt on his face. He reaches out and I stumble back a step. Grief clouds his eyes for a moment before he shuts down. I'm too shocked and confused to even care.

"I told you I was no good; I warned you I would cause you nothing but pain." I can't talk past the lump in my throat; I stand here, staring at him, swallowing continuously. He didn't deny it. Did he really do it? My dad has a smug look on his face—he wanted that little bomb to cause damage and form a wedge between Kai and me. How the fuck did I not know this? My mom told me my dad was the only guy she has ever been with. I peer past Kai to look at mom and find her gaze is already on me, tears again spilling over.

Oh my God! I cover my mouth with my hand, filled with shame and disgust. What the fuck have I done? He told me when I learned who he really is I wouldn't like it, but I didn't listen. Mom moves toward me, and Dad darts his arm out to stop her, but she's furious.

"Move that fucking arm now. You have gone way too far this time, big guy—way too far!" Mom slaps Dad's arm away and moves till she is in front of me. I'm looking at my mom in a new light. She lied to me; I always thought dad was her first and only. I am so fucking confused and disgusted in myself, not to mention embarrassed as fuck. My aunts and uncles just saw me kissing a guy that my mom has apparently slept with! Mom reaches out to touch me but I move back. Sadness clouds her eyes as she drops her arm back to her side.

"Sweetheart I can explain—"

"Explain what, Mom? You lied to me! You told me you had only ever been with Dad. Oh my God, I kissed my mom's seconds. I think I'm going to be sick." I honestly feel like I might hurl.

"Technically, your Dad's the seconds and Kai is the first, but who's counting, right?" I snap shocked eyes to Uncle Dom and watch as Uncle Jax slaps the back of his head and growls at him.

"Dude, what the fuck?" Uncle Dom snaps.

"You're such a dipshit and only making matters worse!" Aunt Soph snarls. Uncle Dom at least has the decency to look at her sheepishly and then turns to me and smiles. This is such a mind fuck. I move over to where Lucian is seated on the couch and drop down next to him. He wraps an arm around my shoulders and pulls me into his side.

"In your attempt to hurt me once again, all you have done is caused your daughter pain." I lift my gaze to see Kai glaring down at my dad, and mom is standing between the two of them with her eyes locked on me—tears pouring down her cheeks.

"Fuck you, Melakai. Out of all the women in the world, you had to go after my daughter?" I flinch at the angry tone in my dad's voice. I'm so angry that Kai hid this from me, but I'm more angry at my mom for lying to me for so many years. I had been told small details about Kai but I never suspected he and my dad fell out because mom slept with him!

"I never went after her!" Kai shouts. Dad, Mom and Kai remain standing as the others take a seat on the other couches. "She came here to me., I tried to fucking send her home, but the portals were locked!" Dad's gaze snaps to me, and all the anger that was in his eyes moments ago is exchanged with concern.

"What the hell is he talking about, Raya?" I drop my eyes to my lap. How the hell do I tell my dad that I lost my magic?

"It's my fault." Lucian blurts out.

"Luce, don't do this, I'm a big girl." Lucian smiles sadly at me.

"He was always going to blame me anyway, cousin." Lucian turns to look at my father again. "Raya and I learned about a potion that was being held near here, and we tried to retrieve it. It was easy. We portaled in, and there it was. Then when we went to leave, we couldn't access our magic. We fought our way out, and I sent Raya to Kai while I led the brothers away." Dad's face changes from concern to anger in an instant, and his angry gaze darts between Lucian and me.

"Why the fuck did you two go after a potion?" I answer him this time.

"Because we thought the potion could help Mom." Dad reels back in shock, and I hear gasps come from the others. Kai looks between my mother and father, concern marrying his beautiful features. Eww, Raya, stop! Sloppy seconds, remember?

"W-what potion, sweetheart?" I push aside the anger I feel toward my mom for now; I will deal with all of those feelings later. Sighing, I follow Lucian's lead and stand so we're both facing my parents and Kai.

"Ever since we learned about your condition, Luce and I have been trying to find a cure. We think we found it, Mom." Hope flares in my mother's eyes before she quickly masks it, and Dad steps forward and grips the top of my shoulders. He bends down till we are eye to eye and says, "Tell me everything, baby girl."

I release a long exhale before gesturing for them to take a seat. Dad and Mom drop down next to Uncle Jax, and Uncle Dom and my aunts occupy the other couch. Lucian settles back down into his seat and as I sit next to him before I realize the seat left available for Kai is right next to me. Fan-fucking-tastic. Kai moves toward me and drops down beside me, and I shuffle over until I'm pretty much plastered on my cousin. I don't miss my father's satisfied grin.

"I so want to hear more about this potion, but then I want to hear more about this awkwardness between you and Kai, cupcake." I cringe, and Kai turns to Uncle Dom and glares at him. I need to bring this conversation back on track immediately.

"Lucian got a tip from one of the rogue fae that he knows. He told us about the potion. We followed the fae's lead and it led us to the vault not far from here."

"What is the potion supposed to do, cookie?" asks Uncle Dom, but Lucian answers for me.

"It's supposed to reverse any spell, curse, or magic toll." Gasps ring out around the room, and Aunt Aurora lets a small whimper escape her. Uncle Jax is on his feet and kneeling down in front of her in the next second.

"What's wrong, love?" Aunt Aurora's gaze jumps from Uncle Jax to my mom and then to me.

"Was the potion green?" Lucian and I exchange a look before turning back to my aunt and answering her.

"Yeah, but how did you know?" Tears gather in her eyes, and then she reaches out to cup her mate's cheek and smiles.

"Because I saw this potion, I believe, I had my first vision in sixteen years last week." More gasps ring out.

"A-are you sure?" Aunt Aurora nods her head at Uncle Jax, and a blush starts to creep over her cheeks when she looks at me again.

"Why are you looking at me like that?" She quickly looks to my parents then back to me and asks, "Did the red dress do the trick?" I squawk so fucking loud that I'm sure the guards outside heard me. My gaze swings to Kai, who is already staring at me with a blank look on his face. We stay locked in this staring match for a few moments before a throat clearing has us snapping out of it.

"What red dress?" My dad barks at my aunt, and Uncle Jax releases a loud growl in warning at my dad to watch his tone when speaking to his mate.

"From the look on Kai and Raya's faces, I think I have had more than one vision," my aunt replies proudly. My aunt lost her gift of being able to see the future and the past when she gave birth, her and Uncle Jax's only daughter. Turns out her visions might be back now, which is freaking epic!

"What look? What fucking dress, Raya?" I recoil at the anger in my father's tone. He never uses that tone with me! I face him and meet his gaze, and there is so much anger swirling in his violet eyes. Mom keeps looking between me and Kai, a small smile gracing her lips. What the fuck is she smiling about?

"Answer me, Raya!"

"Stop fucking yelling at her!" Kai shouts, and Dad jumps to his feet and Kai tries to do the same. I snap my hand out and grip his wrist, and Kai follows the path of my hand to my face and looks to me for an explanation.

"Please don't—he's angry that I kept something from him. I never keep shit from him, and for the first time in my life I did, and now we are all in this situation because I tried to prove I could do something on my own." Kai nods his head and reluctantly takes his seat again. As soon as he is sitting, I withdraw my hand from his wrist. I miss the feeling of touching him immediately. I am so fucking screwed. Dad angrily drops down next to my mom again, who is glaring at him.

"Don't look at me like that, little one."

"Like what, Nico?" Dad throws his hands in the air before turning to face my mom fully.

"Like this is my fault! I had nothing to do with this."

"I told you not to tell her!" Dad's face morphs to pure anger.

"That wasn't your call to make! You're the one who wants to give up and leave me. Our daughter had the fucking right to know that her mother is dying. We're in this situation because you went behind my back twenty fucking years ago and made a blood pack to nullify fucking Randall and the moonstones!" I have never—and I mean never—heard my father talk to my mother like this. Tears are rolling down my mom's face, and Dad is shaking with anger. My heart is breaking for my parents. My dad won't survive losing my mom. My mom is everything to him; they have been together for more than two decades and still my dad looks at my mom like she is his every breath. Of course my mother loves him deeply, but I want a man to look at me the way my dad looks at my mom.

"Dude, too fucking far! That was a fucking dick move, asshole." Uncle Dom snaps at my dad as he makes his way over to my mom and slips into the seat next to her. He wraps his arm around her shoulders and pulls her into his side. "It's okay, love." Lucian, climbing to his feet next to me, draws my attention, and I quickly shuffle away from him until I hit something. I look back to see I am now plastered against Kai. Dad pulls his gaze from me to see what the hell had me moving across the couch so fast, and when his eyes land on a growling Lucian, he stands to his feet.

"Don't make me put you down, boy!"

"Touch my son, Nicky boy, and I'll fuck you up." Dad ignores Uncle Dom, his gaze still firmly locked on my cousin. Dad releases his magic till his hands are covered in purple magic.

"I have warned you time after time, never use this against her! This isn't her fucking fault, Nico, she did this to save my mom!" Some of the anger in my dad's eyes starts to dissipate when he swings his gaze to my Aunt Soph. "We all knew there would be a price to pay; we all accepted the risks. Do not take this out on her, Nico, she needs you." Tears begin to cloud my eyes.

"I am begging you, be there for her now. If you can't be kind and help us, then fucking leave, because I will not allow you to hurt her again!" Lucian sounds like an alpha in his own right. My cousin is fucking strong. Even without his magic, his wolf is still a commanding presence. I don't know all of the details of why my mom entered the blood pact. They said I was too young to understand.

"You have no right—" Lucian cuts my dad off before he can finish.

"I have every fucking right! She is my best friend, and you have distanced yourself since you learned that out of me, her, and Kai, that she was the one to pay the price. You have let your anger towards Kai cloud your judgment. This isn't her fault. Stop being a fucking dick. If she dies, will you be able to live with how you have treated her these past few months?" My dad's magic fades as he stares at Lucian, and tears are rolling down my cheeks at the reminder that my mom could die. An arm wraps around me and pulls me in close, and I rest my head against his chest and weep. I can't lose my mom. She's my best friend, my go-to about everything!

CHAPTER 12

Ryan's dying.

Why her?

Why wasn't it me?

She has so much to live for; guilt is eating away at me. It shouldn't be her, it should have been me! She is a mother and a wife. Me, on the other hand—I am no one. Raya's whimper pulls me from my thoughts. Looking down at her, I feel so much sorrow. She is so young and is facing the possibility of losing her mother. My gaze lifts to Ryan to find her eyes on her daughter. Dom is grinning from ear to ear. Bastard is only grinning like that because Raya is in my arms, and he knows Nico will lose his shit when he realizes.

Nico drops to his knees in front of his wife, and he reaches out and cups her face between his hands. I used to envy Nico—I wished it was me holding Ryan—but now I see how right they are for each other. I was never going to win the girl; fate had already decided she belonged to Nico long before I visited her in her dreams. Fuck, I haven't dream walked in years.

"Little one, I am so fucking sorry. I never should have blamed you for this. If I could trade places with you, I would. I just don't understand why it was you and not...and not—" I save Nico the trouble and finish his sentence for him.

"Me. He's right, love, it should not have been you or Lucian." Nico's shoulders droop and his head drops forward. Ryan's shocked gaze meets mine but her shock quickly gives way to annoyance.

"Don't you dare fucking say that, Kai! You have already given enough for me. You will not give your life for mine again! If a cure isn't found, I'll be okay with this." Raya lifts her head from my chest and looks to her mother.

"How? How can you possibly be okay with this?" Ryan's face softens, and her eyes shine with so much love for her daughter.

"Because I got to love and marry the man of my dreams—literally. But I also got to fall in love all over again when I had you. Being your mother, Raya, has been the greatest gift of my life. You, my sweet, sweet girl, will always be my greatest achievement. You, Raya Stevie Stone, are the best of me." Raya bursts from my hold and runs to her mother, and Ryan is out of Dom's embrace and pushing past Nico to meet her daughter in the middle of the room. Both of them are crying hysterically. Nico looks at his wife and daughter with so much heartbreak as he stands and wraps his arms around both his girls. We all feel awkward being present in this very personal moment, and we look away to give the three of them a minute.

"All right, Luce, tell us about this potion. We don't have long to be away. Poppy has the twins." Lucian snorts and starts cackling like a child.

"Why is he laughing like that?" Soph winces and her gaze darts to Dom, who is trying to mask his laughter.

"The twins and Dom's dad don't really get along. Avery and Kailyn like to pull pranks and they kind of, sort of, may have set Ian's cabin on fire, hotwired his truck, crashed his truck, and stole some of his booze and had a party in the woods with the visiting alpha's kids."

I try really hard, I swear I did, but the moment Jackson breaks out into fits of laughter, I follow suit. Out of all four of us guys, I knew Dom would be the one to end up with kids just like him. "It's not funny! Dom won't punish them because he believes they are just expressing themselves." Soph sounds so exasperated and pissed, but I can't stop laughing. Lucian's comment just makes Jax, Dom, and I all laugh harder.

"They are little shits! They super-glued my ass to the seat when we were having a pack meeting!" I clutch my stomach, and tears leak from my eyes. I haven't laughed like this in decades. My laughter dies when my eyes land on Raya and find her looking at me like a two-horned unicorn.

She pulls away from her parents and moves toward me, ignoring her father's grunts and groans behind her. I stand there still as a statue as she approaches me. The guys have stopped laughing, and everyone is quiet while watching Raya and I. Once she stands before me and looks up at me with those bright green eyes, something inside me cracks. I don't know what it is, but I have never felt this before.

"You look so different when you laugh." Her words have me furrowing my brow. I have no idea what she wants me to say to that. If I were like Dom, I would fill the awkward silence in the room with a wisecrack, but I have never been one for small talk. I can feel everyone's eyes on me, and it's making me feel uncomfortable.

"You don't owe me anything, Kai, but I am asking you anyway. Will you please help us find the brothers and help me save my mom?" I make sure she can see the certainty in my eyes before I answer.

"On my honor, I will help you till we find a cure. First, I need to know everything." Raya nods her head and tells everyone to take a seat, and they reclaim the seats they were once in. I do the same, with Raya beside me. She looks to Ryan, who gives her a small smile and nods her head in encouragement.

"Okay, so after my mom gave birth to me, the spell came to take its price. My mom is strong, and being a fae should make her immortal or extend her life much longer than a human's. The price for the spell she cast to save Aunt Soph is that her lifespan has been halved. Mom has another five years to live. We found out from Mya that from the day my mom cast the spell, that she would be allowed twenty-five years of life before the spell claimed her life as payment."

Shocked, I tear my gaze from Raya to look at Ryan. I can see in her eyes that Raya has told me the truth. I will not let Ryan die. I may not be in love with her anymore, but I still care about her deeply. I look back to Raya. She looks at me differently now, with so much speculation in her eyes. I can't be the one to tell her the truth, though; that is up to Ryan. It's not my place. Sighing, I turn to face Nico, not even shocked to find him already glaring at me.

"We got word from the brothers; they knew we were looking for them and have requested a meeting with us tomorrow." Hope fills Nico's gaze. "Don't get your hopes up. These guys are ruthless and cunning. I have no idea how they have flown under your radar for so long; they are no average fae, Nico. These three brothers are the strongest fae I have encountered, aside from us." Everyone begins hurling questions at me, and I don't know who to answer first. Turns out I don't have to decide after all, as Raya whistles loudly, which has everyone snapping their mouths closed and looking to her.

"Right, now that I have your attention, here is how tomorrow is going to go. Kai, Lucian and I will meet with the brothers—"

"Like fuck you will be going without me!" Nico snaps at his daughter. I have to give Raya credit—she doesn't back down; she squares her shoulders and faces her father head on.

"No, Dad. If we show up with the kings of the fae and wolves, as well as the queens to the wolves and fae, and not to mention Uncle Dom and Aunt Soph, they will see that as a threat. They already know about me, Luce, and Kai. If the three of us go, they won't see it as a threat, and will be more likely to comply and help us." Nico is already shaking his head, and Ryan's face is twisted in concern. The others look downright torn. They know Raya is right, but their concern for their niece and son has them wanting to argue. Everyone begins to shout and yell over each other, and the noise is getting to me.

"Shut the fuck up!" Silence falls on the room, and all eyes turn to me. I can see Raya grinning at me from the corner of my eye.

"Well, shit Kai, with an outburst like that you must have something good to say." I turn and narrow my eyes at a smirking Dominic. Soph smiles at me encouragingly from beside him.

"If you want your daughter and Lucian to get their magic back, then you will stay behind Nico. As Raya said the brothers will see your presence as a threat. If we have any chance of getting Ryan this cure and these two their powers back, we need to play by their rules." I can tell Nico wants to argue, but he knows what I say is the truth.

"Who are these guys, Kai?" I move my gaze to Ryan and answer.

"They are rogue fae, very powerful. I had never heard of them until I moved here, but they haven't caused me trouble as long as I stayed to my side and they stayed to theirs. We have lived in peace for years—until these two ruined it." Lucian growls low in his throat, and Raya is mumbling under her breath about me being an ass. I fight to keep the smirk off my face; she looks cute when she scrunches her nose and furrows her brows.

"How have they escaped my watch? If they are that powerful I would have heard about them." Nico can act as smug as he likes, but he has no idea who these guys are. I don't know their story, but I have heard things, and by the sounds of it, these three haven't had an easy life. I shake myself from my thoughts and answer Nico.

"Look none of that matters now. They have lived their lives and never caused any trouble. I believe they will be reasonable and comply if we explain our situation."

"How do you know that, Kai?"

"I just have a feeling, Jax. If they wanted to cause harm or run me out of town, they could have. They were here long before me, and from the power they wield they could have caused me problems but haven't." Jax and Dom exchange a look. Nico still doesn't look convinced. Aurora seems troubled, and Soph just keeps looking at her son, worry lines mar her pretty face. I turn to Ryan and find her looking between Raya, Lucian, and me. I can't decipher the look on her face.

"Can you guarantee that no harm will come to the kids?" I see Raya bristle out of the corner of my eye at being called a kid by Soph. I understand Sophia's worries; if I had a child of my own, I would feel the same, but children will never be in the cards for me.

"I can't, So-So, but I can assure you that I will protect them with my life. If I thought in any way that this meeting was a setup, I wouldn't even consider bringing them with me."

"Why the hell should I trust you with my daughter's life?" I scowl at Nico, how fucking dare he!

"I have never failed before. Failing isn't in my makeup, but it is in yours!"

Dad and Kai can't seem to stop throwing sly digs at each other. There is so much tension between the two of them, and it's putting everyone in the room on edge. I can see the strain on my mom's face. She gets tired really quickly nowadays. This shit needs to end, and I will not let Dad's jealousy or Kai's anger toward my dad cause my mom to spiral.

"That's enough." All eyes turn to me. "This shit between you both is causing a rift between this family, and it's draining Mom." I turn to Kai and meet his gaze. "I don't know what the story is with you and mom, and I don't care to know. You need to table this shit and get along until we can leave and go home. Then you can go back to your life." I turn back to my dad and see him with a shit eating grin on his face. "Lose the smile, Dad. You need to cut your shit as well. None of this is good for Mom. She's your wife. Everyone should get some sleep and we'll deal with this in the morning."

"And where the hell do you sleep, daughter?" Dad snaps at me, and I narrow my eyes and smile sweetly as I reply.

"Why, in Kai's bed, of course, Daddy." Dad's face is a

mottled red from rage. I can hear the others snickering, and Kai has said nothing to try and defend himself.

"You're fucking kidding right?"

"Of course I am!" Dad releases a long exhale and unclenches his fists. Mom is glaring daggers at dad.

"She is a grown woman, Nico, you can't stop her from having—" Dad plugs his fingers in his ears and starts yelling.

"La la la la la la la." Mom playfully glares at Dad while the rest of us laugh at Dad's childishness. I don't ever think there will be a time where my dad won't see me as his little girl. Truthfully, him being salty to Kai has nothing to do with Kai per se. It's more that he doesn't want me to grow up and date. I love my dad, but he can be way overbearing at times.

Mom, Dad, Lucian, and my aunts and uncles said they would rather portal back to the compound in Alaska and just meet back in the morning, rather than staying at Kai's. Dad put up a huge fuss when I told him I would be staying here and not going with them. It took Mom twenty minutes and a threat of using her magic against him to finally get him to leave with them. When the portal closed and they were all gone, I breathed easily for the first time since they arrived. I spoke too soon, though, as another portal opened and Lucian came stumbling out, rubbing the back of his head. The look on his face told me all I needed to know—this was my dad's doing.

"I swear to God, Ray, when I get my fucking magic back, I am going to fucking burn your father's eyebrows off!" Lucian storms past me and Kai, heading toward his room here at Kai's. When his bedroom door slams shut, a burst of laughter breaks free from both Kai and myself. Lucian is so pissed he only has his wolf and not his magic. He is one strong S.O.B., but without his magic, he is just a regular wolf.

My laughter dies off, as does Kai's, and we both stand here staring at each other. I don't know what to say. Should I broach the subject of him and my mom? Do I act like I don't care? Should I leave?

Kai releases a long exhale and scrubs his hand down his face.

"It's late, you should get some rest." Seriously? That's all he has to say to me after everything I have learned tonight?

"Whatever, Kai, keep your secrets." I turn on my heel and head toward my room, before I round the corner of the hallway, I stop and turn back to him. His gaze is still firmly on me. "When all you have left in your life is your secrets, I hope they make you happy."

I don't wait for his reply. I continue to my room and slam the door shut behind me. That man is so fucking confusing! I promised myself I wouldn't get distracted in my search for a cure for my mom, and yet here I am. I am pining over a fucking guy who has apparently slept with my mom! What is wrong with me? Deciding that I just need to sleep and will deal with all this shit tomorrow, I make my way to the closet and strip out of my clothes. I pull one of Lucian's shirts down from a hanger. I have a thing for stealing shirts; it's a tick of mine, I guess. I like sleeping in big shirts and I prefer to steal guys' shirts. Wait—not steal—acquire is a better word. I pull Luce's shirt on over my head, and I stand here in just my cousin's tee and my panties, wondering why the hell the only guy in the world to captivate me has to be so fucking complicated.

Fuck this. I turn and exit the closet but screech to halt when I see Kai standing in the middle of my room. His heated gaze travels the length of my body, and the look in his eyes and the way he bites his bottom lip has me shivering. Kai is standing here in my room in just a pair of basketball shorts and that's it! Tattoos cover his whole torso, and I can see the ink creeps over the top of his shoulders. His arms are bare, but he did say he has an appointment booked in next week to rectify that. He looks like a badass bad boy, and not even gonna lie—just the look of him has me turned the fuck on.

Stop it! He slept with your mom, Raya!

Clearing my throat to draw his attention, he slowly lifts his gaze from my bare legs to meet my eyes. I raise a brow at him, but he doesn't seem the least bit fazed that he just got caught checking me out.

"Why are you here? Kai?"

"I was gonna go for a run to clear my head."

"That doesn't answer my question." I know I'm being short and bitchy, but it has been a long day and night, and I'm done being mind-fucked.

"I wanted to go for a run to try and clear you from my mind." I reel back slightly, shocked.

"What the hell did I do?" He narrows his eyes at me and stalks toward me till there is only a sliver of space between us. I can feel the heat radiating off of his body, and my hands are itching to reach out and trace the ink that covers his beautiful, sculpted body. Kai reaches out and lifts my chin up so I can meet his gaze, his eyes giving nothing away. I swear, he hides his emotions like a superhero wanting to conceal their identity.

"You have burrowed yourself inside my head, and I don't know how to get you out!" I can't decide if he sounds angry or confused about that. I bat his hand away and take a step back to put some much needed space between us, so I can actually concentrate instead of wanting to lick him–I mean touch him!

"You don't have to worry much longer. As soon as these brothers help Luce and I get our magic back, and we get the cure for my mom, I'll leave." Kai's whole face changes. His eyebrows are raised like Wolverine, and his lips are pulled back in a snarl and his fangs have lengthened. His eyes are like a tornado of angry emotions.

"What if I don't want you to leave?" Yeah, no. He does not get to do this and play me like that. I throw my hands up into the air and storm toward him and start poking him in the chest as I snap.

"You do not get to play hot and cold with me. You want me, then you don't. You have so many secrets and won't share them. For fuck's sake, no one would even tell me shit about you growing up." I stop poking his chest and let my arm drop to my side. I am so tired and don't have the capacity to deal with all of this emotional shit right now. I drop my gaze to the floor and sigh. "Please leave, Kai." He stands there for so long I think he might not leave, but then to my surprise he listens and turns around and walks to the door. I lift my gaze and gasp— his whole back is covered in tattoos as well! Kai pauses when he opens the door, he turns back to face me as he speaks.

"Some secrets are better left unsaid. The past is called the past for a reason, Raya. I wish you well on your journey in this life. If we are ever fortunate to meet again in our next life, I hope I will be someone different so maybe then you wouldn't look at me the way you do." Kai closes the door behind himself while I stand there, gobsmacked. What the fuck was that? How the hell do I look at him? Hell no, he doesn't get to say that and leave! I chase after him, but either he doesn't hear me coming after him or he just doesn't care. He closes his bedroom and not two seconds later I throw the fucking thing open and flinch slightly when I hear it smack the wall and hear a little crack. I think I just put a hole in his wall.

Kai stands there at the foot of his bed, glaring at me. His

chest is heaving, and his fangs are out. Yeah, well, you're not the only one who is fucking angry, Godzilla!

"You do not get to drop a bomb like that and leave! How the fuck do I look at you, Melakai?"

"Leave, Raya, now!"

"Fuck you! I want to know why you're being such an ass. I know you like me, your actions showed that tonight. Why the hell are you pushing me away?"

"I said leave!"

"And I said fuck you!" Before I can even comprehend what the fuck is happening, Kai has his hand wrapped around my throat and my back against the closest wall. His breaths are coming in short, angry bursts, and his eyes are bluer now. His fangs are all the way out and I'm not....scared. I can see it in his eyes; Kai would never hurt me.

"You need to leave, please." I can feel this little pulse in the back of my head, and I have no idea what the fuck it is. The answer hits me full force when Kai's face scrunches in confusion.

"D-did you just try to use your mind control thingy on me?" Kai's eyes pop wide, his fangs retract, and his grip on my throat loosens slightly.

""H-how did you know?"

"I felt it."

"Felt what?" I decide it's better to be honest and not lie just to piss him off.

"This little pulse at the back of my head. I wasn't sure what it was, but then your face gave it away." Kai releases me and steps back, then grips his hair and starts to tug on the strands. "What's wrong?" Kai swings his gaze back to me, so much sadness, regret, and guilt emanating off him.

"I am so sorry, Raya." What the actual fuc—"When this is

over, you need to go back to Farrarie and stay as far away from me as you can."

"Why?" The look on Kai's face is starting to scare the shit out of me.

"Even without your magic, you are able to repel my gifts. You are so beyond special. I left for a reason twenty years ago, and now I finally know what that reason is." I'm so fucking confused; I have no idea what the hell he is on about.

"She's the reason, isn't she?" Both of our gazes snap to my cousin, who is standing in the doorway with a look of understanding in his eyes. Kai nods his head.

"That day in the cells when Mya fainted and you were looking at her strangely, in Uncle Jax's office. It wasn't because you found her attractive, was it?" Kai shakes his head no. "She had a vision, didn't she?"

"Yes," Kai whispers. What the hell am I missing?

"Did you know it was her?" Lucian asks, gesturing to me.

"No, I had no idea until now."

"Can you both tell me what is going on, please?" Lucian and Kai exchange a look before turning to me. I can see it in their eyes—they're both about to lie to me. I raise my hand to stop them both from speaking.

"You know what? Forget it. I don't want to hear either of you lie to me." I push past my cousin and ignore him calling out to me as I make my way back to my room and slam the door closed behind me. This time I lock it.

CHAPTER 14

Malakai

I didn't sleep a wink. I couldn't. No matter how hard I tried I just couldn't get my mind to shut off—not to mention every time I closed my eyes, all I could see was Raya's face. I decide not to go for a run this morning, in case I bumped into Raya. I know she is confused and pissed off, but how do I explain something to her I don't even quite understand myself? The fact that Lucian cottoned on to what was happening last night worries me slightly. I need to get this shit with the brothers over with so I can go to Mya. I need to know if what she saw was really Raya. If it is Raya, then what the hell am I going to do? I can never go through with it—I can't. I would never hurt her like that, no matter how much I hate myself. Because of what I am, I could never do that to her. Twenty years I have been away, all because of what Mya told me, and now that her vision may have come true, I can't go through with it. I used that fight between me, Dom, and Nico as the reason I left Wonder Lake, but that isn't true. I'll be honest, I wanted to get away from there because it was hard to see Nico and Ryan together, but it was also hard to be the king of the race I hated most. I never fucking wanted to be this!

"Why are you up at the ass crack of dawn?" I lift my gaze from the breakfast bar to look at Lucian. At least he looks rested and ready for the day.

"Don't sleep often," is the only reply I give, and he doesn't push for more. He flicks the coffee pot on and whistles as he starts to grab shit from the fridge. I scrunch my face up at the ingredients he has pulled out. Curiosity wins out, so I ask.

"What are you making?" The smug bastard looks at me with a knowing smile and a glint in his eyes.

"I'm so glad you asked. I am going to make spinach and ham omelets for breakfast."

"I'll pass."

"Don't trust my cooking skills?" he teases. I wish that were the case.

"Human food does nothing for me." His face drops, and I know he didn't mean to offend me, so when he begins to apologize, I wave him off. We settle into comfortable silence as I watch Lucian cook breakfast. Since the pair of them have moved in, my house feels like a...home, for the first time. There is finally life in this place, and it's all thanks to them being here. I never realized how isolated I made myself until Raya showed up.

Speak of the devil—Raya comes waltzing into the kitchen wearing the same baggy shirt and nothing on beneath it. She rubs her eyes and avoids looking at me altogether as she greets Lucian and makes her way over to the coffee pot to get herself a cup. She is fucking lucky Lucian is related to her, or I would throw her ass over my shoulder and march her back to her room. She may not be mine, but that doesn't mean she needs to prance the fuck around wearing nothing!

"Have a seat, breakfast is nearly ready." She pauses, lifting her coffee to full lips and quirks a brow at Lucian.

"You cooked?" Lucian bristles and mumbles about her being

an ungrateful little shit. "I'm just shocked, you never cook." Lucian puts his hands on his hips and turns to face Raya. He looks like a father about to scold his child.

"I will have you know I cooked for your mother many times, and she never once complained!" Raya chuckles as she makes her way around the breakfast bar to take a seat next to me.

"Mom was only trying not to hurt your feelings." Lucian scoffs as he turns back to flip the omelet in the pan.

I sit there in silence as they both eat and make small talk. It's not awkward, even though I know Raya has purposely positioned her body away from me. I'm enjoying hearing their banter. It's quite refreshing.

Raya stands and carries her plate to the sink. Cam rounds the corner into the kitchen and pauses, his eyes glued to Raya's bare bottom half. I stand and move so I'm blocking his view of her and growl low in my throat. He quickly snaps his gaze back to me, and I can see a slight blush start to coat his cheeks.

"What?" I snap.

"We need to leave soon, boss, if you wanna stop by the club on your way to meet the brothers." Before I can answer him, the little she-devil brushes past me and stands between Cam and me. I can see the struggle on Cam's face; he is trying so hard to keep his eyes on hers and not let his gaze travel down her body. She moves forward until there is a minimal amount of space left between her and Cam. I growl low in my throat again, and Raya ignores my warning but I see Cam swallow.

"Since we have to leave soon, do you wanna help me pick out my outfit?" Cam loses the battle—his eyes drop to her bare legs, and I snap. I reach out and pull her until she spins toward me then I twist us so my back is to Cam and lift her over my shoulder. She squeals out her surprise, and Lucian averts his eyes so he doesn't get an eyeful of his cousin's ass. I march us to her room with Lucian's laughter following us. She keeps punching my back and slapping my ass.

"Put me down now, Melakai!" That's it. I place a swift slap on her ass. She yelps and her wriggling stops immediately.

"D-did you just spank me?" As I enter her room, I kick her door shut behind us and stand there with her still over my shoulder.

"You're lucky that was all you got after that little display back there," I grit out.

"Jealous, are we, your majesty?" I slap her ass again, and this time she doesn't squeal she...moans.

"Do it again and you just might make me come." Holy fuck, my cock starts to stir at the thought of her coming. I quickly place her on her feet, and once she is steady, I move back and glare down at her. She has a broad grin plastered across her face.

"Don't do that shit with my men!" She moves to stand in front of me and runs her hands down my chest. I am powerless to stop her. When she looks up at me and bats her lashes, I know she is about to deliver a blow that is gonna piss me off.

"What shit? Are you saying I can't fuck Cam?" My restraint snaps, and I grip her throat and use my vamp speed to move us across the room so her back is against the wall. She doesn't even look scared or intimidated. She looks...gleeful.

"This position seems to be becoming our thing."

I growl. "Cut it out, Raya."

"Or what, Melakai?" I crouch down so we are eye to eye. She needs to see how fucking serious I am.

"Cut the shit. You fuck with any of my men like that again, and you won't like what happens to them. Keep pushing me, little devil, and you won't like the beast you awaken, I promise you that." I feel her shiver in my hold, not from fear but from arousal. Fuck, this woman is making it impossible to stay away when her hunger and defiance is calling to the beast inside me.

"Oh Kai, you have no idea the challenge you have just set. It is now going to be my mission to push you until you snap!"

Fuck!

Once we are ready, we all leave to head to Salut. I need to organize my men before meeting the brothers, in case something goes wrong. Raya and Lucian are pissed that we didn't wait for the others to show up, but they can get fucked. Nico doesn't get to just walk into my life and start calling the shots; he's in my territory now, and around here I'm the fucking king, and I call the shots!

After sorting the guys and leaving Cam in charge while I'm gone, I exit my club and climb into my waiting Audi. Lucian and Raya are sitting there, scowling out the window. I know they're pissed, but having their parents there with us will only make matters worse. Ignoring them, I put the car in drive and peel out of the club parking lot. We're twenty minutes into the drive before Raya breaks the silence.

"Where are we going?"

"We're meeting near the canyon."

"Why?"

"Because that is neutral territory. The canyon is the line neither of us cross. They have one side and I have the other; it is how things have always been." She doesn't respond right away. I look out the corner of my eye to see her face twisted in confusion.

"How do you know so much about them if you don't know them, like you say you do?"

"I have heard rumors about them, as I am sure they have

heard rumors about me. They have never caused me any trouble, so I never bothered to reach out before now." The rest of the ride we spend in silence. Soon we pull into the gravel parking area at the canyon. The view here is beautiful, like you are standing on top of the world. No sooner have I put the car in park than both Lucian and Raya jump out, and I follow suit. They're both looking around and spinning in circles, taking it all in.

"This is—"

"Amazingly beautiful," Lucian says as he cuts Raya off.

"Yeah, this view is stunning." I nod my head, but it's not the view I'm looking at. Raya's gaze meets mine, and I'm glad I'm wearing sunglasses so she can't see the look in my eyes. Looking at her is the best view I have ever seen in my life.

"Melakai Cane, we finally meet."

Holy shit!

The three of us stand here looking at the three of them. These guys are not what I expected at all, they look so…young. I expected some old, haggard looking brothers. Don't get me wrong—these three are giving off don't-fuck-with-us vibes, but my God, they are hot!

"You have me at a disadvantage, I don't know any of your names," Kai says. I have never heard him talk with such authority before, and I will admit it's a fucking turn on! The brother in the middle smiles wickedly. He has perfect straight teeth, high cheekbones, piercing blue eyes, and stubble coats his jaw. His black hair looks like a tousled mess but it suits him— this guy is the epitome of a bad boy. The three of them aren't as tall as Kai, but they are built like pro wrestlers; they are filling their plain shirts and jeans puuurfectly. I follow Lucian's lead and round the car so we are standing on either side of Kai. The brother on the left zeros in on me. They all have black hair but at different lengths—the middle brother's hair is long all over, the brother on the right has his just long enough to slick back, while the brother on the left has his short and spiked up on top.

All of them have blue eyes, but each of them hold a different intensity. These brothers are fucking beautiful; I bet their mom is proud.

"I'm Bronx, and this is Boston." He gestures to his left and then to his right. "And this is Memphis."

"It's a pleasure to meet you all, officially," Kai says with a slight tip of his head.

"Why are you looking for us, Melakai?" asks Memphis, the brother on the right.

"We need your help," Kai says in a stern voice. The brothers exchange a look between them and turn back to us, all their gazes on me. The intensity in their eyes has me fidgeting and shuffling from foot to foot.

"You arc the ones that broke into our vault," Boston says in a knowing voice. No point in denying it, so I nod my head. Bronx cocks a perfectly sculpted brow at me.

"Why?" he asks.

Lucian pipes up. "Because—" Bronx snaps his gaze to Lucian and narrows his eyes. Luce stops talking.

"I was asking the girl." Oh no, he didn't.

"The girl has a name," I blurt out before I can stop myself. Boston smirks at me and asks.

"And what is your name?"

"Raya."

"We have heard of you," Boston says to my utter surprise.

"You have?" The three of them nod their heads.

"Raya Stone, princess and only heir to the throne of Farrarie. You are the daughter of Nico and Ryan Stone. Your mother is rumored to be the most powerful supernatural ever." Bronx turns his gaze to Lucian and then continues. "Lucian Silver, heir to the New York pack. You are the shield to Raya's mother and helped her win the battle against her sister and the previous vampire king."

Bronx then looks to Kai and says, "Melakai Cane, first fae to become a vampire, you are the king to the vampires but live away from your homeland in Alaska. I prefer you to the previous king." My mouth hangs open as I stare at the three of them. How did they know so much about all of us? Kai looks dumbfounded as well.

"You knew Randall?" All three of the brothers' faces change to anger, and Kai moves slightly so he is closer to me. Memphis doesn't miss Kai's subtle move.

"We will not harm you; Randall is not someone we care for." Memphis and Boston seem to be calming down, but Bronx still seems pissed. Lucian chooses now, of all fucking times, to be himself.

"So your parents named you all after cities?" I mentally facepalm myself; my cousin is so much like his dad, and he needs a freaking filter and an off switch.

"No, we go by these names now."

"Oooookay. Any reason why?"

"You talk too much." Wanting to break the tension between Lucian and Boston, I step forward, and all three sets of eyes land on me.

"We came here today to ask for our magic back and to ask for your help." The brothers exchange a look before turning back to me.

"Why should we do that?" Bronx asks.

"Because it's the right thing to do."

"Was breaking into our vault the right thing to do?" I drop my gaze in shame. They're right. It was wrong to do what we did, but we didn't think they would just hand it over.

"They had a noble reason to do it. I do not condone their methods, but at the end of the day, what is done is done." I would thank Kai later for saving my ass and not letting me look like a darn fool.

"Why did you both do it? I know for a fact your wolf is still with you," Bronx says.

"Yeah, well, you did give him a run for his money when the three of you chased his ass all over the place." All three brothers smile cockily.

"You have a great wolf; if I had known you were a shifter as well, I would have changed the spell on the vault to remove your wolf as well as your magic." Lucian recoils at their insinuation and growls loudly. The brothers don't seem fazed that Lucian's wolf is so close to the surface. I, on the other hand, am worried that Luce will lose control and his wolf will break free.

"Will you help us or not?" I snap. I'm over standing here trying to beg.

"You have spirit, young Raya, it is refreshing."

"Dude, you look like you're the same age as her," Lucian says to Memphis. The brothers chuckle while we stand there, confused as fuck.

"Oh young wolf, do not let our youthful appearance fool you," Boston says in such a wise, old-man way.

"Why do you need our potion?" asks Bronx. I inhale a long breath and run my gaze over each of the brothers before I answer.

"We need the potion for my mom."

"Why?" I snap my gaze to Bronx and narrow my eyes. I don't fucking like his tone.

"Because, we just do!"

"Not good enough." The three brothers turn to leave, so I blurt the truth out.

"My mom is dying because she is paying the price for nullifying the moonstones that stopped Randall and his army twenty years ago. We need the potion to save my mom...please." I can feel tears gathering in my eyes, I refuse to let them fall. I won't let these three see me break down. I won't let them leave here today without giving it to me. All three of the brothers wear looks of indifference, which just pisses me off. Have they no heart?

"If we give you the potion—"

"And our magic," Lucian cuts in, and Bronx looks at him and narrows his eyes to slits. Lucian mimics zipping his lips and throwing away the key. Dear God that boy's mouth is going to get us in some shit one day.

"If we give you the potion and your magic back... What do we get?" I look either side of me and see both Lucian and Kai with unreadable expressions on their faces. What the fuck could they possibly want?

"What is it that you want?" Kai asks the brothers.

"Randall Cane. We know he is alive, and we want him," Bronx grits out.

"No!" Lucian and Kai say in unison.

"Fine, we'll take the girl instead," Memphis hisses, and Kai grips my arm and yanks me back until he is in front of me.

"Touch her and I'll kill you where you stand." Venom is dripping from Kai's voice, and Lucian is crouched in his fighting stance, growls ripping out of him. He is on the verge of shifting, and I have no magic to help, only my hand-to-hand combat training.

"Enough!" All six of us look toward where we drove in and find my parents, Dom's parents, and Uncle Jax and Aunt Aurora exiting a portal. "You will not lay a single finger on my daughter!" my dad booms out. I hate to say it, but I am so glad my dad and family have come to the rescue, because I doubt we would have won this battle on our own.

The three brothers smile broadly, and each of them mumbles something under their breath then in unison they begin to lift off the ground and rise into the air. Bronx is covered in red mist, Boston is surrounded by green, and Memphis—what the fuck? Memphis is covered by black mist; it looks more like smoke.

I have never seen anyone with different colored magic except for mom, Luce, Aunt Soph and Uncle Dom. Well, Aunt Soph only has different color magic because she can siphon Uncle Dom's magic, but that is her story to tell. Mom rushes forward and then releases her magic to lift her into the air, blue mist surrounding her.

"Little one, no!" my dad shouts. My mom shouldn't be using her magic. Recently, whenever she uses her magic, it takes a toll on her and wipes her out for a few hours. The three brothers glide forward toward my mother, and Mom meets them halfway. The rest of them stand there and stare up at them.

"Well, I believe we are in the presence of greatness." Boston sounds like he is in awe of my mom.

"My name is Ryan Knox-Stone, and I am the queen of Farrarie. You will not harm my daughter, Luce, or Kai. They made a mistake, and I am sorry for their intrusion into your vault, but I assure my daughter and Lucian meant you no harm or ill will—"

"We know that, Mrs. Stone. What we don't appreciate is you all coming here, and your husband throwing around his weight. He may be a king but he does not rule here!" I look at my dad and see his face is a mask of rage. My dad may have a bit of a big–okay, huge—ego. Dad stands there, glaring up at Memphis.

"Then don't threaten my daughter!" All three of the brothers stare down at my dad like he is a nuisance.

"No threat was made. Why are you here? This meeting is only meant for us and the three of them." Bronx speaks with authority; clearly he is the leader out of the brothers.

"Because, contrary to what Melakai thinks, I won't just trust him with the safety of my daughter." Boston cocks his head to the side and stares at my dad. His face is contorted in confusion.

"You have no idea the lengths he will go to, so no harm will come to her."

"And you do?" My head snaps back to Boston.

"Actually, yeah I do." What the hell am I missing here?

CHAPTER 16
Malakai

How does he know?

I only just figured it out myself.

"Mom, please come down, you made your point." I can hear the worry in Raya's voice, and it's then that I notice the strain on Ryan's face. There is more that these guys are not telling me. Ryan swivels her gaze back to the brothers and then reluctantly pulls her magic back inside herself. When she lands next to Nico, she stumbles a couple steps, and Nico catches her before she can fall. Raya, Lucian, and the others rush over to check on her. I remain rooted to the spot and stare at them like a stranger—me leaving was supposed to make it better.

My attention is drawn to the three brothers as they bring their magic inside themselves and land a few feet away from me. They make their way toward me and stand on either side, the four of us stand there staring at the others fussing over Ryan.

"Give us Randall, and we will heal her and her daughter." My gaze swings to my right, and Memphis refuses to meet my stare.

"Why the hell would Raya need to be healed?" We're speaking low enough that the others won't be able to hear, and

Memphis finally meets my gaze with a knowing look in his blue eyes.

"We know her blood is what can set you free." There are very few times in my life where I am caught off guard. Right here, right now, Memphis has stunned me. "Don't look so shocked, Melakai."

"How the hell could you know that when I only just figured it out?" Memphis smirks, his blue eyes glittering with mirth. I turn to my other side when Bronx speaks.

"We are all knowing, and that is all that will be said on the matter. It is your choice, king—you can save the queen and get the girl, or you can watch the queen die and then eventually your beast will break the cage and the girl will die." I suck in a sharp lungful of air.

"Why do you want Randall?" The three brothers share a look before Bronx answers my question.

"It is not of your concern—"

"I will not hand him over for you to set that fucker free. He has taken something from all of us and deserves the misery he is living in now." Anger and rage war inside Bronx's eyes; his shoulders are tense, and his hands clench into fists at his sides.

"The misery he lives in is not enough! He will suffer for what he has taken from us. Do not deny us this, Melakai. We have the power and the means to just take him from you, do not force our hand!" Now it's my turn to stand straighter and allow them to see the power and anger in my eyes.

"You try it, and I will personally make sure the three of you fail." I can hear the threatening tone of my own voice. I move forward a step and turn to face the three of them, who are wearing matching devilish smirks. What the fuck is going on here?

"Your reputation precedes you, Melakai; we'll be in touch soon." With that said, Memphis releases his magic and black smoke surrounds the three of them. Within the blink of an eye, they vanish! I stare around the parking lot for any sign of them, but there is nothing. How the fuck did they do that? They didn't even open a portal or chant a spell, they just...disappeared.

I drove back to Salut while the others portaled. I was glad to have some time to myself. The whole drive to the club I kept running over possibilities. How do they know so much? How could three brothers, who we have never heard of before, be powerful enough to make a potion to reverse a curse? Why is their magic different colors? How have they stayed hidden for so long? So many questions were swirling inside my head as I make my way inside Salut. The club isn't open yet, so it's quiet and empty except for the staff and my guests. They're all seated around the bar with Raya serving each of them a drink. I ignore the fact that I know those bastards won't be paying for said drinks. I need some more time to myself, so I opt to just head to my office.

Once inside my office, I shuck out of my suit jacket and neatly lay it over the back of my chair before sitting down. I stretch my legs out in front of me and lean back in my chair, clasping both my hands together in front of me. I let my mind wander and replay the events of today. Who are the brothers, really? Why do I feel like they are hiding shit? I'm pulled out of my thoughts by a small knock on the door. I look up to see Raya standing in the open doorway. She looks so young; she even dresses like a teenager. Chucks, jeans, a tank top and a thick flannel shirt over the top. She doesn't wait for me to invite her in; she strolls over to my desk and comes around to my side. She holds her hand out to me and offers me a cold bottle of Corona with a lime wedge. I thank her and grab the bottle as she jumps up and sits on my desk. Silence descends. It's not uncomfortable. It's quite soothing being lost in your thoughts but not being alone doing it.

"What happened today, Zilla?" She sounds timid and unsure, like she thinks I will bite her head off for asking such a question. I lift my gaze to her beautiful face, and her full lips tip up in a shy smile and her beautiful green eyes hold so much uncertainty. She has her mother's eyes.

"I was caught off guard by the brothers' knowledge. That won't happen again. I have Cam and Eric both looking into the Masters and where the hell they came from. I underestimated them today." Raya's smile widens, and she tries to hide it by sucking her bottom lip between her teeth. Thoughts of me biting that lip and drawing blood from her.... Fuck no, that can never happen.

"I'll help."

"Why?"

"Because they have a cure that can save my mom. I want to help, and I mean if it helps you out as well, two birds, one stone, and all that." I can't help the smile that breaks across my face, and her eyes drop to my mouth as if they have a mind of their own. My train of thought flees, and the tension in the room skyrockets. As if we are powerless to our own baser needs, we both lean in toward each other. The closer we get, the more her scent overwhelms my senses. When we're a breath apart, she releases a slow exhale. I feel her breath on my lips and want nothing more than to claim those lips as my own. She reaches out and snags my tie, and I allow her to pull me the remainder of the way. When our lips touch...fireworks explode. Before the kiss can go any further, a throat clearing has us pulling apart and me on my feet within a second, Raya placed firmly behind my back. I look to the doorway and see a smirking Dom and Lucian standing there with knowing looks on their faces.

Fuck!

"Thank your lucky stars it was me here and not Nico." Laughter is evident in Dom's voice; I know he is enjoying the predicament that I'm in.

"If Raya wants to save her boyfriend's ass she will be doing my chores." Lucian turns and high fives his father while I stand there and glare at the little shit. Raya moves out from behind me. She moves toward her uncle and cousin with the poise of a gazelle.

She stops in front of Lucian and then says, "Ohhhhhh you didn't just go there?" Lucian pales slightly. "You tell my dad anything, and I tell Aunt Soph you left the twins with Mya, Chase, and Alex so you could bang her enemy's daughter." Dominic chokes on his own laughter and turns shocked eyes to his son.

"You banged Kristy-Lee's daughter?" Dom exclaims. Lucian narrows his eyes at Raya before turning to his father.

"I did it for the team! So then mom can have one up on her mom?" It sounded more like a bloody question; Lucian was grasping at straws. Dom turns to face Raya and smiles sweetly.

"Now, my favorite niece—"

"I'm your only niece!" Raya interjects.

"Well, Jax does have a daughter as well." Raya must have given him a look because Dom quickly backpedals and says, "But you're my favorite, always have been. Let's not let my idiot son's secret get out, eh? Aunt Soph doesn't need to know. For your silence, I promise Nico will never hear a single word about what we didn't see here." I smile and shake my head. Dom is such a fucking con-artist. Raya brushes past the two of them without so much as a glance back at me. Lucian and Dom enter my office and close the door behind them, and I drop back into my chair as the two of them take the seats in front. I don't have to wait long for one of them to speak; Dom has always hated silence and loves the sound of his own voice.

"So, you and my niece, eh?" I refuse to be baited into this inane conversation.

"Was there something you needed, Dom?" Dom, the asshole, just grins at me, and Lucian does the bloody same. It's scary how much these two are alike; sometimes they act more like brothers rather than father and son.

"Well, aren't you grouchy today. Who pissed in your Wheaties?" I ignore his jab and just scowl at him; replying to him would only fuel his stupid behaviour. "So I can't just come to visit my brother?" Now I'm pissed. I scoff and grip the handles on my chair, trying to quiet the rage inside of me.

"You wait twenty fucking years and come here with that bullshit line?" The laughter vanishes from Dom's eyes and is replaced by rage. He sits forward in his chair and rests his arms on his thighs, a low growl rising from him. Lucian tenses in the seat next to his father.

"Whose fucking fault is that, huh? You left us, Melakai! I searched for you for years!"

"Not fucking hard enough, though, eh?" Dom is on his feet in the next second. I do the same, and so does Lucian.

"Fuck you Kai! You left without a fucking word; you never even left a goddamn note. I found you five years later, and I wanted to approach you but then I saw the life you made for yourself and you seemed...happy. I didn't want to ruin that."

"My life has been ruined for fucking years, Dominic! This isn't the fucking life I wanted, I just wanted to—"

"To what, Kai, what did you want?" I'm too wound up to stop myself from spewing my feelings out.

""I wanted to be me! I wanted a family, a home." I can hear the heartbreak in my own voice. I have never spoken truer words in my life. Dom's face is a mask of remorse and guilt— not guilt for himself, but for me. I never had a choice in becoming a vampire, thanks to Ryan's grandmother, who thought she was saving my life. I became this! I drop into my seat and clasp my head between my hands. How has my life become this? How did I let things spiral so far out of control?

"Vampire or fae, you are still one of the best men I have ever known. I didn't know you for shit when Smurf and I came to Alaska, but once you learned who I was, you protected me. I know you hate what you are and hate how you have to drink the blood of others, but that doesn't make you a bad person." I drop my hands and raise my head slowly to meet Lucian's gaze; I can hear the truth in his words. His eyes show me that he meant every word he just said.

"He's right, you know." I turn to Dom. "You have always been the best and most noble out of the four of us. I have always looked up to you, Kai—no matter how far you travel or how often you run, you will always be my brother." Dom's words fill me with a sense of pride and belonging. I haven't had a feeling like this in so long. I make my way over to them and embrace both Dom and Lucian and thank them for their words and understanding.

CHAPTER 17

After leaving Kai's office, I made my way back down to the bar to meet my parents, Aunt Soph, Uncle Jax, and Aunt Aurora. Mom's concerned eyes search my face for an inkling of what's wrong with me, but I avert my gaze and continue to make my way behind the bar. I can feel my dad's gaze burning holes into the back of my head, so I do the only thing I can think of. I make myself a couple of quick fucks— can't go wrong with a bit of Baileys, Kahlua, and Midori. As I set the shot glasses on the bar, everyone goes quiet. I continue to go about my business and make my shots with all eyes on me. Once I'm done, I lift one of them to my lips and down it. It doesn't burn like the hard liquor my dad drinks. I reach for the second, only for my dad to snatch it away and drink it himself. I narrow my eyes at him as he glares back at me. He slams the shot glass on the bar and leans forward.

"Explain now, Raya. Don't leave a single detail out." My dad has his don't-bullshit-me mask on, and I look to my mom for help, but at this moment apparently looking at her nails is more interesting. Sighing, I return my gaze to my dad.

"What do you want to know?" Dad throws his arms in the air and splutters for a bit before getting himself under control.

"How about the bloody truth? I also want to know why the fuck I caught you kissing Melakai! Do you know how old he is?" I scoff.

"Look at the bloody age difference between you and mom!" I snap, and Aunt Soph and Uncle Jax snicker from their seats at the other end of the bar but stop abruptly when Dad pins them with a look. I look to Mom for help, and this time she is looking right at me, so I give her the look to help me out. She sighs then turns to my dad and places her hand on his forearm.

"Calm down, big guy, she is nineteen, not ten. You can't stop her from growing up, Nico. She needs to make mistakes and you can't make those for her." Dad looks at Mom like she has lost her mind.

"You're joking, right? There is no fucking way I am letting her make a mistake with him! She's been gone a few weeks and now look—she is bartending at a shady fucking club and doing shots during the fucking day, love. How is that okay?" Mom turns to me and the look on her face says she is starting to agree with dad. I need to do damage control now—none of this is Kai's fault.

"Melakai has nothing to do with this. Lucian and I fucked up, Kai was nice enough to help us out and offer us protection."

"You could have called us, Raya. We would have come for you." Anger rushes through me—is my dad that dense?

"And go where, dad? I can't go home without my magic, I wanted to fix this mess myself and show you once and for all I can do things on my own. I love you, but sometimes your love is so suffocating." Hurt shines so brightly in his eyes that I cover my mouth with my hand. I wasn't supposed to say that last part out loud.

"Dad...." He raises his hand and I clamp my mouth shut. Tears shine in my mother's eyes. I went way too far. I didn't mean to hurt him; I love him so much, but he can be so overbearing at times. I know he means well, but I want to be young and have fun, not train everyday and learn how to run a realm. I have never been to a club, aside from Kai's. I used to love to dance as a kid, but then dad said no to dancing lessons because it was too provocative. The only way I could take lessons was to get Lucian to sneak me to classes when I stayed with my aunt and uncle. Aunt Soph and Uncle Dom have always allowed their kids to be free and choose their own paths; I have never had that luxury.

"I didn't realize you felt that way." The tone of my father's voice has tears filling my eyes. "I am sorry for smothering you and loving you like I do." Tears fall freely down my cheeks.

"Dad, I'm sorry I didn't mean it—" His eyes meet mine, and the look in his violet eyes guts me. I just broke his heart and hurt him so badly. Guilt is eating at me.

"You did mean it, Raya, it just took you being angry enough to finally admit how you really feel. It seems Melakai has got his claws into you already—"

"I have done nothing!" I turn to see Kai standing at the end of the bar near my parents. His eyes have a storm of emotions rolling through them as he looks at his long lost friend. Dad turns slowly in his chair and faces Kai.

"You never do! You just have to be around, and your presence alone corrupts those around you!"

"That's enough, Nico! He has done nothing but protect both our kids! Show him a little fucking gratitude, you prick."

"Fuck up, Dominic! If it wasn't for your son's stupid-ass idea, my daughter would still be at home safe and out of harm's way." Holy fuck, Dad is taking this way too far now. Everyone begins to argue and shout insults at each other; my aunts and mom are trying to wrangle their men back under control. Lucian is pushing our fathers apart so they don't throw hands. I need to stop this now before someone gets hurt, so I yell the first thing I can think of at the top of my lungs.

"I tried to have sex with Kai, and he rejected me!" All the arguing stops, gasps ring out, and I hear my Uncle Dom mutter "oh, shit." My mom and dad pin me with a look that has me taking a step back, and I try my hardest to smile to lighten the blow that I know is coming, but I fail miserably. My dad is vibrating with rage, his power leaking out around him. Fuck, I am in so much shit—of all the freaking things I could have said, I had to blurt that out. As if my eyes have a mind of their own, they search for Kai, who is standing between Uncle Dom and Lucian. His gaze is firmly locked on me; his mouth is slightly open in shock. I mouth a silent sorry before turning back to my parents.

"Come again?" Oh shit, Dad has his quiet voice on. Nothing good ever comes of him using his quiet voice. I gulp loudly and then swing my gaze to my mom for help, but she's standing there staring at me like a stunned mullet. Sweet baby Jesus, if Mom doesn't get him under control I fear he may actually skin me alive.

"Nico, she is a grown—"

"So help me, Sophia, stay out of this." I turn to my aunt and nod my head, thanking her for trying to save me from Dad's wrath. "Explain now!" I flinch as his voice booms throughout the empty club. I clasp my hands in front of me and twiddle my thumbs as I try to think of a way to save my own ass.

"She lied." My gaze snaps to Kai's—and so does everyone else's. "I was the one who came onto her, and she rejected me." What the fuck? He is so full of shit, why is he lying to save me? I don't get to ponder that question for long, because Dad strikes out and clocks Kai straight across his jaw. I scream and rush out from behind the bar. Uncle Dom, Lucian, and Uncle Jax wrestle Dad off of Kai, and I drop to my knees beside him to inspect the damage. He has a large red mark on his cheek and jaw, his lip is split, and he has blood trickling down his chin. I clasp his face between my hands and turn his head toward me so I can check for any more damage.

"Get the fuck away from him now, Raya!" I spin around so fast I slip from my knees and land on my ass, looking up at my uncles and cousin holding my dad back. Dad has never spoken to me like that before, and quite frankly I'm a little fucking scared of him right now. "Get your shit, you're coming with us back to Wonder Lake. Don't argue with me, Raya— do as you're told."

Tears flow down my cheeks, who the fuck is this man? This isn't my father; my dad is kind, caring, loving, and funny. My dad would never speak to me like this. He would never treat me like this. I feel someone grip my hand and look down to see Kai has placed his hand on top of mine on the floor. I lift my eyes to his, and he has a sad smile on his face, but it's the look in his eyes that has my tears drying.

"Stay." That one word from his lips holds so much meaning —all the sound around us becomes white noise as I stare into his eyes. The spell is broken when a hand wraps around my arm and yanks me to my feet. I turn to see this angry man in front of me Kai is on his feet and glaring at my father. The look on Kai's face is scary as fuck.

"You don't get a say in this; she is my daughter, Melakai. You tried to take my wife from me and sure as fuck will not take my only child from me. She is pure and you are fucking tainted!" I gasp and wrestle out of his hold; once I'm free I shuffle over to Kai.

"How dare you!" I hiss.

"You have no fucking idea who he is, Raya!" Dad is so blinded by his rage that he can't see he is hurting not only Kai but me too. I love him so much, but right now he is out of line.

"I don't need to know his past, Dad! Kai has been nothing but kind to me since I got here."

"Because all he wants is to get in your fucking pa—" Kai cuts Dad off before he can finish his horrible sentence. I stumble back and would have probably fallen on my ass again if Kai didn't grip my arm to steady me.

"You finish that sentence, and you will do more damage to your bond with your daughter than I ever could. I have never tried to hurt you, Nico. I have always tried to protect you and be there for you." He isn't listening to a word Kai is saying; his gaze is on me. His eyes are as round as dinner plates. I guess he shocked himself with what came out of his mouth. I can't believe he would say something so mean and hurtful to me! Mom tries to move toward me, and I shift slightly so I'm partially standing behind Kai. Mom stops and stares at me with so much regret in her eyes.

"He didn't mean it, baby, he's just—" I can't listen to her defend him right now, so I cut her off.

"I don't want to hear it mom. Like dad just said, it took him being angry enough to say how he really feels." I turn to my father, who looks devastated. We have never fought like this before.

"Ray....I....please—" I raise my hand to stop him from speaking. A lump the size of Jupiter is forming in my throat, and the last thing I want to do is stand here and cry in front of everyone.

"We'll call you when the brothers make contact. I think it might be best if you all go now." Dad's shoulder sag in defeat, and the guys release their grip on him. Mom keeps opening and shutting her mouth; she clearly can't find the right words to say to me right now.

"If you don't hear from them by Monday, we will return. It was good to see you, brother." Uncle Jax turns his gaze to me, and his brown eyes soften. "Take care of yourself, cookie, and if you need anything, you know you can call us." I nod my head and give him a sad smile. Uncle Dom turns and opens a portal in the middle of the club. I hope none of Kai's human staff are around.

"Sweetheart, please." I turn to my mom and shake my head. The tears are threatening to fall. I need them to leave now, so I can break down without them around. I can't even look at my dad as the others head toward the portal. When Lucian calls my name, I suck in a deep breath and meet his gaze. He smiles timidly, and I can see the pity in his eyes.

"I'll be back tomorrow night, cousin." I nod my head and smile. Luce is only leaving today so Kai and I can have a chance to talk. I know I'm being selfish in not trying harder to get our magic back, but in truth I'm not sure if I want it back.

"I'm so sorry, Ray." The sound of my father's voice and the hurt I can hear in it causes a whimper to escape me. I hear his footsteps as he tries to approach, but right now I don't want him near me, so I hide behind Kai. I can see from the gap between Kai's legs that he is standing directly in front of him. I feel terrible for the position I have put Kai in, but I can't change that now.

"Just give her time," Kai whispers. I hear a long sigh come from my dad and then he turns and leaves. Just as I think they have all left and it's safe to come out, my dad's voice has me pausing.

"Despite what I think of you Melakai, I know you will protect her. Don't fucking make me regret leaving my world with you." Kai grunts and nods his head but doesn't speak.

"Baby girl, I love you more than life itself, you know that. We'll be back Monday." I don't reply. A few seconds pass before Kai speaks.

"They're gone, little vixen." The dam breaks and sobs wrack my body.

CHAPTER 18

Malakai

I spin around and wrap my arms around her small, shaking body. I don't want the staff to arrive and see her like this, so I pick her up, bride style, and she wraps her arms around my neck and sobs into my chest. I walk us out of the club and nod my head to David. He looks at Raya in my arms and understanding dawns in his eyes. He will run shit tonight for me in the club. I have to pry her arms from around my neck to place Raya in the passenger seat of my car. I fasten her seatbelt then quickly round the car and jump behind the wheel.

We travel in silence, and once we get back to my house, I round the hood and open her door. She makes no move to get out, so I unfasten her seatbelt and carry her inside. I stop in the entryway. I can turn left and take her to her room, or I can turn right and take her to my room. Indecision is warring inside me when a small whimper escapes her that makes the decision for me. I turn right. Once we are inside my room, I kick the door shut behind us and make my way over to the bed. I sit on the edge of the bed with her still in my arms. I have never done something like this before, so I have no idea what the hell I am supposed to do. Do I try to talk to her, or do I just sit here and hold her? If Dom were here, he would know something funny to say to make her laugh. Fuck, even Jackson would know something wise to say that would stop her from crying.

"I...I'm s-sorry for causing y-you so much p-problems." My heart constricts in my chest; she is more worried about me rather than what the fuck just happened between her and her father. This girl is slowly worming herself inside of me, and I don't know if I am okay with that.

"Don't worry about me, little vixen. I'm more worried about you."

"I-I can't believe he said that to me. My dad has never spoken to me like that." Anger courses through me. How Nico can be such a prick to his own daughter I will never know. I know he hates me after everything that transpired between me and Ryan, but that doesn't give him the right to take it out on Raya. She has done nothing wrong except walk into my club and capture my attention.

"He didn't mean it. He isn't angry with you, love. He let his anger for me bleed over to you, and that isn't okay." She pulls away from me so she can look into my eyes.

"Why are you defending him, Kai?" She needs to know the truth. I thought it would be better to come from her mother, but not knowing the truth is causing a rift between her and her parents, and I don't want to be the cause of that.

"Because I am not innocent in this either, vixen; I did some things I am not proud of. Things I knew were wrong, but I was selfish and did it anyway."

"You're not making any sense."

"Are you sure you don't want to hear this from your mother or your father?" She bites her bottom lip and stares at me but not really focusing. She is weighing up her odds; I hope she chooses to hear this from her mom or dad. I don't want to see the look in her beautiful eyes when I tell her the truth. However, luck isn't on my side today, and when her gaze focuses on me, I know the answer before she says it.

"I want you to tell me."

Sighing and needing to buy myself some time I say, "I'll tell you everything, but first I need to get out of this suit, and I'll call Cam to bring you some takeout." She smiles widely, and I pull back in shock.

"You truly know the way to my heart."

"Huh?" She rolls her eyes and playfully bats me on the chest.

"Relax, Zilla, I was talking about the food." Right, food.

Once I have showered and changed, I come into the living room and see Raya has done the same. Cam sits opposite her on the other couch. I don't like the way he looks at her. At least the fucker brought her the takeout she wanted. I head to the kitchen and grab two blood bags from the fridge and quickly down them. I open the trash and hide them under the other junk in there. I know Raya says she doesn't care about me being a vampire, but I care—I hate that I have to drink the blood of others. Her laughter pulls me from my thoughts, and I make my way back to the living room and pause when I see Cam sitting on the coffee table in front of her. Both of them are laughing at something, and it annoys me that I have no idea what the fuck it is. Raya's laughter stops when she sees me, and my worries flee when she smiles brightly at me and pats the seat next to her. I don't hesitate; I move toward them and drop down into the seat. Cam looks from me to her and gets the hint to fuck off.

"I'll catch you later, Raya."

"Yeah, thanks for the food, Cameron." Cam flinches at the use of his full name.

"I knew it was a bad idea telling you my name." Raya just smiles up at him as he turns and walks out of the house. It pisses me off that she smiles at him like that. I want her to only smile at me that way. Wait, what the fuck? Where the hell did that thought come from?

"So you gonna spill the beans now, Zilla?" I roll my eyes and count to three; that fucking nickname is doing my head in. I turn toward her and rest my arm on the back of the couch.

"What's it gonna take for you to stop calling me that?" She smiles wickedly at me and pops a French fry into her mouth.

"For you to fuck me." I choke on fucking air! My eyes are so wide they're starting to water, and she breaks out into fits of laughter at my reaction. Little shit.

"Ha ha," I say dryly. Once she has herself under control and traces of humor vanish from her face, I know my time is up. "What do you want to know Raya?"

"Everything." I release a long breath then jump straight in.

"I have certain gifts, as you know. I control emotions and can persuade people to do things. I also have the gift of dream walking." She cocks her head to the side, confused.

"I think my dad can do that too?" I nod my head.

"Yes, he can. I don't want to go through all of the sordid details so I'm just gonna get to the point okay?" She nods her head, so I continue. "I was tasked with keeping your great grandmother safe, and shit hit the fan and some vamps beat the shit out of me. Your great-grandmother begged Randall—"

"Wait, Randall Cane?"

I nod my head. "Your great grandmother fled Farrarie to marry Randall; she was in love with him." Her mouth drops open in shock. "Anyway, she begged him to save my life, but the only way he could do that was to turn me. I am the first ever fae to be turned into a vampire. I am the original day walker." Raya's eyes are so wide I fear her eyeballs might pop out. "Anyway, years passed and things soured between Randall and your grandmother, I tried to keep her safe but failed. She was locked in a cell and terrible things happened to her. Men raped her."

"What the fuck? Why?" I place my hand on her thigh to calm her down.

"Randall started to get greedy for power, and your great-grandmother didn't like it; she rebelled against him hurting people. So he locked her up, she was placed in a spelled cage so no one could break her out."

"Why didn't you make Randall set her free?"

"Because when Randall turned me, he made me enter a blood oath. I could never rise against him." Understanding dawns in her eyes. "Your great-grandmother fell in love with one of the men who visited her cell. I didn't know they had formed a relationship. I killed him and every other man that hurt her. I just didn't know that she fell pregnant to him. Long story short, I vowed to protect her child."

"Why didn't she portal out if she was a fae?"

"Because Randall made sure she was weak and didn't have enough power to break out of the cell or even heal herself." Disgust is evident in her features. "She had enough magic left inside her when she gave birth to transport her daughter to safety before Randall could kill her. She placed a spell on her baby: anyone who was seeking to harm her could never find her. I found her because I never wanted to harm her. I watched her grow and then marry, then have a set of twins."

"My mom and my aunt?"

"Yes, I watched how your mom was treated, and one night guilt ate at me so I entered your mother's dreams. I knew it was wrong, and I won't lie—I was supposed to kill your mother." Raya gasps and reels back in shock. I push on before she ceases listening. "I knew your mother had the power to kill my world, and I was going to do it until I got to know her. Your mother doesn't have a single bad bone in her body. I lied and told him I killed her—"

"Told who?" Her voice has taken on a hard edge, and I sigh before answering.

"Your father."

"What the fuck?"

"Please let me explain before you go off." She nods her head reluctantly. "Years passed, and your mother and I formed a... bond." Raya shudders. "Your mother had no idea I was real. Your dad figured out that she was alive and started to visit her as well. Your dad was doomed the moment he saw her; I tried to save your mother from this life. I was selfish and wanted her to run away so she wouldn't be in danger, but instead she went to Alaska and found out what she really is and then she met your father." I know I am leaving so many details out, but I don't want to relive those moments. If she wants a play by play of everything, she will need to ask her parents. That is their story to tell their daughter. We sit there in silence for a while; she is lost in her thoughts and I don't want to disturb her.

"So, you and my mom?" I avoid her gaze as I answer.

"Only in her dreams, never in real life." A relieved sigh escapes her, which has me furrowing my brow.

"There has to be more to it. What aren't you telling me Kai?" I smile, she is so much smarter than I gave her credit for.

"I thought I fell in love with your mother, Raya, and my love for her broke the friendship your father and I once shared. What I didn't know at the time was that I was in love with the idea of loving someone. Your mother is an amazing woman, and I do love her still, but not in the way your father thinks. I tried to mend the bridges between your father and me, but I don't think we will ever be what we once were. Your father is also pissed as hell at me, because I knew your aunt was being held by Randall and I couldn't say anything."

"Why?"

"Because I was forced into another blood oath; it was the only way I could protect her. I also knew she was pregnant and couldn't say anything. Your aunt went through hell and I couldn't say a fucking word about it." I hear the anger in my own voice.

"How can you tell me about it now then?" This is where the story takes a turn.

"When your mother came here, I tried to play both sides and feed your mom and dad information from Randall. What I didn't know is Randall knew what I was trying to do, and when I went back, he and your Aunt Stevie tortured me. Before they could really kill me, I finally found a way to set Soph free. While they were distracted, I got her to cast a spell that would make my heart slow so they would think I was dead. I knew Randall would want to gloat and would send me back to your dad, so I made sure to make your mother's blood the key to the spell that would revive me. In order for the spell to work, I had to die first." She gasps and brings her hand up to cover her mouth. "I had to do it so the blood oaths would be broken." Raya reaches out and cups my face in her hands. I sat there, stunned. I expected her to be angry and throw shit or yell but not this.

CHAPTER 19

Sitting here and looking into Kai's eyes, I see so much pain. This man has gone through so much shit in his life, and the fact that he is still standing is a testament to how fucking strong he is. It makes so much sense to me now—Kai hates being a vampire because this was never his choice. I know there is shit he is leaving out for my parents' benefit, but I don't need to know anymore. I still think it's weird and a bit gross that he and my mom…you know…but thank God it wasn't in real life and only in her dreams.

"You are the bravest man I have ever met." Kai's eyes double in size; I just shocked the shit out of Godzilla. Kai begins to shake his head from side to side, and I reach up and cup his other cheek so I can hold his face still between both my hands. I wait till he looks me in the eye before continuing.

"What you did and continue to do for my parents, my aunts, and uncles is so selfless. You didn't need to stick around once Mom brought you back but you did, even though my dad was no doubt an ass to you." Kai chuckles at my attempt to lighten the mood. He reaches up and pulls my hands from his face, but he doesn't release them. His thumbs stroke the top of my hands.

"I appreciate what you said, I really do, but I'm not a good guy, Raya."

"How can you sit here and say that?" Kai drops my hands and rises to his feet; he moves around the coffee table and begins to pace the living room. I recline back into the couch and watch. I have a feeling this is more about how he feels about himself rather than what I feel about him. I sit here and wait for him to sort his thoughts out. I know when he gets his mind clear he will say what he needs to. I have learned that Kai isn't a man of many words and doesn't like small talk. Kai will only speak if he has something to say. Kai runs his hand through his blond hair repeatedly, and he looks like a fucking snack in plain, dark wash jeans and a simple white tee. His clothing may be basic, but I tell ya what...nothing about this man is fucking ordinary.

"I can't be your ever-after, Raya—I'm not that guy. I don't know how to be that guy." My heart hurts for him. How the hell could he think he isn't worthy of love? I stand and approach him like I would approach a wounded animal, afraid I might spook him. He stands there towering over me, suffering evident on his face. I stop when I'm standing a couple steps away from him and crane my neck back so I can look into those beautiful gray-blue eyes.

"Then don't worry about tomorrow. Give me today with you and then we can take every day after that as it comes." I see the moment my words register, and he begins to shake his head. My hope and bravado begin to dwindle.

"Your father will lose his shit, Raya. You don't want to be with someone like me. There are plenty of guys out there your own age who would die to be where I am right now." Hell no, I am not backing down without a fight.

"So it wouldn't bother you if I texted Cam and took him up on his offer to take me out tonight?" I am so full of shit, but he doesn't need to know that. I don't even have Cam's number, I just need to push Kai enough so he will give in and admit he wants this just as much as I do. Before I can even comprehend what the hell is happening, I'm hoisted into the air, my arms and legs automatically wrapping around Kai.

We move like a flash of light—one second we're in the lounge and then the next we're standing in Kai's room. I pull back enough so I can look him in the eye, and I raise my brow in question. He doesn't use words; he walks us slowly toward the bed, placing me ever so gently on my feet at the foot of his bed and cupping my face between his hands.

"Tell me to stop and I will. This doesn't have to go any further, Raya. I'll let you go and never come after you again." I don't hesitate.

"I want this...I want you." That's all it takes. Kai lowers his mouth toward mine and claims my lips in a searing kiss that has me seeing stars. My God, if this is what his kiss can do to me, I cannot wait to see what sex is like with this amazing man. When he darts his tongue out I open for him, and when his tongue enters my mouth and I get a taste of him, I moan. Kai picks me up and I wrap myself around him again without breaking the kiss. He kneels on the bed with me still in his arms and shuffles us toward the head of the bed. He gently lays me down until I rest my head on the pillows, then he breaks our kiss and leans back. Seeing this man between my legs has liquid pooling at my center, anticipation of what's to come sending butterflies into flight inside me. His heated gaze travels the length of my body, and the look in his eyes tells me he is mentally undressing me. He runs his hands from my calves all the way to my face and gently caresses me. I stare up at him in awe. I have no idea what is running through his mind, and I would give anything to be able to read his thoughts right now. He uses his thumb to trace my lips, and my tongue has a mind of its own and darts out to lick his digit. His eyes blaze with desire.

He continues to stare at me, and minutes pass as we stare into the depths of each other's eyes. I feel like he can see past the mask I wear and see into my soul. Can he see the real me? Kai's eyes have the ability to render me speechless. When he allows you to see past his mask, his eyes tell you everything. Like right now I can tell there is a war going on inside his head; his body is coiled tight and his muscles are bunched. He wants me, but something or someone is holding him back. I don't want him to get lost in his own head any longer, so I take charge of the situation.

I reach up and wrap my arms around his neck and yank him down so I can capture his sinful mouth in a kiss that will have all his blood rushing south. I brush my tongue against his, and he releases a small moan, which spurs me on. I lift my legs and wrap them around his waist and use the move that Cyrus taught me in my self-defense training: I flip us so Kai is now on his back and I'm on top. I never break the kiss as I begin to let my hands trace his face and body. I want my hands to remember the feeling of him in case one day my eyes forget.

I know deep down inside of me this thing between us will never last, not because of me, but because of Kai. He thinks he is so unlovable and damaged beyond repair. I don't know what this thing is between us, but all I do know is I want him and I want him to own me—mind, body and soul.

Kai runs his hands down my sides and grips the bottom of my shirt, peeling it slowly up my body. I break our kiss when I sit up straight and finish taking the shirt off for him. He sits forward and wraps his arms around my bare waist, peppering kisses between my breasts. My nipples are rock hard and brushing against my bra. He darts his tongue out and licks a trail from the center of my breasts to the top. He sucks the soft flesh in his mouth, which pulls a loud moan from me. He does the same to the other side and then he runs his hands up my back, pausing when he reaches the clasp of my bra.

He pulls back and looks up at me with lust-filled eyes.

"Last chance. I take this off, we're not stopping." There isn't a moment of hesitation on my part.

"Take it off already." Kai's mouth tilts up into a sexy as fuck smirk, and his fingers make quick work of undoing my bra. He leans back slightly and moves his hands to the straps and pulls the garment away from my body and chucks it over the side of the bed. Kai's eyes are glued to my chest. I'm not a self-conscious kind of girl, but the fact that he isn't blinking and keeps swallowing repeatedly has me worried. I reach between us and grip the bottom of his shirt and lift. He doesn't protest, just lifts his arms in the air and allows me to pull his shirt off. Once I throw it over my head, I snap my gaze back to him and stare at the artwork that covers his glorious body. Ink runs from his collarbone all the way down to his waist. I can clearly see his abs though the ink, and the sight of them has my mouth watering. I reach out and run my hands all over his body. My touch seems to jolt him from his stupor, because one minute I'm sitting on top of his hard cock and the next second I'm flat on my back with Kai between my legs. He doesn't give me a chance to recover; his mouth is on mine in seconds. I run my hands up and down his naked torso, scraping my nails as I go. Kai breaks our kiss and begins to move down my body, kissing, licking and sucking my flesh into his mouth as he goes.

By the time he reaches my jeans, I am a panting, writhing mess. His gaze locks onto mine as he pops the button of my jeans open and pulls the zipper down. I lift my ass up slightly so he can pull my jeans and panties off, and a moment later I lay here bare and exposed to this dominant alpha male. I feel intimidated by his raw sex appeal and the fact that this man is a fucking orgasm on legs, but the way he looks at me now though has my worries slowly dying. His eyes rake over me as he makes his way back up my body, and when he reaches my lips, he captures them in a gravity-defying kiss and grinds his cock against my bare pussy. I moan into his mouth. I want Kai's dick inside me now, I fear if he doesn't fuck me soon I'm going to explode. My body is on fucking fire from all of his teasing, and my pussy is throbbing and I can feel myself dripping. I'm sure when Kai pulls back, the evidence of my arousal will be all over the front of his jeans.

He continues to kiss me and just grind against me, and I'm starting to get fucking sexually frustrated. I need something now! I break our kiss and glare up at him, but the bastard just smirks!

"This funny to you?" I snap, and his smirk turns into a full blown smile. That smile knocks the wind out of me—seeing Kai smile like this is like looking at an angel. Melakai Cane is beautiful. He shifts his weight and moves so one of his legs is between mine and the other on the outside. I feel cold without his body to blanket me. I turn my head to the side to stare at him and ask what the hell is happening.

"As much as I want inside you right now, vixen, you deserve more than some quick fuck." I soften at his words, all traces of my earlier irritation are gone. I reach over and cup his cheek and place a soft kiss on his lips, but before I can pull back, he quickly deepens the kiss and begins to trail one of his large hands down my body. When he reaches the top of my pussy, he uses one finger to slide between my slick folds. I moan into his mouth, and his skilled hand continues to my opening. When he feels how wet I am, he groans. He swirls his finger around my opening then trails it back up to my clit and begins to rub my enlarged nub. I cry out, breaking our kiss. Kai doesn't miss a beat —he leans across me and captures my nipple in his mouth and begins to suck as he rubs my clit. Fuck, this feels so good!

He stops rubbing my clit and releases my nipple with a pop. I don't have a chance to protest before he moves between my legs and buries his face in my pussy. I scream as soon as his tongue flicks my clit. He trails his tongue up and down my wet cunt, and I can't stop the moans from tearing out of me.

"Fuck, you taste so fucking good," he mumbles out. He uses one of his hands to part my folds so he has better access to my clit and reaches up with the other to tweak my nipple. The sensations of him toying with nipple and lapping at my clit has my body tensing. When he releases my folds and inserts a single finger inside me, everything changes. My body begins to overheat as he eats my pussy and finger fucks it at the same time.

"Oh my God, that feels so fucking good." Kai picks up the pace and begins to pump his finger inside me faster. He sucks my clit into his mouth and then I'm exploding. I slam my eyes shut and scream his name to the heavens above, and he stops tweaking my nipple and slows his movements. Shudders wrack my body as I come down from the most intense orgasm I have ever had in my life. Once I'm calmed, feeling absolutely boneless, Kai hops off the end of the bed. I tilt my head forward so I can see what he is doing and fuck me seven ways to Sunday—watching Kai undo his jeans and shimmy out of them has my mouth watering and my pussy clenching. He stands at the end of the bed in nothing but his gray boxer briefs, and I can see his large cock straining against the material. Holy shit, if it looks that big inside his boxers that means it's going to be bigger outside of them.

"Spread your legs, vixen." I reluctantly pull my eyes from his bulging cock to meet his stare and find his gaze is laser-focused on my closed legs. I take a deep breath and give myself a quick mental pep talk before doing as he asked and spreading my legs wide for him. As soon as my legs are open and my dripping cunt is on display, Kai releases a low growl of approval, which gives me the confidence to do what I'm about to do.

I lift both hands and begin to play with my nipples, letting a low moan escape me. Kai's eyes lock onto mine, his eyes burning with unbridled heat. I continue to fondle one of my nipples while I trail my other hand down my body and stop when I reach my pussy. Kai's eyes follow my every move as I run my hand over my pussy, teasing not only him, but myself. I run one finger through my slick folds and sigh at the feeling; my clit is so fucking sensitive from just orgasming. I part my folds and use my pointer finger to rub my clit. This is the hottest fucking thing I have ever done.

"Drop your boxers, Zilla." Kai's eyes snap to mine and blaze with lust. He does as I asked and holy fuck, the sight of his cock has me ceasing all movement and gulping loudly. All my bravado flies out the window at the size and width of that fucking thing! It's like a baby arm is attached to his fucking body! Kai must sense something is wrong.

"Why do you look so terrified?" I dart my gaze back to him and find worry lines creasing his forehead. I take a few calming breaths to gather myself, but that doesn't help because the words come tumbling out of my mouth before I can stop them.

"There is no fucking way that thing can fit inside of me!" Kai throws his head back and laughs—I mean a full-on belly laugh. I lean forward on my elbows and stare at him. I have never heard a more beautiful sound in my life. Hearing Kai laugh is gonna become an addiction, I just know it. Once he gathers himself and stops laughing, he looks back at me and bites his bottom lip. It's so fucking hot watching him nibble on his lip, not even gonna lie.

"Relax vixen, I'll fit." I start to shake my head, but the retort

I had dies in my throat when Kai plants a knee on the bed and begins to crawl up my body. I drop back onto the pillows and stare up at him. I could spend my days getting lost in the depths of his eyes. If I'm not careful, losing my days looking into his eyes might not be the only thing I lose to this man.

CHAPTER 20
Malakai

I can see the fear in her eyes as I look down at her, and I want to wipe the look from her face. So I lean down and capture her lips in a kiss. Kissing her is becoming an addiction really fucking fast, and I'm worried having sex with her will turn me into an addict. She is like a siren calling me to her every day. I can't explain this pull I feel toward her. She has no idea the power she already holds over me; we barely know each other and yet here we are in bed together, because we can't fight the attraction we feel for each other any longer. I pull back and look her in the eyes; I need to see the truth in them before this goes any further.

"Do you trust me?" Her brows furrow as she thinks for a moment before answering.

"In a sense, yes." That's all I need. I lean down and kiss her again and reach down to grip my aching cock and line it up with her opening. As soon as the tip of my cock touches her opening, I break the kiss and look her in the eyes. I don't hesitate — I slam inside of her, and holy fuck, she is so fucking tight. She screams out, but not in pleasure... but in pain? I look down at her and see she has her eyes slammed shut and both her lips are captured between her teeth. Worry begins to settle inside me—what the fuck happened?

"Did I hurt you?" I grit out. It is so fucking hard to be inside her and not move. Her pussy is gripping me like a fucking glove, and by God does it feel fucking amazing. She shakes her head but won't open her eyes, and then it hits me, she is really fucking tight. Oh fuck did I just—

"Raya, open your eyes," I demand, and her eyes snap open and meet mine. I see it in her gaze—what the fuck?

"I'm okay," she whispers, and I stare at her, stunned.

"Are you a...were you a....virgin?" She turns her head to the side to avoid my gaze, but I reach up and grip her chin and turn her head back to me so I can see her eyes. "Answer me."

"Well, not anymore," she sasses back, and I move to pull out of her but she locks her legs around my waist and holds me in place. Her face is a mask of determination now. I glare down at her.

"You should have told me!" I hiss.

"It changes nothing."

"I won't take your virginity, Raya."

She shrugs her shoulders and says, "Well too late, since your cock is the one that broke my hymen." She has the nerve to smile at me! Before I can say anything, she wraps her arms around my neck and yanks me down to her. She uses the monkey grip she has on me to her advantage and starts to rock. Holy fuck! The feeling of her tight little pussy sliding against my cock feels fucking amazing. Fuck it.

I reach up and peel her arms away from around my neck and grip both her tiny wrists in one of my hands and pin them above her head. She opens her mouth to protest but I shut her up when I pull back and slam back inside her. She cries out in pleasure this time, and I repeat the movement and she fights against the hold I have on her hands. I release my hold and lean down to capture her nipple in my mouth, and she moans loud as fuck. I switch nipples and continue to pound in and out of her wet fucking cunt. God, her pussy is gripping me like a fucking dream.

"Kai, please! I want you to fuck me hard!" she shouts. Your wish is my command, vixen. I wrap my arms around her and lean back on my haunches, and she wraps her legs around me and I slam her down onto my cock. She throws her head back and screams. "Holy fuck, you're so deep."

I grip her hips and lift her then slam her down again. Her full tits are bouncing in my face, and she takes over and wraps her arms around my neck and begins to bounce up and down on my cock, and I grip the back of her long hair and pull–hard. Her pupils dilate and she moans low in her throat. Oh, so she likes it rough. I pull her face to mine but instead of kissing her, I go for her neck. I suck the soft flesh into my mouth. I want to leave my mark on her. She doesn't complain, she continues to moan and bounce on my cock. I release her neck and pull on her hair until she looks me in the eyes, I feel her pussy clench, and I know she is close. I maneuver us so she is flat on her back again, then pick up the pace and slam into her so fucking hard I think I might split her in two.

"Holy fuck, oh sweet Jesus." Her pussy starts to quiver, and I slam into her twice more and then she explodes around me, screaming my name like it's a prayer. I don't let up, continuing to pound into her over and over again. Right when I'm about to come, I sit up and pull out of her. I grip my cock in my hand and pump. Her glassy eyes watch my movements; at the sight of me jerking off, she licks her lips.

"Fuck, I'm gonna cum," I grit out, and like the little vixen she is, she drops back down against the pillows and spreads her legs wider so I can get a better view of her pussy.

"Cum on me, Kai!" Her words push me over the edge, and I

come with a roar and watch as my cum spurts out, coating her stomach and tits. I sit here transfixed at the sight in front of me: Raya Stone, covered in my cum, is a fucking sight to see. I rake my gaze over her—her cheeks are flushed, eyes glassy. My gaze pauses on the hickey I left on her neck, and a small smirk graces my lips. She snorts out a laugh. She knows exactly what I am smiling about. My gaze travels lower over her breasts, and I pause to admire those as well. I may have left a few marks there, too. What can I say? I'm a selfish bastard. When my gaze rakes over the ropes of cum strewn over her body, heat begins to fill me. I feel my cock twitch, and I want to fuck her again, but when my eyes land on her pussy, the twitching stops.

"Fuck." I begin to shuffle back down the bed when her concerned eyes meet my gaze.

"D-did I do something wrong?" Guilt fills me. Fuck, she thinks she...fuck. I lean forward and grip her ankles then pull, and she squeals in surprise. I lift her up, and she locks her legs around me and her arms around my neck. I walk us toward my bathroom, and once inside, I place her naked ass on the vanity bench and turn around to start the shower. I come back to her, only to find her gaze is downcast. Shit, I need to talk to her. I wrestle my way between her legs and lift her head until her eyes lift to meet mine. So much defiance shines in her green eyes. Oh baby, I'm gonna enjoy fucking the defiance out of you.

"You did nothing wrong." Surprise enters her features.

"Then why did you say fuck?" I scrub a hand down my face before answering.

"Because you're bleeding, it was your first time, and I wasn't exactly gentle." I feel like a piece of shit for fucking her the way I did, but truth be told, I lost control. This woman has the ability to do that to me. Her snort of laughter pulls me from my thoughts. I look at her in question but she doesn't answer—she just shoves me until I move back and she climbs off the counter.

She reaches up and pats me on the chest but quickly pulls her hand back, meets my gaze and licks her palm. What the fuck?

"You taste good." She turns and heads toward the shower as I stare at her naked ass in shock. Then it hits me.

"Did you just lick my cum?"

"Yep, I rubbed up against your chest when you carried me in here." Oh fuck me, my cock is hard as rock. I have never had this type of reaction to a woman before. I can't believe she just licked my cum. Most woman hate the idea of swallowing cum, and yet this vixen just licked it off her palm like it was fucking candy!

"You gonna join me?" she calls out from inside the shower. How can I say no?

Our shower took forty-five minutes, thanks to Raya. She said she had never given anyone a blow job before and wanted to try it, and I was too shocked to stop her as she dropped to her knees and sucked my cock into her mouth. Holy fuck! She says she has never done it before, but by God, the girl has fucking unparalleled skills when it comes to sucking dick.

The thought of her sucking me off has my dick hardening, and I shift on the couch so my dick doesn't poke her in the side of the head. After our shower, she said she wanted to forget about the brothers and everything and cuddle and watch movies. I have never cuddled a day in my life, so this is all new to me. She currently has her head resting on my lap while she lies on the couch, and I'm sitting here, stiff as fuck, not sure what I am supposed to do. I couldn't even tell what movie we were watching. My attention has been on her the whole fucking time. How does she have me wrapped around her finger after only a few weeks?

"I can feel you burning holes into my head." There's laughter in her voice. She sits up and turns to face me, and her brows furrow in worry. She slides closer to me and then swings one of her legs over me so she can straddle my lap. My hands automatically go to her waist and hold her, and I stare up at her in confusion. She reaches out and traces the worry lines on my face until I stop frowning.

"That's better, now why don't you tell me what's wrong?" I open and close my mouth a few times; I don't know what to say. How do I tell her I know I will mess this up?

"Kai?"

"I'm not a good guy, Raya," I whisper, and her carefree expression vanishes and is replaced by annoyance.

"Seriously? You're gonna say that shit after what we just did?" Now it's my turn to glare up at her.

"I told you I would ruin shit—"

"Don't, Kai, don't fucking turn what we just did into something bad and dirty. We shared something special in that moment, and don't you dare fucking lie and say you didn't feel it either." I can hear the devastation in her voice. I never wanted to hurt her. It was never my intention, but how am I supposed to tell her I just figured out she is the reason why I had to leave twenty years ago? How am I supposed to tell her that in order to get the one thing I want most in life, it means she has to die?

"Boss!" I quickly push Raya off me and stand, I spin toward the hallway, ignoring Raya's mumblings about me being a dick. Cam comes into view a moment later, huffing and puffing worry immediately fills me—something happened.

"What's wrong?"

"The brothers are at the club." Fuck! I nod my head and tell Cam to meet me outside. I turn back to Raya, and she has a deadly look in her eyes. Fuck, she looks so much like her father right now with that frown and the look in her eyes. I quickly shake that thought away.

"I need to go. I'll be back soon—" She is on her feet and jabbing her finger into my chest in a split second.

"I am not staying here, buddy, I'm coming." I grab her hand to stop her from poking me, and she swings at me with her other hand and I catch it just in time before she actually hits me. I stare down at her in fucking shock.

"Have you lost your fucking mind?"

"Maybe, I did fuck an asshole today." Fuck, that hurt, but I also know I deserve it.

"Stop being a brat and wait here, Raya." An evil smirk graces her lips, but her arms go limp so I release my hold on them. She closes the space between us and runs her hands down my chest, stopping when she reaches the waistband of my sweats. She licks her lips. Fuck, thoughts of her on her knees with her head bobbing up and down on my cock fill my mind.

"Either you let me come..." She moves her hand until she is cupping my now hard cock, and I moan at the feeling of her touching my dick. "Or, I follow you anyway and never suck your cock again." I stumble back a few steps and glare at the little shit.

"You do not get to use sexual favors against me." I sound like an idiot, but I don't care right now.

"Why not? You get to use your morbid as fuck line against me."

"What morbid line?" I yell.

"I told you I'm not good." She sounds stupid because she is trying to imitate my voice. Not wanting to continue this ridiculous debate, I turn and head for my room so I can change and then get to the club and sort this shit out.

CHAPTER 21

Raya

As soon as Kai disappeared in his room, I scampered off to my room and quickly changed into a pair of high-waisted jean cutoffs that ride quite high and show off a bit of ass. I paired those with a low-cut crop top that has a slit down the back. To top the look off, I left my long hair down and used a minimal amount of makeup. The key to the outfit is my red, five-inch strappy heels. They make my legs look like they go on for days. When Kai came out of the house and saw me leaning against his car next to Cam, his eyes doubled in size when he saw my outfit. I made sure to keep my expression blank and act nonchalant. He marched over to me, gripped my upper arm, and pulled me around to the side of the car and shoved me into the back seat. The ride to the club was silent and filled with tension. I chose to avoid Kai's gaze every time I felt it on me in the rearview mirror. When we got to the club, I hopped out, only for Kai to grip my arm again and haul me in after him. He marched us over to the bar and sat me down on one of the seats. I glared up at the man-handling asshole, ready to give him a piece of my mind.

"Stay here, I'm not fucking with you."

"And if I don't?" Kai narrows his eyes, but it's the fear I see that has me worried slightly. What the hell could possibly scare him? Is he worried about what the brothers have to say? I reach out to him, but he moves back out of my reach. I won't lie—that hurt. I mask my true reaction and latch onto my earlier anger. "You're a real ass, you know that?"

"I'm trying to protect you!" Oh hell no, fuck that.

"By rejecting me? By fucking with my emotions? Or by being a prick?" Kai has his mask firmly in place, back to being the walled-off, cold asshole I first met a few weeks ago. How the fuck can he look at me like this after what we shared today? I gave something of myself I have never given another, and he treats me like this mere hours later?

Kai moves forward and places his arms either side of me, so I'm caged in with my back against the bar. I can feel the eyes of the staff around us on me but I ignore them. The club will be open soon and it will be packed with patrons. Kai moves his head down until his lips are against my ear.

"I told you from the start, Raya, that I will hurt you and that I am no good. I never lied to you, vixen. I am not your happily ever after, and you need to accept that." As soon as the words are out of his mouth, he pulls back and leaves me sitting there, staring at his retreating form, with tears in my eyes. What the hell have I gotten myself into? How could I be so dumb and allow a man my father warned me about to take my virginity? I am so fucking stupid. I thought I could be the person that could change his mind and show him that there is more to life than living alone. I blink away my tears. I refuse to let Kai's rejection bother me. We had sex, and it was fucking amazing, but that's it. I will listen to my father from now on. I just hope that the brothers are up there now and are willing to return my magic so I can get the fuck out of here and go home. I won't fight my dad anymore; I'll take my role as the heir to the throne more seriously. I will be more involved with all the political bullshit and train hard every day.

"You look like you ate a lemon." I spin around and lean my arms on the bar, a smile spread across my face when I see Cam standing behind the bar. Cam is fucking wicked, the dude has been nothing but sweet and kind since I got here. When Kai was giving me the cold shoulder and wouldn't show me the ropes of bartending, Cam stepped in and helped me. "You look like you could use a drink?" I blow out a breath and nod my head. I could use ten drinks right now.

Cam gets busy behind the bar making me a drink, while I sit here in silence and just watch. His black hair is in need of a cut; it keeps flopping forward onto his forehead and he is forever shaking it out of his beautiful hazel eyes. Whenever he is indoors, his eyes look brown but outside in the daylight you can tell they are green. Cam isn't all that tall, about five foot eleven, I would say. But he is built like a fucking wrestler; I don't need to see him naked to know the dude is cut. Cam finishes making my drink and then hands me a creamy white cocktail with a slice of pineapple and a tiny paper umbrella. Wait, is it a cocktail if it looks like a slushy?

"What is it?"

Cam looks at me with a warm smile and winks. "Don't knock it till you try it doll." I do as he says, and my word it tastes fucking amazing, it's that good I nearly moan.

"Cam, this is delicious! What is it?" Cam smiles proudly and even puffs his chest out.

"It's a piña colada."

"That sounds exotic."

I have no idea how much time has passed, but thanks to the two shots and endless supply of piña coladas, I am feeling myself! Cam has kept me company since Melakai left me here for his stupid meeting with the brothers. I know Cam runs Kai's security, but tonight he has been my own personal bartender, and I really appreciate it. He hasn't once asked me what happened between Kai and me or even brought Kai up once, which I am grateful for. I am woman enough to admit that I just want to go home and cry to my mom and let her hold me and tell me everything is going to be okay. After what happened this morning, I don't know if that is even a good idea. If she and Dad went back to Farrarie, I couldn't even go there, our realm won't allow anyone without magic to enter. It's my world's way of protecting itself from humans. Humans can't handle the truth that we exist; they hate what they can't control.

I thought I would be okay with the loss of my magic, because not having it meant I couldn't rule and wouldn't have so much pressure on me.

But without my magic I feel naked and vulnerable. I have my combat training, but without my magic I am weak. I need it back so I can leave here. I don't want to stay with Kai anymore. With my powers back, I wouldn't need Kai. I could go to the brothers myself and demand the potion for my mother's life. I may be angry as fuck at my parents, but that doesn't mean I would ever wish any harm to come to either of them. I pull my cell phone from my pocket and place my finger on the button to unlock it, and when my phone roars to life I tap on the message icon. I scroll through the messages and click on Aunt Soph's name. My aunt and I are really close. Aunt Soph and Uncle Dom are like second parents to me. Whenever Dad was being overbearing, I would open a portal to their house and stay with them. When dad showed up—and believe me he always found me—Uncle Dom would tell him to fuck off and give me some time. A couple times dad has tried to fight his way past but Aunt Soph would always get in the middle and reason with him, or if all else failed she would call my mom to come get him.

Lucian and I grew close over the years, but the closer we got, the further he and mom drifted. I know Lucian feels so guilty that my mom is paying the price and not him. Mom has tried to reason with him and tell him she is okay, but Luce can't seem to stand being around my mom for longer than he has to. Him pushing my mom away is hurting her, but he isn't doing it to be mean. He spends more time hunting down a cure than anything else; Lucian hasn't stopped trying to save her since he found out she was dying. Dad has been trying, too, but he can't be away from Mom for fear something might happen. What she doesn't know is that my dad is the one funding Lucian's expeditions and paying whatever the cost is for him to bribe people for information about a cure. That's how Luce found out about the vault. He was supposed to go alone, but I eavesdropped on the conversation. They had a shit plan laid out, so I knew I had to sneak out and go with Lucian to help him or risk him fucking this up and losing the cure forever.

Someone tapping on the bar pulls me from my thoughts, and I look up to find Cam staring at me with concern. I smile, trying to reassure him that I'm okay, but I must fail miserably because he says, "You look like you're about to break down." I huff out a breath and choose to be honest.

"I fucked up and lost my magic, lost the only cure for my mother, and oh hang on, I fucked my father's arch enemy."

Cam's eyes double in size, but what he does next shocks the fuck out of me. He throws his head and laughs. I glare at the bastard.

"Seriously?" I snap. Cam takes a few more moments to get himself under control then finally meets my angry glare.

He raises his hands as if surrendering and says, "Doll, anyone with eyes could see and feel the sexual tension between you and the boss." I jerk back in shock.

"What do you mean?" Cam looks side to side to make sure no one else can hear. The club is packed and the music is pumping, so unless you were sitting right beside me you wouldn't hear a word uttered between Cam and I. Well, unless you are a shifter, then you would hear us from across the room.

"Doll, the boss isn't known for being...reasonable. He rules with an iron fist and doesn't give second chances. The fact you broke one of his men's noses and lived to talk about it should say enough." Are we even talking about the same person?

"He can't be that bad," I try to reason. Cam gives me a dry look.

"The Melakai Cane you know is different from the one we know. Don't give up on him, doll; he is a good man at heart."

"Cam, we fucked once."

"So you're telling me it was just about sex and nothing more?" I'm starting to get pissed. Cam has no idea what the hell he is saying. I choose to take a few deep breaths and see how much info I can pull from Cam about his boss.

"Not for me it wasn't, but for him it was." Cam's gaze softens, and he reaches across the bar and places his hand on top of mine in a comforting gesture.

"Don't let him fool you, doll; he cares about you—a lot. If he didn't, there is no way in hell he would be upstairs right now trying to help."

"He is only helping because of who my parents are to him!"

Deep down inside I am latching onto the hope that Cam is right and Kai is really doing this for me.

"Nah, he could have made the right introductions and let your father take the lead, but he didn't. Whether you want to believe me or not, he is doing this for you." I drop my gaze to the bar. I can't let Cam's words trick me into thinking there is more to our relationship. He has told me himself he will never be my happily ever after.

"So do you want my help or not?" I snap my gaze back to Cam's and find him smiling wickedly.

"What did you have in mind?"

"Do you want to make him jealous?" Cam is starting to become my favorite person.

"Can you dance?"

My smile broadens. "Oh this is going to be fun, Cammy."

Malakai

Sitting behind my desk across from the brothers gives me a chance to examine them. They all have the same hair and eye color but their facial features are different, Boston looks like the kind one, Memphis has a dark aura about him, Bronx is definitely the hard ass and the leader of the three that goes without saying. We have been sitting for hours, trying to come to an agreement, but they won't budge. They are willing to return Raya and Lucian's magic, as well as give me the cure for Ryan. All they want in exchange is Randall, and they will not disclose their reasons why they want him. There is no way in hell Jax, Dom, Nico, or the girls will go for this. Ryan will be the first to say fuck no!

"There is one other option." I dart my gaze to Bronx. He has a devilish glint in his eyes which worries me slightly.

"And that option is?" I ask.

"You give us your cure." A growl rips out of me, and my body tenses. I start to feel my fangs lengthening. I will not fucking let them have her!

"I feel for you, bro." I turn and glare at Boston. I don't need his fucking pity.

"Have you told her?" Memphis asks. I take some deep calming breaths and wait till I feel my fangs retract before answering the brothers.

"No." I don't even know why I answered them, to be honest.

"We can fix it." My gaze adverts back to Bronx as I recline back in my seat so I have all three of them in my line of sight.

"How?"

"Before we go any further, stop fucking trying to manipulate my emotions. It won't work on us, so save your bloody strength." My mouth drops open in shock at Boston's words. How the fuck did they know? I have been trying to alter their emotions since they arrived and have had no luck. No one, aside from Raya, has ever been able to resist my compulsion.

"Don't look so shocked, you're not the first to try something and you won't be the last, I can assure you."

"How the fuck can you resist it?" I demand.

"That is not something we are willing to disclose, King." Bronx sounds like a smug prick. "If you give us Randall Cane, we will give you a cure to stop your thirst for the girl."

"Will she be safe from me?" I blurt out before I can stop myself. For the first time since the brothers and I sat down tonight, Bronx's mask slips—longing and loss shines bright in his eyes.

"She will never be truly safe from you. None of us will ever truly be free and safe, because we are all slaves to our demons. All we can offer you is something to quench the thirst that drives you to want to kill her every time she is near you." Before I can answer Bronx, Memphis butts in.

"Or you can drink her dry and finally get what you have always wanted. You would be fae again, and all it would cost you is some young girl's life. I mean, who knows if she is even really your cure." Just thinking about her has my eyes moving toward the security monitors, and what I see has my blood turning to fucking ice. I push back from the desk and stand, and the brothers do the same but look ready for battle. They think my sudden movement means I'm going to attack.

Instead I shock them by extending my hand, and they each shake it and stare at me with questions in their eyes. Memphis darts his gaze toward the huge tinted window in my office that looks out over the club and laughs. "I see what has caught your eye."

"I will be in touch within two days. Let me meet with the others and then I'll get back to you." Memphis is smirking while his brothers stand there stunned. I move to exit my office, and just as I open the door, Bronx's words stop me.

"If she means that much to you, to give up the one thing you want most in this world, then don't let her go. Fight for her, Melakai, because if you choose wrong you will regret it for the rest of eternity, and believe me, forever is a long fucking time." The sorrow in his voice has me looking over my shoulder. Instead of facing me he is looking out the window at the show on the dance floor. I grind my teeth together and march my ass downstairs to wrangle the fucking heir to the throne of Farrarie.

I race down the stairs and head toward the dance floor, but pause next to the bar. Watching her body move and sway to the beat of Chris Brown's "Under the Influence" has me spellbound. The way she drops to the ground and the crowd parts to give her more room to dance is a sight to see. She's like a snake charmer— she has everyone in this club transfixed on her and the way her body moves. She crouches low with her legs spread wide, she runs her hands down her body and stops when they land on her pussy. I dart my gaze away from her to see who she is looking at, and when I find the source of her focus I clench my fists at my side. She never breaks eye contact with Cam as she drops to all fours and then begins to lower the bottom half of her body to the floor so she can thrust her pelvis up and down, flicking her long hair side to side as she does. The way she keeps eye contact and bites her bottom lip has Cam transfixed. Fuck, even I'm standing here in the back of the club watching her every move. I see people in the crowd with their phones out videoing her.

She stops thrusting her hips and then twirls her legs in the air before she does a side split. She moves her arm behind herself to give her leverage and then begins to raise her ass up and down while still in a split. Someone brings a chair forward for Cam and pushes him down into it. Raya rolls sideways so she is on her back on the dance floor, her legs split wide open—thank God she's wearing shorts. She rolls again and begins to move along the ground sideways while thrusting her hips up and down toward him. My anger rises as she nears Cam; she's putting on quite the fucking show for him!

She drops into a split right in front of him and places her hands on his legs as she rises up. She grips the top of his head and pulls him forward so she can grind her pussy against his face for a second before pushing him back and then, straddling his lap, she gyrates against him, giving him the best fucking lap dance of his life!

Fuck this!

I make my way toward them to stop this shit. She's on the dance floor right between his fucking legs. Cam leans forward while she's still on the ground dancing for him, and their lips are a hair's breadth away from each other when I grab the back of Cam's neck and pull him backward till he flips out of the chair. Raya's shocked eyes look up at me as I stand there glaring down at her. I don't wait another second as I move and snatch her off the ground and throw her over my shoulder caveman style and march us both out the fucking club. She will pay for that fucking stunt when we get back to my house! As I near the exit with a raging Raya over my shoulder, I spot the brothers near the corner by the exit. All three of them have knowing smiles on their faces, which just fuels my fucking anger more.

I didn't speak to her the whole way home. As soon as we are inside the house, she storms to her room like the spoiled fucking princess she is. She doesn't get to put on a fucking show like that and then go to her room. I try to take a few deep calming breaths before I trail after her. I don't knock as I throw the door open, and she is standing in nothing but her bra and panties and glaring at me. I move toward her, and she doesn't shy away.

When I'm in front of her, I grip her throat and spin her around so her back is to my chest and she is facing the mirror. Her breaths are coming in short rapid pants, and her pupils are blown wide. She loves it when I manhandle her. I can smell the booze on her, as well, which only angers the beast inside me more. I use my free hand to run it down her arm and then back up to her shoulder, while I hold her gaze in the mirror as I explore her delectable body. I run my hand over her collarbone and then down between her breasts, and a small whimper escapes her as I slowly trail my hand down her body.

"Did you like putting on a show for Cam tonight?" She doesn't answer. "Did you like spreading your legs wide for that bastard?" A whimper escapes her again, and her eyes begin to droop closed as my hands nears her hips.

"Eyes on me, baby, I don't want you to miss my show!" Her eyes snap open and lock onto mine in the mirror, and my hand moves lower until its cupping her sex through her thin lace thong. I can feel her heat against my palm.

She moans at the contact, and I lean forward until my lips

are aligned with her ear and whisper, "This pussy is mine, Raya, and don't you ever fucking forget it." I release my hold on her and leave her room, her rage palpable. She will learn that her petty little games will do nothing but cause her suffering in the end. I will not allow her to use her body as a weapon against me, and as for Cam, he'll fucking get what's coming to him first thing in the morning.

I take a quick shower and yank on some sweats, still furious. I pace my room, angry as fuck at myself for letting her get to me enough to do what I just did. What the fuck is wrong with me? I carried her out of the club like I had some claim on her. Am I not the one who just told her earlier tonight that I couldn't be with her? Then I go and contradict myself by getting pissed at the show she put on for Cam. I tug on the strands of my hair in frustration.

I'm such a fuckup. If she was anyone else, I mean anyone, I would drink from her vein and end her life. I would be free of ever needing to drink the blood of others, and I could go home. I could be free of this godforsaken curse and live a life I could be proud of. I searched for years, trying to find a cure for vampirism, and found nothing. I didn't know twenty years ago that Mya's vision would bring me the cure—all I knew was that if I didn't leave, that the bond I shared between my brothers would be broken for good.

Being near Raya is fucking torture. Every time I am near her I can hear her heartbeat. I can hear the blood flowing through her veins, and all I want is to sink my fucking teeth into her neck. I have never craved anyone's blood as much as I crave her, and having sex with her today and sucking on her neck wasn't just to mark her—it was to see if I could control myself. I nearly lost it today and bit her.

Fucking her and being inside of her was one of the best moments of my life. It felt like I finally belonged, like I could be better than what I am. Then I go and ruin it, because I'm scared that I will hurt her. I know I can never be with her, and that fucking stings more than I ever thought it would. The one woman to stir anything inside of me since I first thought I loved her mother had to be the one person in this whole fucking world that I can't have.

The sound of voices outside of my room has me pausing. Who the fuck is here? I walk toward my bedroom door and throw it open, following the sounds of the voices to the living room. What the fuck are they doing here?

CHAPTER 23

Raya

I stand here staring at my closed bedroom door, wondering what the hell just happened. Kai just had my body thrumming with need then declared his ownership of me and left. He fucking left me standing here feeling so fucking cheap and used. I dash toward the wardrobe and yank on a pair of jeans and pull a plain white shirt over my head and grab my sweater. I feel so fucking dirty and embarrassed. Tears are building, and I don't try to stop them. I race around the room with tears rolling down my face and pack all my belongings into my two suitcases. I don't know where I'm going to go or what I'm going to do, but I can't stay here. Cam's plan worked—I got Kai's attention and got him to show that I meant more to him than some cheap fuck, but once we got home he switched back to being the cold heartless vampire king.

Once everything is packed, I sit on my bed and sob. I know there is only one person I can call who will come get me without any questions asked, so I grab my phone from the nightstand and call.

"Sweetheart, are you okay?"

"Aunt Soph, can you come get me please?" I choke out, and

I hear muffled sounds and then my uncle's voice comes over the speaker.

"Where are you, cupcake?"

"I'm in my room at Kai's house." Before I can say anything more, a portal opens near my bedroom door and my aunt, uncle, and Lucian walk through it. I drop my phone and jump off the bed and run to my aunt, who wraps her arms around me as I bury my head in the crook of her neck and cry. She rubs her hands up and down my back, trying to soothe me, but I can't talk. She holds me for so long that when I finally pull away to look at her, my eyes are stinging and I can feel how puffy they are. My uncle takes one look at me and begins to growl low in his throat.

"What happened?" he demands. Aunt Soph wraps her arm around my shoulders and pulls me into her side. I don't want to tell my uncle what happened, and Aunt Soph must sense this because she speaks for me.

"Dom, get her bags. Luce, grab her phone and whatever else she has left here, we'll meet you in the living room." Aunt Soph doesn't wait for their answer; she leads me out of the room and toward the living room. When we get there, she turns me till I'm facing her and cups my face between her hands. I can see so many questions swirling in her violet eyes, but Aunt Soph won't push me to talk.

"You will come with us back to the compound, but when we get there sweetheart I am going to have to tell your mom and dad that you're there." I don't want Aunt Soph to lie for me and get in trouble, so I just nod. She pulls me in for another hug and holds me until Uncle Dom and Luce arrive a minute later.

"We got everything, cupcake." I pull out of Aunt Soph's hug and smile weakly up at my uncle. He is livid, but his anger is not directed at me. Before either of us can say anything, the sound of a door slamming open has our attention snapping to the right to see a shirtless Kai standing in his open doorway. I thought today couldn't get any worse, but how wrong could I be?

"What the fuck is going on?" Kai turns his gaze to me but Lucian steps in front of me to block me from his view. I peer around Lucian to see Kai has his upper lip pulled back in a snarl and his eyes narrowed. He storms toward Lucian but is stopped when Uncle Dom steps in front of his son.

"You even try to take a swing at my son and I will fucking take you down!" Uncle Dom's tone has me quaking; he sounds scary as fuck.

"Why are you here, Dominic?" Kai snaps.

"Because my niece called my wife, crying her eyes out. I never expected the cause of her sadness would be you." Uncle Dom shouts the last part, and I flinch.

"What makes you think it was me?" Kai sounds like an arrogant ass now, which has the tears flowing faster down my face.

"Don't be a fucking prick, Kai, your scent is lingering on her! You're fucking lucky she called Soph and not Nico, because he would fucking kill you for what you have done to his little girl!" I drop my gaze to the floor, not wanting to hear Kai's reply. I can't take anymore today. A minute passes before Kai replies.

"Leave. I'll be in touch in two days to discuss the brothers' terms." A sob breaks free before I can stop it, and Aunt Soph curses under her breath before releasing me and turning around. She chants under her breath and a portal begins to appear.

She turns back toward me and Luce and says, "Take her back to her parents, son, your father and I will follow you both shortly." I don't protest when Lucian wraps his arm around my shoulders and leads me toward the portal.

"Stop!" Lucian and I both pause at the sound of Kai's voice. I don't have it in me to turn around and look at him—it hurts too much.

"Let her go, brother, you have done enough."

"Fuck you Dominic, stay out of this," Kai yells, and I hear a scuffle behind me but still don't turn.

"If you really care about her, Melakai, you will let her go. Do not force her to stay when she needs to leave; you know better than to force a woman to do anything." No one says a word as Aunt Soph's words start to sink in. I feel Lucian tense beside me and hear Uncle Dom growling.

"I'm sorry, vixen. I told you from the start I would only wind up hurting you." The grief in Kai's voice has me choking back another sob. I inhale a few breaths to force the lump in my throat down so I can speak.

"I believe you now." I break free of Lucian's hold and step through the portal with Kai's shouts following me through.

After I came through the portal, Lucian was two seconds behind me. He led me through Uncle Jax's compound to the room next to his. Mom used to tell me stories about how they would all spend more time here than at their own houses. She said Uncle Jax's compound became the team's headquarters. The room I am in has a queen bed, window seat, bathroom, wardrobe, fireplace, and that's it. Lucian started a fire for me before he left to go and retrieve my bags. He and Uncle Dom are able to communicate through their mind link. All wolves from the same pack can do that except Uncle Jax, who is the king of the shifters. He is able to communicate with all wolves, if they are in a close enough radius to him. I always found that so freaking cool but so weird. I would hate to have someone be able to read my thoughts all the time. Luce reckons that once you learn to block your mind, they can only access thoughts that you allow them to. After Luce left, I decided to hop into bed and close my eyes. They are so sore and sting from all the tears I have shed.

I am such a fool for thinking I could be the one to tame Melakai Cane. A knock at my door has me sitting up. I call out to come in, thinking it's Luce with my bags, but it's not. It's my mom and dad, and the sight of them both and the look of concern on their faces breaks the dam open again. Sobs wrack my body as my mom and dad rush toward me and engulf me in a bone-crushing hug. Mom whispers words of love, while Dad whispers threats of death to whoever hurt me. I don't have it in me to talk. I don't even think I can tell them the truth. Dad is going to be so mad at me.

"Baby, can you tell us what's wrong?" The worry in my mom's voice has my chest constricting. How do I tell her the truth without sounding like an idiot?

"I promise I won't get mad, baby girl." I can hear the truth in his voice. I move out of their hold and scoot to the top of the bed so my back rests against the headboard. My dad moves to sit at the end of the bed and tugs mom with him. He perches her on his lap, wraps his arms around her waist, and rests his chin on her shoulder. Seeing how much my parents love each other has a feeling of longing hitting me straight in the heart. I have always envied the love my aunt and uncles shared, but most of all, I envy my parents' love. My mom can't make a move without my dad noticing. Whenever Dad is out of control, Mom is the only one who can calm him. I want that type of love. I want the type of love that you can feel in your bones. I want to feel safe, cherished, and most of all, I want someone to look at me the way my dad looks at my mom.

"I did something so stupid." I can't even meet their gaze as I say that.

"What did you do, baby girl?" I can hear the strain in my

dad's voice. He is trying so hard not to nut out and demand an answer from me.

"I think I fell in love." I hear both my parents gasp, and I feel movement on the bed. My mom sits next to me, wraps her arm around my shoulders, and pulls me into her side. I wrap my arms around her and cry.

"Let it out, my girl. We're right here." Minutes pass as I cry, my mom holds me through it all. I never realized how much I needed my mom until this moment. Being in her arms makes me feel like everything will be okay. I can't lose her.

"Who, Raya?" I stiffen in my mom's embrace. Judging from the sigh that she lets loose, she already knows the answer.

"Who do you think, big guy?"

My Dad curses under his breath and then says, "Raya, baby, I need to hear it from you." I sniff and pull out of my mom's hold. I use the sleeves of my jumper to wipe my tired eyes and nose before meeting my dad's gaze.

I hold my chin high as I say, "Melakai."

Dad jumps off the bed and starts pacing, tugging at his hair as he goes. He keeps mumbling things under his breath, then he'll stop, look at me, shake his head, and then go back to pacing.

Five minutes later my mom sighs and says, "I think you broke him, baby." Mom and I both chuckle at her attempt to lighten the mood.

Dad stops pacing and turns to pin us both with a look that has us shutting our mouths. "You've been with him for what? Four weeks? And you think you're in love with that good-for-nothing son of a bitch?" I flinch at his harsh tone.

"That's enough, Nico!"

"No, Ryan. He tried to take you from me, and now he wants my daughter. Do you even know what he did, Raya? Do you even know the man you think you're in love with?" I grind my teeth together and give my dad the filthiest look I can muster.

"I know exactly who he is. He told me everything." Dad doesn't seem shocked. He scoffs and narrows his eyes to slits.

"Oh, I bet he told you his version of things."

"Then why don't you tell me yours? Why the hell do you hate him so much? He isn't a bad guy." Dad throws his hands into the air and turns to my mom.

She shrugs her shoulders and says, "Don't look at me, she gets this from your DNA, not mine." Dad rolls his eyes and shakes his head. My mom reaches over and grabs my hand, threading her fingers through mine. I stare at her in question. She smiles meekly at me and my resolve crumbles a bit. My mom is on my side. She isn't angry at me like dad.

"Oh hell no!" Both of us turn to Dad to find his gaze locked on our joined hands. He points an accusing finger at my mom. "You do not get to pick sides in this, little one. You know as well as I do that he is no good for her. He is a piece of sh-"

"Stop!" He snaps his mouth close and stands up straighter. Mom releases my hand and jumps off the bed to go stand in front of him. "You do not get to tell her who she can and can't love. How many people told me not to trust you or love you?" Dad reels back, shocked, and I must say I'm a bit blown away to hear this, too.

"That's different and you know it."

"How? Because it was you? Because you're so noble and honest? You lied to me and hurt me, Nico, and don't you dare fucking say you didn't!"

"He isn't good enough for her!" dad yells. Mom moves forward and places both her hands flat against his chest and looks up at him with a ghost of a smile across her lips.

"No one will ever be good enough for our daughter in your eyes, Nico. But you have even said it yourself. Kai is noble, kind, and fiercely loyal to those he loves." Dad cups Mom's face between his hands.

"He tried to take you from me, love."

"But he didn't, big guy. He tried to save me from a life of misery and pain. Kai never loved me, Nico. He thought he did, but that is in the past. He is a good man, and you cannot say otherwise. He saved our asses time and time again. I mean, for God's sake, Nico, he nearly died for me!" Dad groans as he steps away from Mom and turns to face me. He moves around the bed and sits on the edge near me. He reaches out and clasps my hand in his. I meet his gaze and hold it; I am nineteen years old, I am not a child anymore. I will take whatever my father has to say in stride and then move on.

"You, Raya Stevie Stone, are everything to me. I never thought I could love anyone as much as I love your mother, but that all changed the day you were born. I love you, Ray, and I don't want to ever see you get hurt. I won't lie, I want to smash his ugly face in for hurting you." Mom stomps her foot on the ground. Dad smiles cheekily at me and flicks his brows up and down. I roll my eyes playfully. "I can't say I support you being with him. He has a lot to prove to me before I even consider the idea of my daughter being with the likes of someone—"

"What your father is trying to say is that he will not stand in your way, right, dear?"

"Right," Dad grits out through clenched teeth. I launch myself at him and wrap my arms around him. He catches me and returns my embrace.

"I love you, Daddy," I whisper. His hold on me tightens.

"I love you too, baby girl."

"What the fuck did you do, Kai?" Normally, I would be pissed at getting blamed for something, but this time Dom is right to blame me. I did fuck up, and to make matters worse, I think I may have let the best thing that has ever happened to me in over century walk right out of my life. I turn around and march into the living room, dropping down onto one of the couches and clasping my head between my hands. Not a minute later, I feel the couch dip and an arm wrap around my shoulders. I can tell it's Sophia without even looking.

"What happened, Kai? Why is Raya so distraught?"

"Because I fucked up, So-So," I mumble out. She moves and pries my hands from my face so I'll look at her. The look in her eyes guts me. There is so much sadness and pity. I don't want or need her pity. I knew things would never work with Raya, but a fucking tiny sliver deep inside of me hoped. I haven't felt hope in such a long time that I latched onto that small tendril and thought just maybe, maybe, there was a small chance I could find happiness again.

"Dude, you did more than fuck up. I could smell you all over her. You should be fucking praying Nico doesn't pick up your scent." Truthfully, I couldn't give a flying fuck what Nico has to say about it. I didn't sleep with Raya because I wanted to scratch an itch. I'm not the type of guy to just sleep with anyone to get off. Raya means something to me. That's why I slept with her.

"Dom, that is not helping."

"Sorry, babe, but you know I'm right. We have enough shit going on with Ryan and our son losing his powers. Now our niece has gone and started a war within our own family." Hearing Dom blame Raya pisses me off. None of this is her fault.

"Don't blame her. She didn't do anything wrong." Dom throws his hands into the air and marches down into the living room and sits on the couch opposite us.

"Melakai, she lost her powers, her mother is dying, and Nico is going to see it as you took advantage of his confused and distraught daughter. Her being attracted to you is one thing, but her sleeping with you is a whole different ball game." I know he's right, but I'll be damned if I admit that to him.

"She isn't a fucking child, Dominic." He pins me with a death glare.

"No, but she is his only child."

"Come back with us, Kai, and talk to her." I start shaking my head. I won't chase her. She is better off without me. I care about her enough to know that. I will bring her nothing but pain and misery.

"Don't be a fucking coward, Kai. Fix this!" I'm on my feet in a second, and so is Dom. I flash across the room and stand in front of the growling bastard.

"I am no fucking coward, Dominic. She is better off with her parents. They can keep her safe and alive. I can't." Dom's growling stops, and the anger vanishes from his eyes as he looks up at me.

"You stupid bastard. You have no idea the damage you are causing yourself. If you want to hide out here, fine. You left twenty years ago because you hated yourself, not us. You can use that as an excuse as long as you like, but you and I both know the truth. You ran from yourself. If you ever change your mind, you know where to find us."

Dom moves toward Soph, grips his wife's hand in his, and chants to open a portal. I used to be able to open portals. Just before they leave, Dom stops and turns to look at me. "As you know, we have twins, Avery and Kailyn. We named Kailyn after the hero that saved his mother." I stumble back, shocked. They think I'm a hero?

Four days!

Four fucking days since Raya left. I have tried to make contact with the brothers, but haven't gotten a reply. I'm starting to worry now that something has happened to them—or worse, they changed their minds. I texted Jackson and lied, telling him that the brothers said they needed more time to make the potion. I have sent my men out to search for them, but they can't find any trace of them. I sit here behind my desk at the club, flipping my phone around in my hand, debating if I should try calling Raya.

What would I say if she picked up? Would I feel worse if she didn't answer? Memories of her have haunted me every day since she left. I can't even sleep in my own bed without thinking of her. Her scent clings to the sheets, and I don't have the heart to change them. I don't even shower in my ensuite anymore, because the memory of her on her knees plays on repeat. Before

I can decide, my office door bursts open and Cam walks in. I growl at the sight of him. The black eye I gave him has faded now. The fucker overstepped when he allowed Raya to put on her show.

He walks toward my desk and plops down on a seat in front of me.

"Nice ink, boss." I moved my appointment forward and got both my arms tattooed. The one on my right arm has something special added to it. No one but her would know. I don't know why I added it, but I always wanted to have a piece of her with me.

"What do you want, Cam?" I snap.

"Lucian is downstairs asking for you." Why is he here? I push away from my desk and exit my office with Cam on my heels. I march down the stairs and head toward the bar, where I can see him sitting. The club isn't open today, so it's empty except for my men. When I approach, I notice the rings beneath his strange eyes. His gray and black hair is a mess, and his clothes are wrinkled and look slept in.

"What are you doing here, Lucian?" His tired eyes meet mine, and concern fills me at the blank stare he gives me.

"She's gone, Kai."

"What? Who?"

He growls low in his throat. I see from the corner of my eye David and a few others move toward us. I raise my hand to stop them. Lucian is no threat to me.

"Raya, you dumbass! She's been missing for two fucking days." I reel back, shocked. How the fuck could Nico let this happen?

"What happened?" I demand.

"I woke up two days ago, and my magic was back. I burst into Raya's room to tell her and see if she had hers back, but she wasn't there. We have searched for her everywhere. Nico and

Smurf are out of their minds with worry. Jackson has his best trackers trying to find her, but nothing."

"Why are you coming to me, Lucian?"

He narrows his eyes. "Because my dumb ass thought you might actually give a fuck about my cousin and offer to help. It's the least you could fucking do!"

"Fuck you!"

"You broke her fucking heart, Melakai. I am hoping that because she loves you, you will be able to use the link between the pair of you to find her."

"How am I supposed to do that?"

He looks at me as if I'm stupid. "By going to her in her dreams."

I haven't dreamed walked since Ryan.

"Do her parents know about this?" Lucian shakes his head, so I release a long sigh and say, "Take me to them."

CHAPTER 25

Malakai

Lucian, Cam, and I exit the portal at the front of Jackson's compound. As soon as we take one step toward the main door of Jackson's huge building, wolves, fae, and witches come at us from every angle. Lucian releases his magic and stands in front of Cam and I. The little shit has my respect for that move. He didn't need to protect me but he chose to, and that loyalty goes a long way in my book.

"Stand the fuck down now!"

"Who is that with you, Lucian?" Some guy shouts.

"Melakai Cane, king of the vampires and brother to the alpha of New York, king of the fae, and alpha of all alphas" I look past Lucian to see Ryan, Nico, Dom, Soph, Jax, and Aurora standing by the front door of the compound. The warriors withdraw and disappear a moment after Ryan's words register. Before getting into it with the others, I turn to Cam.

"Go to Eric and tell him I'm back. Get him to gather all of the men and start searching for Raya Stone." Cam nods and takes off at vamp speed to the mansion.

"I don't need your help to find my daughter!"

Sighing, I move to stand beside Lucian, who has pulled his magic inside himself.

"Why is he here, Lucian?"

"Because he can help us find Raya."

"I don't need him!" Nico roars, and I move till I'm halfway toward the six of them. My gaze lands on Ryan, and I see tears welling in her eyes. She breaks away from the others and comes to stand in front of me. Nico, of course, follows her and stands directly behind her. Ryan reaches out and clasps my hand between both of hers.

"Help me find my little girl, Kai, please." I yank her forward and wrap my arms around her, ignoring Nico's grunts and groans. A moment passes and I pull back, resting my hands on top of Ryan's shoulders. I crouch down until I'm eye level with her.

"I'll try my best."

"How the fuck do we know you didn't set this up?" I drop my hold on Ryan and stand tall, glaring at the fucker who once again questions my loyalty.

"What would I have to gain out of kidnapping your daughter, Nico?"

"It wasn't just her! Randall is gone too, you dumbass." I wheel around and pin Lucian with a look. He stands there rubbing the back of his neck and looking everywhere else but at me. "You didn't tell him, did you?"

Lucian finally meets my gaze. "I wasn't sure if you would come if you knew the truth." It all clicks into place now. I spin around and look at both Ryan and Nico.

"I know who has her. I need to lay down now."

Nico brushes past Ryan and stands so we are chest to chest. "Who has my daughter?"

"The Masters brothers."

"Where are they?"

"I don't know. That's why I need to lay down," I grit out.

"You wanna take a fucking nap right now?"

"No, you fuck face. I need to see if I can enter Raya's......dreams." I have no time to prepare when Nico's fist clocks me straight across the jaw. I don't hesitate to throw a punch of my own that has him stumbling back a step.

"You will stay the fuck away from my daughter!" It's now or never. If I do this there will be no going back. Can I live without her? It doesn't take me a second to know the answer.

"I can't do that, Nico."

He releases his magic, and two energy balls form in his hands. Ryan tries to stop him but is too late. He throws one after another at me. I try to dodge them but can't. Those fuckers burn! One hits me in the chest and the stench of my own burning flesh fills my nostrils. The other got me in the thigh.

"Enough!" Ryan releases her magic and wraps Nico in a bubble. He thrashes against her hold, but he isn't strong enough to break his wife's magic. No one aside from Lucian has ever been able to.

"Let him try please, Nico," Ryan begs. Minutes pass as we all stand in silence waiting for Nico to calm. When he nods his head, Ryan drops the dome.

I look at her in shock. "You're not weakened."

She shakes her head. "I woke up the morning Raya went missing and found a note and potion beside the bed, telling me to drink it." How the fuck did they not put two and two together?

"You will not go anywhere near my daughter. Ever since she came to you she has been in danger."

Anger courses through my veins. "I never put her in danger!" I yell. Dom and Jax move toward us, ready to intervene if we go at it again.

"Yes you did. Raya has never been in trouble before. She

sure as fuck has never given anyone a lap dance before she came to you!"

I cock my head to the side confused. "What?"

Dom is the one to answer me. "Raya's little dance at the club was uploaded to YouTube. Daddy dearest over here saw his daughter doing her thaaaang and isn't impressed by her moves." Nico glares at Dom, and I can't help the chuckle that escapes me. Nico tries to move toward me but is stopped by both Dom and Jax.

"What the fuck are you laughing at? I watched you carry her out of your fucking club!"

"Exactly, you dick. I stopped her from going any further. I never made her do that."

"But you are the cause for her doing it, though, are you not?" I scowl at Jackson. What a douche bag throwing me under the bus like that!

"Yes!" I grit out.

"What did you do to my daughter, Melakai, and don't fucking lie to me!"

"Oh, this should be good, Nicky boy."

"Fuck up, Dom," Nico snaps.

I dart my eyes to Ryan and scrunch my face in confusion. She is smiling at me like she already knows what I am about to say. I take a deep breath and meet Nico's angry violet eyes. I walk—well, limp—toward him thanks to the pain in my leg. I'll heal in a couple hours. That's one bonus to being a vampire is that we heal fast. I stop when I am a foot away from Nico.

"Raya is a free spirit, Nico. She was being herself when she was with me. You know why she wasn't in a hurry to get her magic back?" I carry on, not giving him a chance to answer. "Because she knew when it came back that she would have to go home and be the princess. She couldn't be herself anymore. All she has ever wanted was to be free, but you are so blinded by your control freak ways you couldn't see your own daughter suffering."

"Don't you fucking dare pretend to care!" he yells.

"I do care," I yell as I pound my fist against my chest.

"You fucking hurt my daughter. She came back here a mess. You broke her heart, Melakai, and I will never forgive you for that!"

I drop my gaze from his as I say, "I never should have let her leave. I know I will never be good enough for her, Nico. That's why I tried to push her away, but she is so fucking stubborn, like you. She wormed her way inside me, and now I can't get her out of my head. I could never hurt her. That's why I pushed her away. It was better I break her heart than ruin her life. I will help you get her back, then I promise I will leave and she will never see me again." I hear the girls gasp, but I don't acknowledge them.

"Look at me." I do as he asks and meet his gaze. "Swear to me that you will leave and never come back."

"Fuck you, Nico. You can't do that to him. You're a–"

I cut Dom off. "I swear."

We all make our way inside. Ryan and the others refuse to speak to Nico. I don't blame him, though. If I was him, I would want to keep my daughter away from a guy like me, too. We enter a room, and I'm immediately assaulted by Raya's scent. She must have stayed in this room. I push past the others and make my way to the bed. On the nightstand, I see a letter with my name on it. I drop down onto the side of the bed and pick it up.

"Don't touch that!" I turn and pin Nico with a fucking glare that has him shutting his mouth. I agreed to his terms. I agreed to leave the only family I have ever known for him, so the least he can do is shut the fuck up while I read the letter his daughter wrote. I focus back on the letter and open it.

Kai,

I hoped you would come.

I'm sorry, but when the brothers came to me and told me their terms, I agreed. I cannot let my mom die.

I know everyone must be angry with me, but I had to do what needed to be done. The brothers assured me that Randall would never go free. Please trust me and tell my mom and dad that I'm okay.

Love,

Raya xoxo

I fold the letter up and place it in my pocket before lying flat on the bed. Her scent engulfs me. I close my eyes and wait for the pull that I haven't tried to feel for in so long. I don't even know if this will work, but I am praying that it does. Minutes tick by and still nothing happens. I search deep within myself and try to find the tether that will bind me to her. Just as I'm about to give up, I find it. I latch on to it and pull.

CHAPTER 26

Either I'm very brave or stupid.

When the brothers came to me the other night, they offered me a deal. If I give them Randall Cane, they will return my power and Lucian's. They will also give me the cure for my mom. I told them there is no way I can access the cell he is being held in. The brothers gave me a spell and a pair of gloves that would mimic my Uncle Dom's magic signature to get the elevator to work to take me down to the cells. They assured me that Randall wouldn't be able to put up a fight. I have heard stories about what a monster this man is. I knew he hurt my mom and Aunt Soph. He kept Lucian a prisoner for most of his life, until Mom and Luce broke free. The last thing I want is for a monster like him to be set free, but I also know there is no way my mom will do what needs to be done so she can live. I did as they asked and followed their instructions. I got the sickly looking vampire from his cell and brought him to them. How I didn't get caught sneaking him out is a mystery for the ages.

Randall Cane looks like microwaved death. His face is gaunt and his eyes are sunken in. He has no weight on him whatsoever. He is literally skin and bone. His eyes are dull and black, and he has no hair at all, not even eyebrows. I think he was left in that cell to desiccate.

"You okay?" I turn to the side and watch as Boston sits on the log next to me. I have no idea where in the world we are. Once I met them in the woods behind Uncle Jax's with Randall, they transported us somewhere. I began to panic until the brothers told me why they took me with them. I turn back toward the fire and blow out a breath. We're camping in the middle of nowhere. All you can see is mountains and open land for miles. The night sky is so bright and filled with stars. It's cold as shit, but the fire helps.

"I just want this to be over so I can go home," I reply honestly.

"I promise you will get home safely, Raya. I will not let any harm come to you." I don't know why, but I believe Boston. He and his brothers have been nothing but kind to me. They didn't force me to come with them. When they told me why they needed my help, I offered to come.

"No harm will come to you, Raya." I look up to Bronx taking a seat and smile at him. Memphis joins us a moment later.

"What are you going to do with him?" I dart my gaze over to the large wooden box. There are bars on one side of the crate that allow air flow and for Randall to see out, but that's it. He has been locked in there for two days.

"Don't concern yourself with that. It will give you nightmares." I shudder at the double meaning to Memphis's words.

"Okay, so then let me ask you all this: How did you know about Kai?" The three of them exchange a look before Bronx answers me.

"We have a friend. She is similar to your aunt. Our friend can call on visions. She doesn't just randomly get them. She saw what you are to Kai. When we found out there was a cure, we decided to help." It still doesn't make sense, though.

"Why would you three offer to help me? You don't even know me." Sadness shines in all their eyes.

"Because you remind us of someone we lost so long ago." I can hear the sorrow and pain in Boston's voice, and my heart hurts for them. Clearly they have lost someone they all cared for.

"I'm so sorry for your loss." I hope they can hear the sincerity in my voice. I am eternally grateful to these three males for what they have done for my mom and what they are trying to do for Kai. I don't even know if Kai knows that I'm gone. I left him a letter, hoping he would come. After the brothers explained everything to me, I knew why Kai pushed me away, and my heart ached for him. Even if Kai doesn't feel the same way about me, I still want to help him and give him his life back.

I try to keep my eyes open longer but can't fight the pull of sleep. I bid the brothers goodnight and head to my little pup tent. I shuck off my shoes and climb inside the sleeping bag, zipping it up behind me. As soon as I get comfy and close my eyes, sleep pulls me under.

A rustling sound has me snapping my eyes open. I sit up and look around. Worry and fear seep inside me. Where the hell am I? I'm lying on the bank near a lake. Trees and mountains surround me, but I have no idea where the hell I am. I look down and notice I'm no longer in my jeans and shirt. I'm in a pair of cutoffs and a tank top that barely contains the girls. What the fuck is going on? I hear the rustling sound again, this time behind me. I jump to my feet and spin around, scanning the woods. I try to

call on my magic, but it doesn't come. Fuck. As the sound draws closer, I drop into my fighting stance and wait. When I see the figure emerge from the trees, I gasp.

"Kai?" He struts toward me, worry lines marrying his beautiful face. As he gets closer, relief shines in his gray-blue eyes. He wraps his arms around me and lifts me off the ground, holding me against his chest. He buries his face in the crook of my neck and inhales. I stay still in his arms. He releases me a few minutes later, then holds me at arm's length and runs his eyes up and down my body. Not in a sexual way, but like he is checking for injuries or something. When he finally meets my gaze, he cups my face between his hands.

"Where are you?" Huh?

"I'm standing right here, Kai."

He shakes his head. "Vixen, you're dreaming. Remember I told you I'm a dream walker?" I nod my head. I do remember him saying something like that. "You're dreaming, Vixen. I need you to tell me where you are so I can come for you." I pull out of his hold and shake my head no.

"I can't, Kai, I need to do this so you can finally be free!" He growls and then spins around and begins to pace the bank. Can't he see I'm doing this for him? Or is he worried that I will use the cure against him?

Before I can ask, he comes to a stop in front of me and asks, "What have they told you, Raya?"

"The truth."

"They lied to you, Vixen." I scowl up at him.

"No, they didn't. You did. Why didn't you tell me the truth?"

"How was I supposed to tell you that in order for me to get what I wanted most out of life, you had to die?"

I stumble back. The brothers told me all Kai had to do was feed from me at the peak of the blood moon, not kill me. "What do you mean?"

Kai sighs then gestures for me to take a seat on the ground. I do.

Kai sits close enough next to me that our thighs are pressed against each other. "Raya, all I have ever wanted since I was turned into a vampire is to become a fae again. I spent years searching for a cure. There isn't one, vixen."

"Is that why you left?"

Kai shakes his head and looks out over the lake. "No, I left because Mya told me that if I didn't, I would tear our family apart. I didn't understand what she meant until I met you."

I reel back shocked. "What did I do?"

"Your blood calls to me, vixen. I can hear the thrum of your pulse, I hear the beat of your heart, and feel the heat of your veins your blood calls to me. Being near you is the worst and best form of torture."

"But when we...you didn't bite me...you sucked my neck."

Kai's eyes cloud with shame. "I was seeing if I could over-come it. I nearly bit you, Raya. If I taste your blood, I won't stop. I'll keep going until I drain you dry. I'm sorry, Vixen. I thought you were mon salut."

I have no idea what that means, but hearing those two words come from his mouth sounds so fucking hot. "The brothers can fix this, Kai."

His eyes soften as he reaches out to tuck my hair behind my ear. "There is no cure, mon salut. Tell me where you are, and I'll come for you. We have tried to track you, but they have spelled you so no one can trace your scent or your magic."

I shake my head. I trust the brothers, and they have no reason to lie to me! "I can't, Kai. I believe them. They have no reason to lead me astray."

Kai's face hardens. "Where is Randall?"

I sigh, no point lying. "In a cage."

"What do they plan to do with him?"

"I don't know. I swear." Kai curses beneath his breath. "What's wrong?"

"You have to go, Vixen. I'll come to you next time you sleep, and I'll bring you home." Before I can say anything, he leans forward and captures my lips in a heated kiss that has my insides turning to mush and my pussy clenching. Before I can further this kiss, he pulls back and rests his forehead against mine. "Stay alive, vixen. I'm coming for you."

Everything goes dark.

I wake panting and dripping with sweat, then scream bloody murder.

"Ray?" The three brothers are crouched around the open flap of my tent. All of them look concerned, and that sets me on edge. I quickly sit up and ask. "What's wrong?"

"You tell us, Raya. You were the one screaming in your sleep." I cock my head to the side and look at Boston. I can see in his eyes that he is serious. I don't know why, but I feel like I can't tell them the truth. What if by a small chance Kai is right and they are lying to me? Kai said they spelled me, and not once have they mentioned that to me. With all that said, I decide to lie.

"I'm sorry. I had a nightmare."

"About what?" Bronx sounds suspicious, so I have to think fast.

"I have been getting them a lot lately. I keep dreaming that my mom is dying, and I can't save her." All three of the brothers' shoulders droop, and understanding enters each of their gazes.

"I'm sorry, Ray." I look at Bronx in shock. He doesn't seem like the type to ever say sorry.

"It's okay. I'm gonna try to get some more sleep, if that's okay." They each nod and wish me goodnight. Boston and Bronx turn to leave, but Memphis stays behind and zips the flap.

Before it can close fully, he pops his head in and says, "I like you, Raya, but if you put either of my brothers lives in danger, you will pay the price." I gulp loudly and nod my head in understanding. Once the flap is closed, I flop back down and start to wonder if Kai is right.

CHAPTER 27

Malakai

I bolt upright in the bed and clutch my head. Before I even have a chance to get my bearings, questions are being shouted at me. I can't even hear myself think, let alone answer their questions.

"Shut up!" Aurora bellows. I drop my hands and lift my head to look at Aurora. Out of all of us, she is always the quietest. So, to hear her shout has us all stunned. I notice then that Jax has his arm around her waist and looks like he is supporting her weight. Did she have a vision? Aurora breaks away from Jax, moves toward the side of the bed, and sits down next to me. I just sit here staring at her, wondering what the hell she is up to. "They pulled her out of the dream, didn't they?" Everyone remains quiet as I nod my head. "Melakai, you need to find her."

Before I can answer, Ryan asks Aurora. "Is my daughter in danger?"

Aurora doesn't take her eyes off me as she answers. "Not really."

"What does that mean?" I ask the seer.

"They won't harm her, Kai, but they are not telling her the

truth either. They are giving her half-truths. They need her for something, but I don't know what."

"What did you see, Aurora?"

"She isn't being held against her will. She willingly left with them, because they promised her a cure for you, along with healing her mother and regaining her and Luce's magic." Growls sound out around the room, and I can feel all their eyes on me. Guilt is weighing heavy on my chest. She put her own life in danger for me. She has no idea what the fuck she has gotten herself into.

"Something isn't adding up. Why do they need Randall? Why are they promising Raya a cure for me? What could they possibly have to gain from any of this?"

"I don't know, Kai. We need to figure out who the hell these brothers really are. I have never seen or heard of anyone who has that much power. They could have killed us that day at the canyon, but they didn't. We need to find out why." Jackson was right, something isn't making sense, and I don't like being in the dark. I climb off the bed so I can get out of here and clear my head.

Ryan darts her arm out to stop me. I look down at her in question.

"Is she okay?" she whispers. My shoulders sag. I can see the worry and fear in her eyes for her daughter. Ryan is supposed to be the strongest supernatural in the world, and not even she can locate Raya, and it is killing her. I can see it in her eyes.

"She's her mother's daughter. She is resilient and strong. Three asshole brothers won't break her, Ry."

"W-will you go to her again?" I nod my head. She releases a relieved sigh. "Thank you, Kai, for saving our asses once again."

I have no words for her, so I nod my head and exit the room. I push the front doors open and exit Jackson's compound. I need air. Being in that room with all of them was suffocating. I can feel their eyes judging me. I know I'm not a fucking saint, but I'm also not the fucking bad guy here. All I have done is try to help and be there for my brothers and their wives, but the only one who seems to not hate me is Jackson. I hate the divide between me and Dom. I hate the rift between me and Nico more. I know I fucked up years ago by going to Ryan, but I was blinded by my need to save her. I thought manipulating her emotions would do the trick, but I was wrong. Her love for Nico brought her here to Alaska anyway, and all my efforts proved futile. Will there ever come a time in my life where I am needed or wanted? Have I let myself go too far and closed myself off so much that I can't let anyone in? My phone vibrating in my pocket pulls me from my thoughts. I fish it out and answer it.

"Eric."

"Your majesty, I hear you are back."

"I am."

"Cam has said you need the men dispatched and searching for the princess of the fae?" Sighing, I decide it will be better to hold off. If the brothers are up to something and they are found, there is a chance they will hurt Raya, and that is not a chance I am willing to take.

"Stand down for now. If anything changes, I will let you know."

"Sir, may I speak freely?"

"Yes."

"Is it true that Randall has been freed?" Wow, good news really does travel fast.

"Yes."

"What does that mean for us?"

"Him being freed changes nothing. He will be captured again and imprisoned. How many others know about this?" I can't afford for the men to go on their own hunting mission.

They want Randall dead for all the horrible things he did to them.

"Pretty much everyone, sire." Fuck that is not the answer I wanted to hear.

"No one is to go after him. Do I make myself clear?"

"Yes, sir." I end the call and dial David. By the looks of things, I will be away longer than I thought.

"Hey, boss."

"David, I need you to take care of the clubs. I have a meeting set with the manager of Salut Miami tomorrow, and I won't make it. I need you to take the meeting and make sure everything is running smoothly there. The preparations for the build in Arizona have been approved, so I need you to get in touch with the contractor and give them the green light." I can hear him scribbling down everything I am saying. David is not only one of my head of security, but he is also my go-to for shit like this.

"Got it, boss. Anything else?" I need to stay true to my word. My word is my bond.

"Find someone to take over the day-to-day runnings of the club in Colorado and find us an isolated location to lay low for a while."

"Why?" I can hear the shock in his voice, but I don't need to explain myself to him.

"Just do it. I'll be in touch when I'm on my way back. Have everything ready to go once I get there."

"Yes, boss." I end the call and pocket my phone. I hate to say it, but leaving Colorado is going to be harder than I thought. I made a home for myself there. I actually laid down roots for the first time since becoming a vampire over a century ago. I don't know where I'll go, but I know if I stay in Colorado she will find me again, and I don't think I will be strong enough to push her away.

"You know she will just hunt you down, right?" I spin around to find Soph, Ryan, and Lucian standing a few feet away. "My cousin isn't known for taking 'no' for an answer." I sigh and run my hand through my hair.

"What would you have me do, Lucian? I gave Nico my word that I would disappear and stay gone once Raya is home."

"Fuck your word, Kai." I turn to Ryan, shocked. Her voice is laced with so much anger. "I know my husband is lashing out at you because of our past, but I am begging you—please don't do this to my daughter!"

I growl in frustration. "I can't be with her, Ryan."

She takes a couple steps forward and scowls at me. "Do you love her?"

I suddenly feel awkward having this conversation with her. "It doesn't matter. I must go."

"Bullshit. Why are you running again?"

I glare at Sophia. "I never fucking ran. I told you all the day we captured Randall that I was leaving. I am tired of always being the one to blame for shit."

"Cry us a fucking river, Kai." I snap my gaze over the girls' heads to see Jax, Dom, Nico and Aurora making their way toward us. I see out of the corner of my eyes that we are gathering a crowd of onlookers from our raised voices. "You left because you were pissy."

"I left because you and Nico blamed me for both your wives being hurt!"

Sophia and Ryan both turn toward their husbands, and each of them places their hands on their hips.

Both Nico and Dom glare at me. Fuck them. They deserve what's coming to them.

"So help me God, brother, if you and Dominic made him leave, I will fucking cause you both harm!"

"How you gonna do that, little dove?" I wince. Dom should learn to shut his fucking mouth and stop baiting his wife.

"Ryan and I will take a two-week vacation and leave you and Nico with the twins. Oh, and I'll withhold sex for a month." Dom's eyes double in shock.

"Yeah, what she said."

Nico turns and glares at his wife. "Don't you two dare gang up on me and stop talking about fucking Soph. You're my little sister. I don't need to have that mental picture in my head!" Nico shudders visibly while Dom just laughs and pats him on the back.

"Dude, you have two nephews and a niece. How do you think they were made?" Nico growls and pushes Dom away from him.

"Tell me the truth now, Nico. Did Kai leave because of you?"

Nico's gaze finds mine as he answers. "Partly."

Ryan gasps and then turns to Dom. "Did you have anything to do with it?"

Dom starts to rub the back of his neck and averts his eyes.

"Dominic!"

"Fuck. Yes, okay? I was angry and worried because you all spelled us in a fucking room, and I was worried Soph would get hurt, so I lashed out. I couldn't take the words back once I said them, and when I went to say sorry, it was too late. He was gone."

"I am so fucking angry at you right now, Dom. He saved my fucking life!"

Dom turns to Soph, and I can see the regret in his violet eyes. His silver hair flops forward onto his forehead, but he ignores it as he looks at his wife. "I know, Soph, I'm sorry."

"Don't apologize to me. Say sorry to Kai, and you better

fucking pray he forgives you, Dominic. If it wasn't for him, I would be fucking dead."

Nico and Dom both recoil at her words, I see Lucian tense as well. I don't need them to say sorry. The damage is done, and all we need to do is move forward now. I can't take all of their emotional shit.

"Save it. I don't want to hear it." I turn around and head for the woods, ignoring them calling out to me. I don't want their half-assed apology and fake feel sorry for me bullshit stories. I will always care for them and protect them, but that doesn't mean I need to be around them.

I laugh when I spot the stream up ahead. Of course, I had to find my way here. This stream seems to be the spot me and my brothers go to when we're out of sorts. We first found this stream when Nico and Ryan had a massive fight, then when Dom found out Soph had hidden the fact he was Lucian's father from him. Now here I am alone and sitting on the wet grass by the stream. What a predicament. I can hear voices from behind me. Their conversation becomes clearer the closer they get. When I register who the voices belong to, I groan–here we go again.

"So help me, you better fucking move, Nico!"

"Why, Dom? I don't even want to be here."

"If the both of you don't get your asses out there and make this right, both of your wives are going to kill you."

"Fuck off, Jackson, you brown nose. Nicky boy, I will say it once more: if my wife withholds sex from me because of you, I will fucking ruin your life!" I hear a thwack then Dom starts cursing. "Hit me again, you little bitch, and see what happens."

"That's my sister!" I've had enough of this shit. I stand and turn to see the three of them standing at the edge of the tree line. The three of them hold two bottles of whiskey each. I shake my head. Dom and Jax look sheepish, but Nico just looks like he would rather be anywhere else than here.

"Just leave. I will help you get your daughter back, and then I'm gone. I have made the arrangements. I will keep my word." Dom shakes his head, and Jax looks annoyed, but Nico...Nico looks pleased.

"Don't leave, Kai. We have lost twenty years with you already. My kid doesn't even know her uncle. Dom's twins don't even know you, and he named his son after you!" I grip my hair and tug on it in frustration.

"What would you have me do, Jackson? Those two made it clear how they felt. I did what they wanted. I never asked for any of this. Raya came to me!" I shout. I'm so fucking angry that I can feel my fangs tearing through my gums. I need to feed and soon.

"That didn't mean you had to sleep with her!" Oh shit. Dom's eyes double in size, and I'm sure mine do the same. I look at Nico and wince. His face is contorted and his hands are glowing purple.

"What the fuck does Dominic mean, Melakai? Did you sleep with my daughter?"

CHAPTER 28

Raya

I wake the next day and feel like I didn't sleep a wink. My body is achy and sore, and my back hurts from sleeping on the ground. I didn't realize how much I would miss a bed until now. I guess Kai is right; I am a spoiled princess. I hop out of my sleeping bag and riffle through my backpack for a spare change of clothes. I pull out my last clean pair of jeans and my last shirt. I need to do some laundry soon or I'm gonna be reusing clothes, and that is not appealing. I quickly tie my long hair into a messy bun on top of my head and exit my tent.

The three brothers are standing by Randall's cage, and when they hear me approaching, they all turn to me. I pause under the intensity of their gazes. Something feels off this morning. Bronx moves toward me, and I stand my ground. My father has always instilled in me that you never back away from a man. You stand your ground, or they will see you as weak. Bronx stops a few steps in front of me. I notice now that he has changed clothes, as well. I keep my gaze locked on his. I keep my mask of indifference in place. His eyes scan me from head to toe, then he searches my face for what I have no idea.

"Sleep well, Ray?" I hide my confusion, smiling politely and shrugging my shoulders.

"Not really. My back is stiff and sore." Bronx nods his head but says nothing further. Something is going on here. I can feel the dynamic between us has shifted.

"How long before we get this cure?"

"Why?" I can hear the suspicion in Memphis's voice, but I choose to play dumb and ignore it.

"Because I want my own bed. My back is killing me, and I'm out of clean clothes." Memphis opens his mouth to respond but stops when Boston pins him with a look. "You guys okay?"

Boston looks at me and smiles. "Yeah, Ray. My brothers and I are just not seeing eye to eye this morning." I can tell he is lying to me but don't call him on it. "We'll sort out your laundry for you, and I'll take you down the stream later to bathe." I nod and thank him before making my way over to the platter of food they have set up near our tents. I'm going to need energy for what this day is to bring, I'm sure, so I load my plate with a bit of everything, then take a seat and scarf it all down, chased by a glass of juice. I can hear the brothers behind me talking in hushed tones. Is Kai right? Are they using me for something? Did I walk into a trap? Half an hour later the three Masters brothers stand in front of me, each of them wearing a look of disappointment.

"Spit it out." The three exchange a look before they focus back on me. I wait patiently for one of them to spill the beans.

"How long has Melakai Cane been coming to you in your dreams?" I hide my shock and meet Bronx's eyes. I won't lie to them. They will be able to tell, and right now I need them to trust me, so I can find out what the hell is really going on.

"Last night was the first time."

Bronx looks caught off guard that I actually told the truth— good. "What did he say?"

Now, this is where I need to be careful. I can't tell them the whole truth, but I can skirt my way around the full truth. "He wants me to come back. I told him I couldn't. He said that there is no cure, and I told him he was wrong."

"Was there anything else?"

I meet Bronx's gaze and decide to play the sex card. "Well, there were some other things, but words were not exchanged, if you get my drift."

"Eww." The three brothers jump back a step like I'm toxic. They all look horrified. What the actual fuck? Why the hell are they repulsed?

"What's your problem?" I snap.

"He's a vamp–"

Boston cuts Memphis off. "Nothing. It's just we were surprised that you and Kai are together."

"We're not together." It annoys me to say that out loud, but it's the truth. Kai has made his feelings clear, but last night he did kiss me, so now I'm more confused than ever.

"So, you're just sleeping together?"

I glare at Boston. "Are you my father? That is none of your business."

Boston kept his word and sorted my laundry out. Fuck knows how he managed to wash and dry my clothes, but I'm grateful nonetheless. He also took me down to the stream so I could bathe. My hair smells and feels so much better. At least the brothers were smart enough to bring some toiletries with them. I tried to ask Boston some questions, like why we're not staying at their house, or how long till I get the cure. The guy is like a vault. He just stares at me but won't answer a single question. The day passed by at a snail's pace. We're all sitting around the fire, once again eating dinner. Movement from Randall catches my eye. I turn toward him and just stare. How could this husk of a man have caused so much pain and trouble?

"Don't let the near-death look fool you, Raya."

I turn back toward the guys and ask, "How did he manage to cause so much pain?"

Each of the brothers faces take on a hard edge. They go silent for so long I think they won't answer me. Finally, Memphis answers. He reminds me so much of Kai. He doesn't like mindless chit-chat, and he doesn't need to fill the silence if he has nothing to say. "He is a manipulative piece of shit. He uses others' pain and agony and capitalizes on it. If he senses a weakness, he will exploit it. He killed Jackson Marshall's father, he killed your grandfather, and blamed the fae. He is also the reason your aunt is dead. Do you need further explanation?"

I'm irritated at the way Memphis just spoke to me like I am a toddler.

"That explains why I should hate him, not why you hate him." Memphis narrows his eyes at me. I'm dying to see him release his power. I haven't seen them use their magic except for transporting us. These brothers intrigue me, and I'm dying to learn what their story really is.

"Our secrets are our own. We will not disclose our reasons for wanting him dead with you. All you need to know is that in order for him to die, we need to cure your boyfriend." I grind my teeth together at his jab. He knows damn well Kai isn't my boyfriend. He only said that to piss me off.

"You know what? I didn't have to come here and help you all, but I did. I have been nothing but kind to the three of you, and all you have done is treat me like I'm an idiot all day. I don't know what has changed since yesterday, but I actually thought the three of you were cool. I even told Kai that last night. I will help you get whatever you need for this cure, and after that we can go our separate ways. I'm sick to death of men and their secrets." I stand and storm off to my tent, shaking with anger. I zip the flap up behind me then drop down on top of my sleeping bag. I don't know why I am so upset. I think deep down inside it's because I know Kai is right—the brothers are playing me, and they sure as fuck are hiding the real reason why I'm here.

I don't know what the hell is taking so long and why they can't just make this cure. Unlike my mom, who is half witch and half fae, I can't cast spells from nature. I am full fae through and through, like my dad. My magic may have hints of blue through it like my mom's, but that's about as good as it gets. I know if it came down to a battle of magic between me and the brothers, I would lose. They don't even need to have their magic for me to feel how powerful they are. I asked Bronx what supernatural race they come from, because they are way too powerful to be just a fae. I know they aren't shifters, vampires, or warlocks either, so Bronx's answer confused me more. He said they are their own race, whatever the hell that means. I hear rustling outside my tent, then someone calls out knock knock before the flap on my tent opens. I scowl at Boston. Once the flap is open fully, he squats down outside my tent so we are eye to eye.

"You want the truth?"

"Yes!" I growl out.

Boston takes a deep breath before he speaks. "We are waiting for the blood moon. It reaches its peak in four days' time. When it is at its highest peak, Randall will die, and Kai needs to drink the cure then. After that, you will be free to go on and live your life and never see us again."

I'm shocked. "So, you lied. You already have the cure, don't you?"

"Yes, but we just need one last ingredient."

"What is it?"

"A drop of your blood."

I reel back shocked. "Why my blood?"

"Long story short, we just do. That is all I know. Your blood needs to be mixed with the cure. And it's not really a cure—it's more like a new life potion. Anyway, get some sleep, and we can talk more about it in the morning." Boston stands and begins to close the flap of my tent, but he stops when I say his name.

"Thank you for being honest with me. I appreciate it."

"Sure, Ray."

Nico has murder in his eyes. His body is coiled tight and ready to spring into action. I could lie, but Jackson, the living lie detector, would pick up on it, so I have no choice but to speak the truth.

"I was joking, Nicky boy. He did—"

"Enough, Dom."

Dom snaps his mouth closed and mouths an apology to me.

"I won't lie to you, Nico."

"I want to hear you say it before I fucking kill you!"

I throw my hands up in the air. "See, you're doing it again. You suffocate her like she is a child!"

He pounds his glowing fist against his chest, for a second I think the bottle of whiskey might shatter. "She is my child, Melakai."

Fuck this, fuck him, and fuck all of their judgment. I am finished with this shit. I throw my head back and roar. It feels good to let it out.

A moment later I look to Nico again, and some of the anger had evaporated from his eyes. "What do you hate more, Nicky boy, the fact that your daughter fell in love or the fact that it was me she fell for? Or are you just fucked off because I am the only one who can reach her? I never set out to fucking hurt her, Nico. I tried to send her home, but the portals were locked. What did you want me to do? Throw her out on the streets or hand over to the brothers? I did what I thought was right. I didn't mean to fall in—I never meant to hurt her, Nico, I swear."

Nico's hands stop glowing, but his eyes are still burning with anger. I'm panting from blurting all of that out.

"Stop! You two go as far back as hairlines and fat crayons. Let this go."

"Shut up, Dominic. You kept this from me."

Dom has the cheek to stand there and look shocked.

"I told him to tell you." That lying little shit!

"The fuck you did."

"Well, I did imply it at least." I glare at the bastard.

"We need to get back, now. Chase and Alex are here." Jax doesn't wait for us to respond. He turns and runs back toward the compound.

"I still love the pack mind-link."

I ignore Dom as I take off after Jax, and he and Nico are hot on my heels.

I follow Jackson into his office. Nico and Dom stumble in after me. Ryan, Soph, Lucian, Aurora, Chase, Alex, and Mya are all sitting on the couches in Jackson's office. This place still looks the same. He even has the same huge-ass wooden desk and worn leather chair behind it. Being in this office brings back memories. The four couches are still the same, they just have new cushions. The bookcases behind his desk have more books now.

Children's artwork hangs on the wall beside his desk. I notice that he changed the large bay window to French doors. When my eyes turn back to the artwork on the wall, that's when a thought hits me.

"Where is your daughter and Dom's twins?" Jax faces me, and I can see I shocked him with my question.

"Ah, Rora and I sent Lily to stay with the twins in New York. We thought it would be safer for her there." I nod my head; that was a smart choice. I feel for all of them having to be away from their children. Lucian is old enough to stay with us, and truth be told, by the time Soph and Dom learned who he really was, the boy was already seventeen. Out of the corner of my eye, I see Alex and Chase make their way over to us. It's been a long time since I have seen the Knox brothers. Out of all of us, they are the only ones who have aged slightly. Witches and warlocks age like humans. Fae can live for hundreds of years, as can shifters. Vampires are already technically dead, so we don't age at all.

Chase and Alex smile wide when they stand in front of me. Alex's jet-black hair now has a few grays running through it, and his blue eyes hold more wisdom. He looks like he still hits the gym daily. He extends his hand and I shake it. I turn to Chase next and smile. Chase has always been the jokester out of the two, and God knows he loved to give Nico shit. Chase's blond hair has a few grays through it now, as well. His sky-blue eyes have laugh lines on the side of them. Both of the Knox brothers look like they're happy, and that makes me proud. I extend my hand to Chase, but he knocks it away and wraps me in a bro hug. I return the gesture. He steps back and grins at me. I just know he is about to say something stupid that is going to piss Nico off.

"I was hoping you would have duked it out with Tink and kicked his ass." I snort. Nico growls, and Dom the idiot fist bumps Chase. I shake my head and brush past the brothers. Mya stands when I approach the couches. Her muddy brown eyes hold so much sympathy for me. Where the Knox brothers have aged, Mya hasn't. You wouldn't be able to tell if she had gray hair. Her hair is naturally white-blonde, almost silver like Lucian and Dom's. Mya may look tiny and innocent, but this woman is just as tough as some of my men.

"Hello, Kai."

"Mya." The tension in the room has skyrocketed. I want to demand answers from her, but I can't even formulate a sentence to get the words out.

"You did good, Kai. You gave her a chance to live before you claimed her." I stumble back, shocked. She fucking knew!

"You lying little witch!"

"Hey, calm the fuck down!"

I turn and glare at Alex in warning. "Stay out of this. This is between me and her." I turn back to Mya, whose eyes still look at me with pity. This is all her fault! "You knew it would be her, didn't you?"

"Yes."

"Why didn't you tell me the fucking truth?" I yell. Alex and Chase move toward us but are stopped by Dom, Jax, and Lucian. I can see Nico has joined the girls, and they all stare at us in curiosity.

"Would it have changed anything if you knew? You brought that girl to life, Kai. She was suffering silently in her world and was being weighed down by the pressure put on her. She isn't your cure, Kai."

"What?"

"I was wrong when I had that vision twenty years ago. I saw you and her, but something changed. Her blood is the cure, but not for your vampirism per se."

I growl. I'm getting fucking frustrated. "What the fuck are

you talking about, Mya?" Mya turns to face Nico, and I do the same. I see confusion in his eyes, but when I look at Ryan, her eyes have doubled in size. She knows.

"You left because Mya had a vision." I nod. "What was the vision, Kai?"

"Tell them," I demand.

Mya sighs but does as she is told. "I had a vision twenty years ago. I never told Kai the whole truth."

"Why?" Nico asks.

"Because I knew he would go deep underground and your daughter would never find him." Nico tries to speak again, but Mya raises her hand to him. "Please just let me finish. I told Kai he needed to leave or in nineteen years he would do something that would tear his family apart, and there would be no coming back from that. What I didn't tell Kai is that I saw him with Raya. Her blood calls to him. I thought she would be his cure, but I was wrong, it's for a different reason."

"And that reason is?" Nico snaps.

"Her blood is the key to linking Kai to Randall. The blood moon will be here in four days, and when it is at its peak, if Randall and Kai have her blood in their system, all vampires will die." I look at her in shock, the whole room is deadly silent. But I feel like Mya is hiding something. She keeps darting her eyes around the room. I look at Jax, but he isn't scenting the air, so he can't help me out here.

"How?"

"All vampires are linked to their king. So, if Kai dies, so do all his subjects. I don't know what Randall has to do with this; the brothers could just kill him and be done, but for some reason they don't want that."

We've all been sitting in Jackson's office for hours, trying to come up with a solution or figure out why the brothers are doing this. Mya having that vision has helped us. Raya thinks they have a cure, but the truth is they just want me linked to Randall so they can wipe out my whole race. Why? What do they have to gain from this? It can't be power so it must be...revenge?

"We need to dig into their past. We need to find out what vampires or Randall did to them."

"What do you mean?" Jax asks me.

"Think about it. They could have killed me or Randall, but they haven't. They need me alive for their plan to work. Why do they hate vampires so much?" I pull my phone out of my pocket and dial Cam. He picks up on the third ring.

"Yeah, boss?"

"I need you to pull all the old vampire history books from the basement and bring them to me at Jackson's."

"All of them? There are like a hundred boxes!"

I grind my teeth and count to three. "Unless you want another fucking black eye, Cam, do as you're told!"

"Yes, sir."

"And bring me some bags of O-negative and some clothes."

"Yes, sir." I end the call and toss my phone onto the coffee table. I scrub my hands down my face. I am so fucking tired, and I need a stiff fucking drink.

"Why did you give Cam a black eye?" I drop my hands to my lap and find everyone staring at me. "Come on, dude, don't leave me hanging."

I glare at Lucian. He is just as fucking annoying as his father. "He pissed me off."

"Bullshit. You gave him a black eye because of Ray, didn't you?" I growl low in my throat as he, Dom, and Chase chuckle.

"You should have broken the fucker's nose." I snap my gaze to Nico and grin.

"I did, and I broke some of his fingers." Nico reaches over from his couch and extends his fist. I bump mine against his, we both smile at each other for a moment, and then reality comes crashing down on us. We quickly drop our hands, slink back into our seats, and look everywhere but at each other. Ryan snags my attention when she jumps to her feet and moves toward the middle of the seating area. She glares at me and Nico, and I dart my gaze to him to find he is looking at me with the same confusion.

"This is stupid!"

"Love–"

"No, Nico, we're all leaving the two of you in here by yourselves to sort this shit out. We'll be back when Kai's people get here with the stuff, and by God, Nico, you better make shit right!"

"Babe, come on we–" Ryan pins him with a look that has him shutting his mouth. I cover my mouth with my hand to hide my smile. Ryan turns to me and pins me with a look.

"What?" I snap.

"Don't you dare think that you are innocent in this! You could have come to us about Mya's vision, but you didn't. You're just as much to blame as him. Sort your shit out. I can't be worrying about you two trying to kill each other while I search for my daughter." I drop my gaze. She's right. This shit between me and Nico is petty compared to the danger that Raya is in.

As soon as Dom shuts the office door, the room is engulfed with awkward silence. I can feel the tension rolling off Nico in waves. I don't know what to say, so I remain quiet. Minutes tick by as we both sit across from each and avoid eye contact at all costs. After another ten minutes pass, I get fed up and finally break the silence.

"I never meant for things to go this far with Raya."

Nico finally lifts his gaze. I can't get a read on his emotions from the look he is giving me. "How did they get this far, Kai? Out of all the women in the world, why did it have to be my daughter?"

I release the breath I didn't know I was holding and answer him truthfully. "When I first saw Raya, she stirred feelings in me I haven't felt in so long. When she told me who she was, I tried to send her away. When I found out the portals were locked, I kept her with me to keep her safe. Then the more she was around and I got to know her, it just...happened. I tried to fight it, I swear. I pushed her away so many times and stopped her advances until one day...I didn't. I won't lie to you, Nico. I did sleep with her."

Nico growls and then runs his hands through his black hair and then starts to scrub his face. I wait for him to unleash his anger, but it doesn't come. "I can't support this, Melakai. She is just a child. She has no idea what she fucking wants. She has a right to live and being with you will stop that—"

"Making her train every day and take on her role as the heir isn't the same thing?"

He glares at me. "I'm preparing her for life. I want her to be ready."

"You're suffocating her, brother. She doesn't have the heart to disappoint you. She told me so. Lucian said she never told you about the vault because you wouldn't listen to her. She is smart, Nico. She is so bright and talented and just wants to be free of the burden of her future while she can. I know you love her and want her to be safe, but we are in this position because she couldn't come to you out of fear."

Nico deflates and drops back into his seat. Silence descends once again. I give him time to process what I have just said and wait for him to speak.

"I will let her live her life how she wants, if you promise me one thing."

"What is it?" I can tell from the look in his eyes that I am not going to like his answer.

"You leave her alone. You don't pursue her or chase after her once she is back. If you want her to have her freedom, then she needs to be free of you, as well. She is young and needs a chance to live, Kai. Don't take that away from her."

I feel a sharp pang in my chest and reach up to rub it. I've never felt this pain before. I take a few deep breaths and answer him. "What if she comes after me?"

"She won't."

"What if she does?" I insist.

"Then she does. I won't stop her. But I just want you to give her some space, and if this is what she chooses, then I guess we'll deal with it then."

"You have my word. Does that mean I don't have to move?"

Nico smiles a cunning smile. "Would I be pushing it if I said no, so it would be harder for her to find you if she did want to?"

We both laugh, and it's good to sit here with him and not want to punch his face. Before we can say any more, the door opens, and the others walk in. I see Cam, Eric, and a few others come in behind them carrying boxes. Before I can greet them, I feel the pull inside me.

"Shit, I need to lay down," I announce to the group.

"Why?" I can hear the panic in Nico's voice.

"Raya is going to sleep, and I promised I would come to her. While I'm under, you all need to dig through those boxes and find something. Cam, Eric, and the others will help you." I lay down on the couch and close my eyes. A minute later, I'm being pulled toward my dream land with Raya.

This time, when I emerge from the woods, she doesn't seem so scared. She still looks apprehensive, but that's better than how she looked yesterday. Once I'm in front of her, I pull her toward me and wrap my arms around her. She rests her head against my chest. I keep one arm around her waist as I run my other hand through her long tresses. She has the most beautiful long hair.

"I missed you." Her words have me pausing my movements. "Please don't push me away again." Hearing the vulnerability in her voice shatters me. I hate that I have made her feel this way. That was never my intention.

I pull back and hold her at arm's length; she seems unsure and that worries me.

"What's wrong, vixen?"

She pulls out of my hold and moves to sit down at the edge of the bank. I follow and do the same. I stare at her, transfixed. She is beyond beautiful. Her full lips are begging for me to kiss them. Her chest rises and falls, causing her ample chest to strain against her tank top. My gaze travels down to her legs. Fuck, I need to get my head on straight. All I seem to think about when she is around is being inside her again.

"I think you might be right."

I shake my head to clear my thoughts. "Right about what?"

She shocks the fuck out of me when she moves and straddles my lap. My hands have a mind of their own and grip her waist. She reaches out and cups my face between her small hands and tilts my head till I meet her gaze. I groan at the look in her eyes. Her gaze is filled with lust. She begins to grind on my cock, and an involuntary moan escapes me. I tighten my grip on her waist and hold her steady. She growls and tightens her grip on my face, which causes me to smile.

"I asked you a question, vixen."

"And I'll answer all your questions, if you make me come."

I shit you not, I choke on air. I start coughing and spluttering, and the whole time she just sits there and grins at me. I have never met a woman in my life that is as forward as Raya Stone. I don't know whether I find it endearing or frightening.

"Vixen, we can't."

"Why? Surely you can't bite me in my own dream, right?"

I groan. "No. Well, I can, but it won't do anything to you."

She cocks a brow at me and smiles seductively as she begins to run her hands down my body. "So, what's the problem then?"

Fuck, my willpower is waning.

"We just shouldn't because—" The rest of my sentence dies in

my throat when she bends down and captures my lips. I have zero control left. I kiss her back with such hunger that she gasps. I'm going to hell anyway, so I may as well sin a bit more before I go. I run my hand up her back and grip the nape of her neck to hold her in place. My other hand wraps around her waist, and I pull her forward until she is sitting right on top of my cock. She moans into my mouth the moment she feels my hardness between her legs. She wraps her arms around me, and in a move I never expected, she somehow rolls us so now I'm the one on top of her! I pull back and grin down at her. Her face softens, which makes me pause. "What's wrong?"

"Nothing. You should just smile more. It suits you."

"I never really had a reason to smile about anything until recently." I see her eyes mist. I refuse to allow her to pity me, so I lean down and capture her lips in a heated kiss. I grind my hips against her, and a small whimper escapes her, which just fuels the beast inside me. I pull back and grip the bottom of her tank top and peel it off, chucking it to the side. She's wearing one of those bras with the clasp in the middle of her breasts. I unsnap the clip and groan when her tits come into view. I don't waste any time. I lean down and capture one of her nipples in my mouth and tweak the other with my hand. She grips the back of my head and holds me in place. For a woman who was a virgin a few days ago, she sure as shit knows what she likes, and that turns me on even more. I release her nipple with a pop and then switch sides, paying the other one an equal amount of attention. She begins to thrust her hips up to try to grind against me, but I use my hand to push her waist back down.

She growls. "Kai...please!"

I release her nipple and look up at her. Her gaze is locked onto mine. Keeping my eyes on hers, I begin to slide down her body. I sit back on my haunches, pop the button of her cut-offs open, and peel the zipper down slowly. Her pupils begin to dilate. I grip her shorts and yank them down her legs, chucking them over my head. She lies down on the grass in nothing but a purple thong. Purple might just be my new favorite color. I drop down, run my nose against her panties, and inhale. I can smell how wet she is. I sit up again and look down at her. Her green eyes are filled with lust.

"Look at you. So innocent and pure but wet as fuck for a monster." My words elicit a moan from her.

"I'm always wet when you're around."

I growl out my approval and dive back between her legs. I run my finger along the side of her thong and pull it to the side to expose her beautiful pink pussy. I use my fingers to part her slick folds, and her pussy is slick with her arousal. I blow against her enlarged nub, and she cries out. I dart my tongue side to side, pulling another moan from her.

"Kai, please. I need more."

Who am I to deny the princess what she wants?

I bury my face in her sweet pussy and eat. I eat her like I haven't eaten in days. My thirst for her blood is no longer an issue. I don't crave her blood here in her dream like I do in the real world. She shakes beneath me and mutters sweet nothings as I suck her clit into my mouth. I insert two fingers inside her and begin to pump. She screams out in pleasure. I continue to finger fuck her tight cunt and lick her clit. I never slow the pace. She reaches down and grips my hair, and I feel the walls of her wet cunt gripping my fingers, and I know she is close. I pull my fingers out and sit back as her shocked eyes meet mine.

"You're not coming on my fingers, Vixen; you're gonna come on my cock." Her mouth pops open to form an O. I pull my shirt off then make quick work of getting out of my jeans. I line my cock up with her opening and don't give her a chance to prepare. I slam inside her. She screams my name. This time, though, it's in pleasure, not pain. My cock is balls deep inside her pussy, and it *takes everything inside me not to come right fucking now. I keep still to not only give her a chance to adjust to my size but to stop myself from coming. A few seconds pass before I move. Her eyes roll back as I pull out of her and then slam back in. Her moans and the way she breathes my name causes something inside me to break. I look down at her as worry seeps in.*

"Let go, Kai. I can take it. Give me everything you got, Zilla." Fuck, I'm going to hell a fucking happy man. I lean down and capture her lips. She kisses me back with such hunger it steals my breath. She locks her legs around me and pulls me deeper inside her. I can't hold back any longer. I remove her legs from around my waist and sit back. I don't pause. I grip her legs and place each of them on my shoulders and lean forward to get a better grip. I grasp each side of her face and fuck her—hard.

"Oh, fuck, I'm gonna come!" She screams her release, and I follow her a moment later with a roar and her name on my lips.

I sit back on my haunches, panting, my cock still deep inside her. Her pussy is clenching the shit out of my cock, and I love it. Her cheeks are flushed, and her chest is heaving. Her hair is a mess, and the sight of this beneath me has me wanting to fuck her again. She looks beautiful with the thoroughly fucked look on her face.

CHAPTER 31

Raya

That was the most incredible sex I have ever had!

Okay, granted, I have only ever had sex twice, but still. That was fucking Earth-shattering and mind-blowing. I had no idea where he began and I ended. We became one, and it was fucking epic! I'm lying here wrapped in Kai's arms, tracing the tattoos on his chest, when it hits me. I sit back and look down at him.

"You got your sleeves done?"

Kai smiles wide and nods his head. I turn and lift his left arm, inspecting it. Dragons, wizards, orbs of different colors, and trees. There are so many different things inside this one tattoo. I look at him in question. He sits up, and before I can even protest, he wraps his arms around me and sits me between his legs, my back to his chest. I can feel his sticky cock resting against my ass. I grin because I know his cock is sticky from fucking me, and that thought alone fills me with pride. I and my body are the reason this beast of a man found pleasure; Kai found his release inside me.

"I got these to remind me of where I have been and how far I have come. Each of these tattoos means something." I point to the wizard on his arm and he chuckles.

"That fucker represents Dom." I point to the dragon, and that causes him to have a proper belly laugh. I turn and look at him over my shoulder. Seeing him laugh is becoming one of my favorite views in the whole world. Kai is drop-dead gorgeous. He looks like he could be a male model on the front of GQ. "Can you keep a secret?" I smile and nod my head. "The dragon represents your father; you know, 'cause he's a moody bastard." It's my turn to laugh. I laugh so hard I have tears falling down my face. I look down at his arm again, but my attention is snagged when I notice a tattoo on the top of his thigh. How have I never seen that before? I run my hand over it, mesmerized by its beauty. Kai stiffens beneath my touch. This tattoo means something important to him. There is a crescent moon, a lake surrounded by mountains, and trees and stars line the sky.

"What about this one?"

He's quiet for a moment before he answers. "That one...I got that one for...it serves as a reminder...of my past." Hearing Kai flounder so much, I get who this one is for. I save him the trouble and answer my own question.

"This one is for my mom, isn't it?"

Kai releases a long sigh before he answers. "Yes."

"Oh." We sit here in awkward silence. I didn't feel uncomfortable before laying here naked with him, but now I just feel so exposed. I know he said he didn't love my mom, but then why get a fucking tattoo for her? I scoot forward and try to stand, but his arms snake around my waist and haul me back against him. I huff out my annoyance. He leans forward and runs his nose against the crook of my neck, which causes my skin to goose pimple.

"Don't be mad, vixen."

"I'm not," I snap.

"You're a terrible liar."

I snort. How can he expect me not to be fucking mad?

"Your mom...helped me, in a way. She showed me I could be more than a day-walking leech." I flinch at the harsh tone in his voice. "I am the first ever fae to be turned into a vampire. With my fae blood in my system, I am able to walk in the daylight. No other vamp was able to until Randall figured out why I could. He would then capture fae and drink from them, but it never lasted. Anyway, that was a long time ago. The tattoo may represent your mom, but to me it is a reminder that she helped me heal. Your mom is a good woman, and she never judged me for what I am. For that, I will always be indebted to her."

"Do you still love her?" I blurt the words out before I can stop myself. I clench my eyes shut and mentally slap myself.

"No, vixen. I love her as a sister, but that is it. I mistook her kindness for love and allowed myself to fall in love with the idea of love, but that is it. I was never really in love with her. Would I go to war for her? Yes. Your mother has done more than earn my loyalty and trust, she is someone I will always care for like I do your aunts and uncles."

I reach up and scrub my hands down my face. This is all such a mind fuck. The one guy who sees me, the real me and causes me to feel things I have never felt, of course has to come with complications. Can I let go of the fact that he fucked my mom in a dream like he just fucked me?

"Tell me what you're thinking?"

I sigh. It's better to be honest than sit here and lie to him. "I'm confused, and I'm hurt and angry. What if this is the same as what you had with her? Is any of this real to you, Kai?" He maneuvers me so I am now straddling him; I look down into his gray-blue eyes and see so much pain. It hurts my heart to see that look in his eyes. I run my hands through his blond hair and relish in the feeling of it. He cups my face and brings my gaze back to his. I feel a lump form in my throat.

"This is nothing like that. With her it wasn't real. I never let her see me, the real me, but somehow you haven't given me a choice. You see me, Raya—not the king or the millionaire club owner, you just see me. I have waited years for someone to see me as a man and not anything else. I like who I'm becoming, and that is all thanks to you." His words pierce me right in my heart. I lean forward and kiss him, pouring all my feelings into this kiss; with this kiss I am showing him that I don't want his money or his title—I just want him! His cock starts to harden beneath me, and I grind down onto it, and he moans into my mouth. I lift up but don't break our kiss, and reaching between our bodies, I grab his hard veiny cock and line it up with my entrance. I start to slowly impale myself on him. When he is deep inside me, we both sigh in contentment. He places his hands on my waist and begins to guide my movements. Having him inside me this way, he feels so much deeper. I moan as the friction starts to build inside me. I deepen our kiss and start to pick up my speed as I bounce on his cock.

"Oh fuck!" I shout. Oh my God, he has only been inside me for a few moments, and already I want to come on his fat cock. He tightens his grip on my waist and begins to thrust up inside me each time I slam down on him. I'm two seconds away from coming.

"Look at me when you come on my cock, vixen." I snap my eyes to his and hold his gaze. My pussy begins to clench his cock; the coil inside me is tight and ready to snap. One more hard thrust sends me over the edge, and I hold his gaze as I scream his name and come all over his cock. He slows his thrusts to allow me to come down from my orgasmic state slowly. "Get on your knees, Vixen." I do as he demands and hop off him and kneel. He stands in front of me and begins to pump his hard cock in my face. I dart my tongue out to moisten my lips. I want to taste my cum on his cock. "You want to suck your cunt juices off my cock?" I moan at his dirty words and nod my head. "Interlace your fingers behind your back and keep them there." I do as he says. "Open your mouth." I open my greedy mouth, and he slams his cock inside my mouth, and I gag. He grips the back of my hair to hold me in place. I can't breathe, but I don't give a fuck; suffocating to death on Kai's cock would be the best fucking way to go. He pulls out, and I drag in a lungful of air before he slams inside my mouth again, and this time I savor the taste. Tasting myself on his cock is euphoric. I love the tangy taste of both our essences mixed together.

"You want my cum down your throat or on you?" he rasps out. I can tell he is so close from the sound of his voice. He pulls out so I can answer him.

"On me. I want you to mark me as yours." His eyes round and his pupils dilate. I've just stroked the beast inside him. He fucks my mouth for another minute before he pulls out and begins to stroke his cock fast. I watch in fascination. This is such a turn-on, watching Kai make himself come.

"Oh, fuck, Vixen! Here it comes!" he roars. I open my mouth as the first spurt lands on my cheek, then another on my tongue. I lean back slightly so he can cum on my tits. And he does, his face is contorted in pleasure. I swallow the dollop of cum on my tongue and moan. Fuck, he tastes good. When his eyes land on the mess he has made on my face and tits, his eyes darken. "You have never looked better." He crouches down in front of me and runs his finger across my chest, smearing his cum all over me. Then he trails that finger down my body until it reaches my greedy cunt. "Spread your fucking legs, Vixen." I moan and do as he says. He reaches up and swipes the cum off my cheek then proceeds to push his cum-covered finger inside my tight hole. I moan out my pleasure. He grips my hair with his free hand and pulls me toward him before he smashes his lips against mine. He pulls back a couple of minutes later and looks down at me with such hunger in his eyes. "This body, these lips, and especially this greedy cunt belong to me, Vixen. Do you understand?" I nod my head. "I ever see another man touch what is mine, I will fucking kill him, you get me?"

"Yes."

"Good girl." He pulls his finger out of my pussy and brings it to my mouth. "Now be a good girl and suck the cum off my finger." I do exactly as he says and enjoy every fucking minute of it.

I bolt upright on the couch in Jackson's office and dart my gaze around the room to see everyone is still here except for my guys. When my gaze lands on Dom, I narrow my eyes. He's looking at me with a shit-eating grin. Bright light catches my attention. I see Nico is inside a blue dome. I dart my eyes to Ryan to see what the hell happened. Nico is pounding his fists against the dome. What the fuck happened?

"What's going on?" Jax, Chase, Lucian, and Alex won't even look at me. Sophia, Mya, and Aurora keep flicking through the books in their lap. Ryan is trying to calm Nico, so my last option is Dom. I meet his gaze and raise a brow.

"Dude, you sleep talk." I scrunch my face in confusion.

He sighs then says, "You moaned the princess of fae's name…out loud, sexually dumbass." Oh fuck. I stand then turn toward Nico and smile sheepishly. He roars and runs at the dome, hoping his sheer force will shatter it—it won't.

"You bastard! You promised you would leave her alone." I need to think fast before shit gets out of control.

"Technically, I didn't break that promise. You said when she gets back I had to leave her alone." Nico glowers at me.

Ryan gasps and then looks between the both of us before settling her gaze on me. "Explain," she growls out.

Sighing and running a hand through my hair, I try to think of a way out of answering, and I'm shocked when Nico takes over answers for me. "We had an understanding. When Raya comes back, he will leave her be. He doesn't have to disappear; he just has to back off and let her live."

Ryan drops the dome and then stands in front of her husband. "You have no right to make that call for her."

"She's my daughter, and I will do what is best for her."

"Fuck you, Nico. She is our daughter, and she has the right to choose who she loves. You do not get to choose for her."

I don't want them fighting over this, so I butt in. "Ryan, I agreed to the terms. I will help get her back, and then I will leave. If she chooses to come to me, then he said he would back off and deal with it."

Ryan spins around and faces me, shock clear on her face.

"I call bullshit. There is no way he is ever going to be okay with his best friend banging his daughter." The three of us turn and glare at Dom, and it gives me great satisfaction to not only see Jackson but Lucian as well slap the back of the fuck face's head. "What the fuck!"

"You deserved it, Dad!"

"And you're the load your mother should have fucking swallowed!"

We all burst out laughing—well, everyone except Sophia and Nico. If looks could kill, Nico would have murdered Dom six times over. Sophia walks over to Dom, places her hand on his shoulder, and then knees him right in his junk. Dom crumples to the floor, hollering in pain and shouting death threats at his wife as she stands over him.

"The next time you say something dumb like that to my son

or call him your sperm again, I will make sure I break your fucking dick next time."

"You love my dick," Dom wheezes out, and Nico groans.

"Baby, that's what dildos are for. You are easily replaced!"

"Mom!"

"Sophia!" Nico and Lucian shout at the same time. Soph ignores them.

"I swear to God, Little Dove, you get a vibrator or a dildo, and I will make your life fucking hell."

"Promises, promises," Soph says as she makes her way back to her chair.

When I turn back toward Nico and Ryan, her gaze is already on me. "I'm only going to say this once, Kai, so listen good. You already hurt my daughter once. If you leave and you hurt her again. I will be the one coming after you. Not Nico, not the fae army...just me. Do I make myself fucking clear?" I respect Ryan so much more at this moment. She is an amazing mother.

"Crystal."

She nods her head and then goes to join the girls and Lucian. Hopefully, they have found something in the history books from the mansion. Nico comes to stand in front of me, and the murmurs in the room stop.

"If I ever and I mean fucking ever hear you say my daughter's name like that again, I will fucking rip your heart out and feed it to Dom's wolf." I can't stop the grin that spreads across my face. "You're such a fucking prick, Melakai," he says as he brushes past me.

Everyone decided to call it a night and get some sleep. Jax told me to use Raya's room, which just pissed Nico off more. I was glad to see Cam had brought me a bag of clothes and some blood bags. I was famished and needed to feed. Four bags later, I finally felt like myself again. I took a quick shower, shaved, and hopped into a pair of sweats, ready to call it a night. Just as I was about to lay down, a thought hit me. Before I left Raya, she said that she would be back by the blood moon. My train of thought is cut off by the sound of someone pounding on my door.

"Come in." I'm shocked to see Aurora and Jax, and the look on Aurora's face tells me everything I need to know—she had a vision.

"They plan to kill you."

I knew it. But Mya pretty much said that earlier, so why is she so upset about this vision? "So, the potion I'm supposed to drink on the blood moon...what does it do?"

She shakes her head. "I can't see what the potion does. All I know is they plan to kill you the night of the blood moon." Fuck. I need to see Raya again to find out more. "Kai, I need to ask you something." I dart my gaze to Jax to see he is hesitant, which worries me slightly. I nod my head. "I want you to take me with you next time you go to Raya. I need more information from her in order to piece this vision together." I can hear the frustration in her voice. Aurora has only recently started having her visions again, so she is a little out of practice.

"When?"

"How soon can you go to her again?"

I close my eyes and feel deep inside myself. I can feel a tether inside me which links me to Raya's dreams. She's still sleeping.

"We can go now, but we need Dom to put you under with me." Aurora turns to Jax who nods his head and leaves the room. The two of us are left here standing awkwardly in silence.

"For what it's worth, I think you would be perfect for her and her for you."

I snap my gaze back to her, shocked. "Why do you say that?"

"Because you will push her to go after what she wants, and she will make you see that you are more than what you think."

I see it in her eyes. "You knew, didn't you?"

A sly smile breaks out on her face. "My visions returned a while ago. I just never said anything." The devious little shit. "But yes, I have seen the two of you, and so has Sophia." Fucking Soph. So-So has the gift of being able to see others' love lives. She thinks that gift is useless, but I think it is an honor. "Don't worry, we haven't told anyone else." I nod my head and thank her just before Dom, Jax, Nico, Ryan, and Sophia walk through the door.

"I'm here. I'm shitty and I'm tired, so this better be good."

I quickly speak before Aurora does. "The brothers are gonna kill me, and Raya has no idea they are going to use her to do it." That wakes Dom the fuck up. The others all wear looks of shock and confusion.

"How?"

"When"

"Why?"

I ignore their questions and speak directly to Dom. "I need you to put Aurora under with me, so we can go to Raya."

Nico steps forward and looks me directly in the eyes. "I'm coming, too."

I knew he wouldn't let this go without a fight.

"Me too."

Fuck let's just make this a family gathering, then. I look at Dom and the look in his eyes tells me all I need to know.

"He can't put that many of you under. Only two of you can come." Ryan and Nico exchange a look between each before Nico nods at me. I walk over to the bed with Aurora and Nico trailing me. Aurora jumps between me and Nico and interlaces her fingers through both our hands. I know this must be hard for her, because she never touches people unless she has to. It brings on visions.

"Okay, I don't know how much time you will have. If I start fading, I'll get Ryan to maintain the link and bring you both back." Dom doesn't have to worry about me, because I am already linked to Raya. "Let's do this. Saleepa draminga entare, solacer takenga."

We're back in the woods. I look to make sure both Nico and Aurora are okay. Once I deem that they are fine, I start to lead them toward where I know Raya will be. We break through the woods and I see her sitting by the edge of the lake. Nico's voice has her jumping to her feet and spinning around to face us.

"Seriously? You brought her to Lake fucking William?"

I ignore him and make my way to Raya. As soon as she is in front of me, I wrap my arms around her and hold her against me. I ignore Nico's groans and muttering. She pulls back and looks up at me with uncertainty in her eyes.

"What's going on, Kai?" I'm shoved out of the way by her father as he wraps her in a bone-crushing hug. I see some of the tension drain from his body as he holds her against him. I have never seen Nico like this except for when he is with Ryan. He releases Raya, and she moves on to hug her aunt.

"Dad, why are you and Aunt Aurora here?" I move so I'm standing beside Raya.

"I had a vision, honey. Are the brothers planning something for the blood moon?" Raya nods her head, confusion colors her

features. "Honey, whatever they have planned is going to backfire-"

"No, they are giving me the cure to change Kai back!" She defends against her aunt. Aurora darts her eyes to me.

I sigh and spin Raya so she is facing me and meets her gaze. "Vixen, they lied. They plan to kill me the night of the blood moon. There is no cure."

She shakes her head and tears begin to gather in her eyes. "No! That's not true! I gave them Randall so they would cure you and mom! They promised!"

"Baby girl, they lied."

Raya turns to face her father. "How do you know, Dad?"

Nico briefly darts his gaze to mine then focuses back on Raya. "Because Uncle Dom and I spent years hunting for a cure for Kai. Your mother has been looking for a cure for the past twenty years with the help of your uncles, aunts, and cousin. I even help her from time to time." This revelation shocks the fuck out of me, I had no fucking idea they were doing this for me. Why didn't they tell me?

"Oh my God, Dad, what have I done?" I can hear the horror in her voice. Nico pulls Raya to him and wraps his arm around her.

"We can fix this, honey, but I need your help."

Raya's eyes look at me as she answers her aunt. "What do you need me to do, Aunt Rora?"

We spend the next twenty minutes discussing what Raya has learned from the brothers. I can see she is apprehensive. I know she thinks the brothers aren't bad. They have brainwashed her into thinking they mean me no harm, but they are liars. We try to get her to describe her surroundings, but she hasn't seen any clear landmarks to narrow our search down. I can see the frustration on Nico's face. He wants his daughter home with him and safe.

Nico clutches his chest. I look at him and Aurora and see the strain on their faces.

"We need to go. Dom's power is fading."

Fear clouds Nico's violet eyes as he looks to his daughter.

I knew he wouldn't want to leave once he got here. "We need to go now. The longer we stay here the harder on Dominic it is." The thought of hurting Dom snaps Nico out of his stupor. Aurora embraces Raya and tells her that she will do everything in her power to change the vision she had. Nico turns to his daughter, fear etched in his features. I can't imagine what he is feeling. If I was him, I don't know what I would do in this situation. He reaches out and wraps his arms around her.

Raya clutches her father and begins to shake. "I'm so sorry, Daddy. I was so stupid," she hiccups out.

"Shhhh, it's okay, Princess. I won't let anything happen to you. I swear to you on my life I will find you. Be strong, baby girl. We raised you to be a warrior, and I need you to channel that now and be the warrior I know you can be." I look at my brother, proud as fuck. Nico is a control freak, so I know this is hard for him to do. He releases Raya and holds her at arm's length as he leans down and places a kiss on her forehead. "I love you more than all the stars in the sky. You, my baby girl, are my and your mother's everything."

"I love you too, Daddy. Tell Mom I'm sorry," she sobs. Nico meets my gaze over the top of her head, and I nod. I move toward them, grab Raya, and pull her toward me. I wrap my arms around her and hold her against me as Nico and Aurora head back toward the woods. Raya calls for her dad to come back. I see Nico stiffen, but he doesn't slow his pace. I hold her sobbing form until I feel that their presence has gone from this land. I turn her toward me and look her in the eyes. Tears are running down her face.

"You can do this. You're stronger than you think. Your father is the most stubborn motherfucker I have ever met, and your mother is the strongest woman I have ever known. You have both their blood running through your veins. You can do this, vixen." Before more can be said, I feel her fading. She is being woken up. Shit. "You have to go now, vixen. I'll come to you when I can." Panic fills her eyes. Before that look shreds me, I move back and release my hold on her dream.

CHAPTER 33

Raya

I wake to find the three brothers looming over me. Each of them wears a look of betrayal. I open my mouth to say something, but no words come out. I feel myself start to panic. I look to Boston, who seems to be the easiest of the brothers to reason with. The look he gives me has any hope of getting through to him fading.

"We offered you a cure, we tried to help you, and then you go and betray us!" Anger flares inside me. They are the ones who lied to me from the start. I feel so fucking foolish for ever thinking I could trust these three. Kai and Dad are right; I'm impulsive and reckless. My stupid decision has not only put me in danger but the people I love. I need to try to find a way out of this situation. I am Raya Stone, and I am no meek female. I am heir to the fucking throne, and I have trained to fight since I was three years old. My magic isn't weak, either.

Just the thought of my magic has it surging to the surface. I take some calming breaths before I begin to glow and the brothers see that as a threat. Boston shakes his head. So much disappointment shines in his eyes. I don't know why I feel guilty, since they are the ones that led me astray, not the other way round.

"You don't get to look at me like that, Boston. You all lied to me."

Boston snaps his gaze back to me, disappointment is replaced by anger. "What did he say to you?" I flinch at the coldness in his tone. Boston sounds like a heartless bastard.

"Answer him, Raya!" Bronx demands.

"He told me that the three of you plan to kill him the night of the blood moon." I search each of their faces, hoping to see shock or something, but I don't see that. Memphis has a cruel smile on his face. Bronx and Boston keep their expression blank.

"He's right, isn't he? You three used me to get Randall." I can hear the hurt in my own voice. I thought I could trust them. I don't understand why I am so hurt that they lied to me. I don't even know them, but their betrayal stings like a motherfucker.

"They need to be wiped from this Earth."

"They?" I question, and Bronx narrows his eyes and nods. "Who are they?"

"Vampires. They are a fucking weed in this world, and their whole race needs to die!"

I gasp, and my hand comes up to cover my mouth. They don't just plan to kill Randall and Kai. They want to kill the whole vampire race! "Why? What did they do to you, Bronx?"

Bronx glares down at me. "They took everything from us." Bronx's facial expression gives nothing away, but the heartache in his voice tells me everything I need to know.

"Randall did it, didn't he? You said I remind you of someone you used to know. Is that why you helped me cure my mom?" Bronx won't meet my gaze, Memphis is vibrating with rage, and Boston looks lethal.

I try to reason with them, hoping I can get through to them and change their minds. "Not all vampires are bad. Some of them—"

"Don't you dare try and defend your leech lover to us! He is just as fucking bad as the rest of those bloodsuckers. He will die, along with Randall and the rest of his race. You will help us whether you are willing or not."

"Fuck you, Memphis! I won't help you with shit."

Memphis smiles wickedly down at me. "Oh, my sweets, all I need to do is hold a knife to your throat, and he will drink the potion willingly. Your lover would die in a heartbeat to save you. The fact that you haven't realized that until now is comical."

No, I will not let Kai die for me. I need to find a way out of this now. "Just kill Randall. He's the one you want, not Kai," I plead.

"Once he drinks the potion, it will link him to Randall. You see, when Melakai became king, it joined him to every vamp in existence. We just need him to drink the potion. Then, when we kill him on the night of the blood moon, it will kill everyone linked to him. When Randall sees that his precious vamps are all dead, he will die slowly."

Tears flow down my cheeks. Memphis is fucking crazy. Whatever Randall did to these three must have been bad. He has turned them into monsters.

"Please......don't do this."

Bronx scoffs and turns to leave my tent. "You have three days, then we travel back to Alaska. We brought you here hoping to convince you to see the harm these cockroaches have done to the world. Instead, you went and fell in love with one of them. We only need your blood, and then you're free to go. I meant what I said when I told you no harm would come to you, Raya." Hearing those words out of Boston's mouth stings—has he no heart?

"Take my blood now and let me go."

"We can't. It has to be done on the blood moon."

"Why, Boston?"

"Because it has to be done then for the spell to work."

Boston follows Bronx's lead and leaves me alone in my tent with Memphis. Out of the three of them, Memphis is the one that scares me. He stands there staring down at me in a way that makes me uncomfortable.

"I would never hurt you. Do as you are told, and you will be back with your family sooner than you think." With those ominous words said, he turns and leaves, zipping the flap shut behind himself. I break down, wrap my arms around my middle, and sob. I am such a fuck-up. How could I have been so fucking stupid to think these three brothers were ever noble? I actually fucking felt sorry for them. I need to suck up my hurt feelings and do some digging. I need to find out how the fuck these three are so strong. They ooze power, and believe me, when you are inside a small tent with the three of them, it's fucking suffocating.

Once I see the daylight pierce through the tent, I change and brush my teeth. I need to get answers before tonight. I know they are not going to willingly tell me what I want to know, so I need to be sly about it. But how? I decide I need to channel my inner Uncle Dom and use sarcasm as my shield. My daddy didn't raise me to be weak, and my mom is the baddest bitch in the world, and I will not let them down. I open the flap and step out of my tent to see the three of them already sitting around on the logs by the fire. I take a few deep breaths and make my way over to the table that holds the food. I pile my plate high, then go over and sit on the empty log between Memphis and Bronx. I can feel their eyes on me but choose to ignore them. My dad taught me that silence is better than words. It makes people uncomfortable. If I sit here and talk, I'll show them all my cards and give them the upper hand. If I sit here quietly and appear unaffected by their stares, it gives me the upper hand because they will be trying to figure out what I'm up to.

"We didn't think you would come out today."

I shrug my shoulders in answer to Boston and continue to shovel food into my mouth. I see a bottle of water on the ground next to Bronx. I swallow my mouthful then turn to him and ask in the sweetest voice. "Can I have that water please, Bronxy?" Bronx jerks back, shocked. I hear Memphis spluttering behind me. "Never mind, I'll get it myself." I reach down and grab the bottle. Unscrewing the cap, I take three big gulps before capping it and placing it down beside me. I can feel their eyes burning holes into me but ignore them and continue to eat. Once my plate is finished, I stand and take it to the trash bag then turn and face the brothers. All three of them are staring at me like I'm a fucking unicorn or something–perfect!

"What are you up to?" I can see the skepticism in Bronx's eyes.

I smile sweetly and shrug my shoulders. "What's the plan today? If you don't have anything on, I would love to spar. I haven't let my magic out in ages." The three of them exchange a look before turning back to me.

"You want to spar...against us?"

I turn and grin at Boston. "Why not?"

"Because we would kill you in battle."

I meet Memphis's smug look and pout. "But you said you would never harm me."

Memphis narrows his eyes at me and stands. Before he can take a single step Boston jumps to his feet and says, "I'll spar with you!"

What in the name of all that is fucking holy was I thinking?

I'm standing here drenched in sweat, panting like I ran a fucking marathon while Boston stands in front of me bouncing on the balls of his feet, ready to go another round. Memphis and Bronx stand by the tree in the shade with their arms crossed in front of their chests. We have been doing this for the past hour. I cannot for the life of me land a single energy ball on Boston.

"You need to be quicker than that, Ray."

I glare at the smug prick. "I'm going as fast as I can."

"No, you're not."

I throw my hands in the air, exasperated. "How the fuck would you know?" I snap.

"Because you're limiting yourself. You're trying to control the magic inside you. Let that control go and get out of your head. You're taught to be ready always. Don't do that. You need to be in the moment and anticipate my next move, not guess." I can hear the truth in his words. I have always been taught to be ready and prepared. I have never fought the way he is telling me to, but what if he is right?

"Let your control go, Raya. You're trying too hard, and you're getting lost in your own mind. Let your instincts take over and guide you." I'm shocked that Bronx is actually willing to help me; he and Memphis haven't said a word since we came out here. I nod my head and straighten. I call my magic to the surface and allow it to course through me.

"That's it, Ray. Now, open your eyes and stay out of your head." I do as Boston says and watch him. "Everyone has a tell. Something to indicate what their next move is. You just need to find mine." I nod my head. Boston begins to allow his magic out, and I stare in awe as he releases his green magic. I have no idea why his power is green or why Bronx's is red and Memphis's power is black. I'm pulled out of my thoughts when Boston begins to build a ball of energy in his hand. I don't lash out with one of my own like I have been doing. I stand and wait. I watch him like a hawk and see if I can find his tell. Dad had told me the same thing once. If I find Boston's tell, then I can beat him.

He moves around me, and I follow his movement as he passes the energy ball from hand to hand. I see a flicker in his eyes and wait. He moves left then jumps back to the right. I have just enough time to dive out of the way before the ball hits me. I roll on the ground and jump to my feet, a purple energy ball of my own in my hand. We circle each other, and that's when I see it again. His eyes flicker, then he launches another ball. I dodge it–barely—then, before he can recover, I launch mine and it hits him in the chest. I jump for joy and clap my hands, then I'm sent sailing and land face first in the ground.

What the fuck just happened?

I roll over to my side in pain and stagger to my feet. My back is aching, and I feel the breeze hitting my exposed flesh from where the energy burnt me. I turn and glare at Bronx and Memphis.

Bronx grins at me and says, "Always be aware of your surroundings. If this was a real battle, you would be dead."

I glare at the fucker. "That was a dick move, and you know it!"

"That dick move will save your life one day. Now go again, and this time don't fucking celebrate." I glower at the bastard. I block the pain in my back from my mind and face Boston again. We do the same thing and circle each other. This time I don't hesitate. When I see his eyes flicker, I drop to the ground and send one of my energy balls straight into his stomach. When he drops to his knees, I turn and send the other one to an unsuspecting Bronx. It hits him straight in the shoulder. I gloat at the fact I got the bastard, and I erect another ball and wait for Memphis to attack. To my utter shock, he doesn't. He looks from me to Boston and then to Bronx and breaks out into a fit of laughter. Bronx turns angry, cold blue eyes to me and points an accusing finger.

Before he can go off, I speak. "Always be aware of your surroundings, Bronxy."

Memphis laughs harder. Boston joins his brother and laughs while Bronx and I stand there and glare at each other.

"She got you! She actually got you!" I can hear the laughter and awe in Boston's voice. I want to look at him, but I'm smart enough to know not to take my eyes off Bronx. I make sure I keep all three of them in my line of sight.

"You little shit. Now it's you and me." I gulp at the threat in Bronx's voice. Oh, no. I think I may have just pissed him off. I can see from the way Memphis and Bronx protect Boston that he is the youngest and least powerful out of the three. I have yet to determine who is stronger out of Bronx and Memphis. Something tells me that these two would be evenly matched. Bronx makes his way toward me, and I'll be honest, I want to shit my pants. The look in his cold eyes tells me he won't go easy on me like Boston did.

"Bronx, don't. Leave her alone."

Bronx ignores Boston's pleas and comes to stand in front of me.

"It's about time I teach this leech lover a lesson." I keep my mask in place and don't let him see how much his words hurt me. I thought I was getting somewhere with them today, but I guess I was wrong; they will never change their minds. After today, I only have two more days to figure out a plan to stop them from killing Kai. Boston is the strongest supe I have ever battled against, aside from my mom. My mom could take them on in a one-on-one fight, but there is no way she could take all three of them on at once. I need to find out how they got so powerful. Bronx moves away from me and stops when there is a good distance between us. I block out my worry and focus. If I lose concentration for even a second, I know Bronx will pounce, and I worry he won't stop. I call on my magic again. Going up against Bronx, I will need to access more magic than I ever have. I pull more to the surface and allow it to wrap around me like a blanket. I watch Bronx release his and stare. His red magic swirls around and clings to its master. His whole body is covered from head to toe in red mist.

"Bronx, she's just a kid."

Bronx turns to Boston, but I refuse to take my eyes off him for even a second.

"She isn't a weak child. She has been coddled her whole life, and now she is about to learn a harsh lesson." His gaze swings back to me, a wicked glint in his eye. "You can surrender."

I square my shoulders and raise my chin. "Not in my nature."

"Very well, but I will not go easy on you like Boston did. It's not in my nature to hold back." I nod my understanding, and Bronx begins to circle me. I move so my back is never to him. I study every one of his movements to try and find his tell. His face is a mask of indifference. I form two energy balls in each of my hands and hold them at the ready. Bronx cracks a ghost of a smile, but that's it. He still won't release any more magic or form any energy balls. Before I can take my next breath or even blink, Bronx is behind me with a red energy ball hovering in my face. His free arm is wrapped around my throat. I stand as still as a statue, stunned. How the fuck did he just do that? "I could end your life right here, right now."

"Then what are you waiting for?" Why the hell did I just

say that? I feel Bronx's chest rise and fall behind me. We both stand there breathing hard and fast.

"I told you, I will never harm you, Raya." He releases his hold on my throat, and the energy ball he had in his other hand disappears as he steps back. I spin around and face him. His eyes hold so much sadness that my chest aches for him. What happened to these brothers? "Don't look at me like that."

"Like what, Bronx?" He scowls down at me, then storms off back toward the tents. Memphis and Boston move to where Bronx was just standing.

"He's like a 5000-piece puzzle. Don't try to put him back together, Ray. You did good. No one has ever been able to find his tell." I nod my head, but truthfully, my mind is whirling with thoughts of Bronx.

"How are you all so powerful?"

Memphis doesn't hesitate to answer me. "That is a secret we will never share with you. All you need to know is the price was worth the outcome in the end." What price did they pay? Did they sell their soul to the devil or something?

"Come on, let's get some lunch, and I also need to feed that fucker." The guys have been feeding Randall a half a cup of blood a day. I had no idea where they were getting the blood, and I sure as fuck didn't ask, either. The three of us head back toward the camp to see Bronx tugging on his hair and swearing. When his gaze snaps up to ours, I freeze. He storms toward me and wraps his hand around my throat, lifting me off the ground. I claw at his hand and try to breathe. Memphis and Boston try to pull him away from me, but Bronx blasts them back with his magic. His cold emotionless eyes meet mine, and I feel my eyes starting to bulge from lack of oxygen.

"Where the fuck is he?" he screams in my face. I try to shake my head but can't move due to the grip he has on my throat.

Tears stream down my cheeks as fear sets in. I might actually die. What the fuck happened to cause Bronx to switch like this?

"Let her go, Bronx. She's done nothing."

"He's gone, Memphis. He fucking escaped, and the only one with any feelings toward the leeches is her!" My eyes start to droop shut. I try to gasp for air but fail miserably.

"Let her go now before you kill her!" That's the last thing I hear before everything goes black.

CHAPTER 34

Malakai

Nico was a mess after we got back last night. I haven't seen him at all today. I know last night was fucking hard for him. I wish I could have helped him in some way, but there was nothing I could do or say to make this situation any better for him. I feel so responsible for Raya being gone; if she had never met me, she would never have gone with the brothers to find a cure that doesn't exist. Sitting here in Jackson's office combing through all these books from the mansion has proved useless so far. We haven't been able to find a single thing that links the brothers to the vampires or Randall in any way. If we can't find the link between them, then we're fucked, plain and simple. We have all hands on deck except Jax, Ryan, and Nico. Jax has pack shit to sort out, and Nico and Ryan are God knows where. The rest of us are here combing through these dusty old books.

"What do we do if we can't find anything?"

I turn to Sophia. I can see in the way her body is wound tight that she doubts we will find anything.

"We have to keep trying, Little Dove. If we don't, our niece could be in some serious shit."

Soph sighs and goes back to reading through the book she

has. I know Dom is just as worried as she is. To make matters worse, we have no idea what kind of link we are looking for.

"What if the link isn't between the brothers?"

"What are you saying, Chase?"

"Think about it, Alex. When you hurt someone, they will get over it eventually, but if you hurt someone they care or cared about, then they would want revenge for all eternity." I hate to admit it, but Chase may have a point. Have we been looking at this all wrong?

"So, what are we looking for then?"

"Any ties between someone mentioned in these books and the brothers. If we find that link, Rora, we will find their Achilles heel." I had to give Chase props. I really think he might be onto something here. Jax joined us and began to help sort the mass of books.

We spend the next few hours going through these books with a fine-tooth comb, hoping that something will pop out, but we have no such luck. I can feel myself starting to lose hope; if it becomes a choice between Raya or me, I will gladly go to my grave for mon salut. She deserves to live and experience life. I know everyone thinks I have a hero complex, but I really don't. I just know that her life is worth more than mine. I have lived a long life, and she has barely started hers. I need to find a way out of this for both of us. I want to experience life with her and watch her grow, whether she is with me or not.

"Hey, I think I found something." All eyes turn to Jackson.

"What is it?"

"I think I just found our trump card, Dom. I think they have a sister." Hold the fuck up, since when? All the rumors I have heard about them only mention the three of them, not a sister. "It says here that in 1982 Randall met a young girl by the name of Storm Masters. He kidnapped her for her abilities as a seer." What the fuck?

"I would have known that. I was with him in the year 1982, and I never met a seer while I was with him."

"That's what it says here, Kai. Who wrote these books? Maybe we can speak to that person and find out more?" I release a long sigh. The person who wrote those books is dead. Randall killed Raphael about fifty years ago. We need to do more digging.

"Wait, what the hell would Randall want a seer for? What use was this Storm to him?"

"If he had a seer, Aurora, he would be able to see the outcome of any battle and know whether he would win or not. We need to dig more into this and find out everything we can about her."

"That's gonna be hard, Kai. They didn't have the internet back then, so we will need to do this old school and go through the newspaper archives or something like that." Fuck, Sophia had a point. Jackson linked his pack and got a few of his men to head into town to the local library and collect newspapers from that era and whatever else they could find that would help us.

"We need to go through the rest of these records from 1982 onward and find out what the hell happened to this woman. We need to know who exactly she is to the brothers. If we can find that out, it might just help us save both Kai and Raya. Sorry, Mom, but I don't give two shits if they kill Randall. I'll gladly stand by and watch as they torture that son of a bitch to death." I can hear the venom dripping from Lucian's tone. He has wanted to kill Randall for years, but Sophia wanted him caged and to suffer like he made her suffer. I want the cunt dead just as much as everyone else in this room. He is a vermin that needs to be exterminated from this fucking Earth.

Jax's guys turned up with boxes filled with newspapers, death records, police reports, and a whole lot more. We took a break to get some lunch before we all dove back into it. I refused to eat with the others; I didn't like them seeing me feed from a blood bag. I didn't like anyone watching me eat. It was something that I always did alone. I met the others back in the office and we all went through the boxes. Hours passed with no success. Everyone's spirits were low. We had hoped that it would be easy, but nothing in life is ever fucking easy. It was now getting dark, and still Ryan and Nico hadn't joined us. I was starting to worry that something might have happened.

"I got something." I spin around and face Alex who is pacing behind my sofa with a manila file opened in his hands. "Storm Masters was reported missing on the 9th of October 1982 by her brothers. It is believed that Storm was taken outside of Lady Duke's Pub on the night of the 8th of October. Her purse and one of her shoes was found in the alley beside the local pub. Her brothers are offering a reward of $5,000 for any information regarding their sister. This is from a newspaper article in 1982. We need to check the police records for any missing persons filed back then. If we find this woman, we may be able to bargain with the brothers for Raya's freedom without Kai having to ingest that bloody potion." I appreciated Alex. I knew he and Chase had the Knox coven to run, but instead of going home, they chose to stay here to help me and of course find a way to save their cousin, as well.

"Okay. Aurora, Sophia, Mya, and I will start on the missing persons. Alex, Chase, Lucian, Dom, and Kai—you guys keep going through the books from the mansion and the newspapers." Jackson was in his element; that asshole loved to take charge and boss people around. Nevertheless, we all did as he said. Time moved so much quicker than what we did. Combing through each article or record book, we came up empty. Was this a dead end?

"Guys, it's nearly midnight. Maybe we should call it a night and pick it up again tomorrow?" Everyone agreed. I hated that we were stopping, but my eyes are burning, and I think coming back tomorrow with a fresh pair of eyes might do us a world of good.

After showering, eating, and getting into the bed, I finally start to relax. There is no way I will be able to go to sleep if I don't calm the hell down. I lay there and take a few deep calming breaths then close my eyes. I try to feel for the link between Raya and me, but I feel...nothing! I bolt upright in bed and try to rub the panic from my chest. Maybe I'm just tired? I know deep down inside me that that isn't the case, but I tell myself that to try and ease the panic inside me. I take a few more calming breaths then lay down again. I close my eyes and try to feel for the tether that binds me to her...nothing. What the fuck is going on? If I can't feel a connection to her then that would mean...she is...no longer living. I sit up again, grab my phone from the nightstand, and send out an SOS text to the gang. I even include Nico and Ryan in that message. They need to know.

Ten agonizing minutes later, everyone shows up. Jax and Aurora look like the walking dead, Dom and Soph look like they just fucked, Lucian, Mya, Chase, and Alex look like they were up to something, but Ryan and Nico...they look hollow.

"What's with the 911 text, Kai?" I stop pacing the end of the bed and look at each of them. My gaze lands on a distraught Ryan. I look at Nico next; he has bags under his eyes, his hair is a mess. He looks...broken. Seeing that look on his face guts me. I keep my eyes on his as I answer Dom.

"I tried to find Raya, but I can't feel the connection to her anymore." Ryan gasps, tears clouding her eyes. Nico's grip around her shoulders tightens.

He clenches his jaw as his eyes take on a hard edge. "What does that mean?"

I really wish I didn't have to answer him, but he deserves to know the truth. I square my shoulders and lift my chin. "If I can't feel the tether that binds us, that means she might be gone." A sob tears out of Ryan, and tears cascade down her cheeks.

Nico drops his arm from around his wife and moves to stand in front of me. His eyes shine with unshed tears. The look he gives me is beseeching me to be wrong and tell him it was a joke. "What do you mean gone?"

I can hear the rough edges in his voice. He is fighting his urge to crumble and break down.

"It means that she could be......dea—"

"No!" Nico and I both turn to face Mya. She is as pale as a ghost. "The vision I had. You had to stay away from her for nineteen years–you did that. I saw it...you and her...she can't be...gone." Mya darts her gaze to Aurora. I follow her line of sight.

Aurora has tears leaking from her eyes. So does Sophia. Mya seems more panicked than upset. Aurora and Sophia you can tell are distraught, but Mya...I can't explain it, but something doesn't feel right.

"What are you three not telling us?" I can hear the anger in my own voice. I have had a feeling since I arrived that Aurora, Sophia, and Mya are keeping something from us. Aurora and Sophia confirmed my suspicion when Mya arrived. They all look guilty right now. The three of them exchange a loaded look, and Nico comes to stand beside me.

"Answer him!" Nico yells, the three women flinch and for once, Jax and Dom don't say anything in the girls' defense. They are both looking at them skeptically. Minutes tick by as we all stand there silently waiting for one of the girls to say something....anything.

"Please, whatever it is or whatever you have done, I don't care. Please just help me get my daughter back." To the shock of everyone in the room, Nico drops to his knees. The king of fucking Farrarie, and one of the baddest motherfuckers I know, is on his knees. "I am begging you. Tell me where my daughter is or tell me if she is...gone." A strangled sound escapes Nico. Ryan rushes over, drops down in front of her husband, and wraps her arms around him. Everyone in the room is staring at Nico. None of us can believe what we have just witnessed. A growl draws my attention back to the others.

Lucian is facing the women. "What have you done, Mom?"

Sophia drops her gaze to the floor. "I knew the moment Ryan found out she was pregnant that she would have a girl and that girl would become Kai's other half." Aurora already told me this.

"Why didn't you say anything?" I ask.

Sophia snaps angry violet eyes to me. "How could I, Kai? You left, so how the fuck was I supposed to tell you?" I don't get a chance to answer.

"I had a vision after Ryan gave birth. I knew then why Kai had fled." Jax looks at Aurora in utter shock.

"I had a vision twenty or so years ago that Kai would destroy this family if he stayed. I told him he needed to leave after Dom and Soph got married. He didn't question my reasons, just said okay and left. When Raya was fourteen, I had another vision. This time, I knew I couldn't stop it. The first vision I had was of Kai killing Raya. At the time, I didn't know who Raya was, just that him killing her would tear this family apart. The vision I had when she was fourteen showed me that Kai needed Raya and vice versa."

"What the fuck did you three do?" This comes from Dom. All three women drop their gazes to the floor. Dread begins to stir inside me.

"We had no idea who they were. I overheard Luce and Raya talking about going to Colorado to this vault. I found out who the owners are, and we sent an anonymous tip to them that their vault would be robbed. We knew Lucian would go to you for help, and that way, Raya would finally be able to meet you. We didn't know that the brothers would do any of this."

I look at Sophia like I don't even know her anymore. I know they meant well, but what the fuck? Raya could be dead because of them. Their meddling could have cost Ryan and Nico their daughter. Ryan stands beside me, glowing bright blue. I take a step back and shudder. The look on her face scares the shit out of me. She is vibrating with rage. The glare she sends each of the girls has them stepping back toward the back wall.

"Why the fuck would you do that to my little girl?" The anger in her tone has me looking at Lucian. He is moving toward the three girls, ready to defend them if he needs to.

"We never meant for this to happen, Ry." Ryan scoffs and glares at her sister in law.

"You know this whole thing for me has been like a bad fucking dream! My daughter goes missing, and I get her back. Then she leaves willingly with them, and I come to find out she would never be in this position if it wasn't for you three interfering!" Ryan throws her head back and screams. A wave of power pulses out of her, shattering the windows and destroying the furniture in the room. I blink my eyes open to see Lucian has formed yellow domes around everyone in the room to protect them from the blast. He moves toward a raging Ryan. The magic has stopped pulsing out of her, but she still stands there glowing. Lucian raises his hands like he's about to surrender.

"Smurf, let me help you."

"Can you bring my daughter back, Luce?" Lucian flinches slightly at the harsh tone in her voice but keeps moving until he is standing in front of Ryan.

"Smurf, if there is anyone in this world who would be able to tell if Ray is really gone...it would be you. Feel inside yourself, Smurf. Follow that mother's intuition, and tell me what you feel." Ryan stares at Lucian for a long moment before she closes her eyes. Her power begins to fade, and once it has disappeared completely, Lucian releases us from his magic. Everyone stands and stares at her like she is a circus act. Nico climbs to his feet and wraps his arms around her from behind.

"You can do it, little one. Find our little girl," he whispers in her hair.

"I...I don't feel empty. If she was gone, I would feel empty, right?"

Lucian smiles warmly at her even though her eyes are still closed. "Yeah ,Smurf, that's good. It means Ray is still alive, and Kai is wrong."

I bristle at the little shit's words but say nothing. I look at the three women and find Mya's gaze is still locked on me. Something isn't right with this woman. She is hiding something from us, and something inside me is urging me to dig more into her background. If I do this, though, I need to be careful. Mya isn't some weak witch; she is powerful. The fact that she looks torn and scared doesn't sit well with me.

CHAPTER 35

Malakai

Nico, Ryan, Dom, Jax, Lucian, and I are standing in my new room. Jax gave me another room since Ryan destroyed the one I was staying in. I asked these guys to stay behind because I need their help. I don't know if I'm right, but I just have this feeling inside me that won't go away, and the more I think about it, the more I'm starting to think I am on to something. I know it's late and everyone is tired, but I'm too fucking wired to sleep and I know for a fact there is no way Ryan and Nico will sleep again until Raya is home safe and sound.

"I need your guys' help, but I need this to stay between us."

"By us you mean we can't tell the girls?" I nod my head. I know this will be hard for Dom and Jax. They're both angry at their partners.

"The girls did what they thought was right. I don't agree with how they did it, but I do believe they were coerced into it." Five pairs of eyes turn to me like I've lost my ever loving mind, and fuck, maybe I have.

"What the hell do you mean?"

"Hear me out, Nico—I know you're pissed at So So and Rora, but I think we have overlooked a huge piece right now."

Nico nods his head for me to continue. "What exactly do you all know about Mya?" The five of them exchange looks, and all of them seemed confused.

"What are you getting at, Kai?" My gaze softens when it lands on a defeated looking Ryan. She hasn't seen or heard from her daughter since she left with the brothers. This must be so fucking hard not knowing what to do, my heart aches for her.

"Mya told me about the vision she had twenty years ago, and how she described that vision tonight isn't what she told me back then." Dom throws his hands into the air and narrows his eyes at me.

"Dude, it was twenty years ago. Anyone's bloody memory would be a bit foggy, cut her some slack." My anger begins to build inside me; why can't they see we have let a snake into our family?

"I don't think she is innocent. If it's proof you need, I will find it, but I think Mya knows a fuck load more than what she is telling us."

To my utter surprise Nico moves toward me, slaps a hand on my shoulder and says, "What do you need me to do, brother?" I swallow a few times, shocked as fuck.

"I-I need you to help me dig into her background and find out everything we can. We need to go over all the newspapers and records that Mya went through—I have a feeling she is hiding a key piece of information from us that will lead us to the discovery of Storm Masters."

It's nine in the morning, and Lucian and Ryan are both passed out on the bed with books scattered around them. Dom, Jax,

Nico, and I are sitting on the two couches with books and newspaper clippings scattered everywhere. We have all been sipping coffee like it's the air we need to live. My eyes are burning from lack of sleep, my body is stiff and aching in the wrong places, and I can feel a headache coming on. Jax linked one of his pack members to bring the three of them breakfast and to bring me some bags of blood, I lied and told them that I wasn't hungry, but they know me better than that. A soft knock sounds at the door and Jax stands to open it. A young boy wheels in a cart that has plates with a variety of food, plus a container on the bottom shelf that has three bags of blood. Jax thanks the boy and he disappears out the door as quietly as he came. The guys each grab a plate and pile them full with food. I ignore the grumbling in my stomach and try to focus on the words in the book. I hear Nico sigh before he speaks.

"Don't hide it, Kai." I look up and see sadness shining in his eyes; that look pisses me off.

"I don't need your pity, Nico!"

"You know what? That's it!" Dom whisper-shouts so he doesn't wake Ryan and Lucian. "None of us fucking pity you, never have. Just because you hate what you are doesn't mean we do! Pull your head out of your fucking ass and own what you are. You're a fucking king, you dickhead, now act like it. I was pissed at you for hiding shit about my wife from me, not because you couldn't set her free. Nico was pissed 'cause you sought Ryan out when you knew you shouldn't have. Our anger was with what you did, not what you are! Now get the fuck over yourself so we can go save your girl." My eyes met Nico's, and to my utter surprise, he didn't say anything about Dom's my girl comment. Jax reaches over to the cart, grabs a bag and passes it to me. I stare at it for a moment before grabbing it from him.

I hold the bag in my hands, and I can feel the three of them watching me. I know Dom is telling the truth. I guess, deep down inside, I always knew that was true, but my hatred of what I have become overshadowed everything else. I thought because I hated it that they would hate it too. I tear the top from the bag and then bring it to my lips. I look to each of them to see their reaction and they're all...smiling.

"About time, you big fucker, now let's get back to work." Jackson's words fill me with warmth, and my eyes cut to Nico. He smiles wide and nods his head.

After another hour of combing through the boxes and newspapers that Mya has gone through, I start to lose hope. What if I am wrong and Mya is innocent? I have been feeling for the tether that binds me to Raya, but I still feel nothing. I try to push my worry away and focus on the task at hand. A loud gasp has us turning to the bed, Lucian is sitting up and Ryan is staring at him with worry in her eyes. Lucian's gaze cuts to mine, and the look in his eyes has me on edge.

"What if you can't reach her because they have blocked you?" I open my mouth to say something but then snap it shut. Could that happen?

"Could they do that, Kai?" The hopeful look in Ryan's tired eyes has me wanting to lie but I can't.

"I don't know, no one has ever done that before." Nico runs a hand over his chin, a worrying glint enters his eyes as he looks at me.

"Can you go to the brothers?" Huh?

"Come again?" Dom asks.

"Shut up, Dominic. What if they blocked her because they want you to go to them instead?"

"I have no idea, I've never tried to go to someone I'm not linked to." Nico deflates.

"What if the four of us go? Dom can cast a spell that will put us all under, and we can try it that way?" Jackson may be onto something.

"No, if the four of you are going then so am I." Nico opens his mouth to protest, but a scathing look from Ryan has him shutting his mouth.

"I don't know if I will have enough pow—"

"I'll help. If you teach me the spell, I'll ground the five of you from this side and bring you back if I feel your power weaken."

"You can use mine as well, I'll help in any way I can." Dom looks from his son to Ryan, remaining silent for a moment, pondering if this could work.

"If Luce stays here and uses his magic to keep us grounded, then I can try channel Ryan's to give us more time there." Everyone agrees at once.

CHAPTER 36

Raya

Am I dead?

I start to slowly blink my eyes open, then snap them shut. The sun is bright in the sky and stings my eyes. My throat feels like sandpaper. What happened? As I sit up, I notice that I am on top of my sleeping bag, outside near the fire pit. My gaze moves to my left, where Memphis and Boston sit on the logs, staring at me. Boston shakes his head then quickly jumps to his feet and heads toward the tents. Seconds later he returns with a bottle of water. He crouches down in front of me, and the look in his eyes worries me.

I open my mouth and try to ask what's wrong but then quickly snap it shut. My throat is so fucking raw and sore. Boston takes the cap off the bottle then hands it to me. I take it and gulp the water down. I cough and spit water all over Boston's shoes, but he doesn't seem to care.

"Take it easy Ray, your throat is going to be sore for a while." Memphis pushes Boston out of the way and takes the spot he was just in. He raises his hand toward me and then places it on my throat. I stiffen as the memories come flooding back. Oh my God! Bronx Masters tried to fucking kill me!

"I'm gonna fix your throat, try to relax." I stare at Memphis with narrowed eyes and jerkily nod. His eyes harden, and I don't know whether he is pissed off at me or pissed at what happened. He begins to chant in a language I have never heard before, and in seconds my throat begins to warm and I'm able to swallow properly. A few moments later, Memphis removes his hand and the pain from my throat is gone.

"How do you feel?" What a loaded question if I ever heard one.

"Like you all lied to me and used me." Memphis drops his gaze to his shoes, and Boston won't even look at me. "Where's Bronx?" Both their gazes snap to mine.

"He won't hurt you again, Raya, you have our word!" I scoff.

"Excuse me if I don't believe that, Boston—if I recall, he tried to fucking kill me!" Both of the brothers flinch. I don't care, they all swore they would never hurt me and yet Bronx did! I don't know why I feel so hurt and betrayed. I need to remember that they are the enemy; I can't trust them.

"Bronx took off, I'm sure he'll be back later."

"Why did he do it?" Memphis sighs and runs a hand through his hair.

"He thought you let Randall out." I reel back, shocked.

"I did no such thing!"

"We know, Ray. Memphis locked him in a new cage down by the creek. Bronx didn't know we moved him. Memph and I couldn't stand to look at him every day after what he's done, so we moved him." Anger flares inside me, and I rise to my feet and glare at both the brothers. Memphis climbs to his feet and moves back to stand by his brother.

"I could have fucking died because of the two of you!" They both lower their heads. "I am so fucking mad right now!" Boston lifts his gaze to meet mine, his anguish evident.

"Bronx wouldn't have done that if we had remembered to tell him. It wasn't his fault Ray, Randall took—"

"Took what? What the fuck did he do to warrant you three committing genocide? What did that man do to make you three kidnap me and then threaten to kill someone I care about?" Neither of them answer me, and I'm vibrating with rage. I feel my magic begin to course through me. If they don't start talking I'm about to start throwing energy balls and ask questions later.

z"He took our sister." I spin around to see Bronx walking toward us from the trees. As he gets closer, I move backward until I smack into Boston and Memphis. The two brothers part so that I can slip behind them. I can see Bronx from the gap between the two brothers, and the look on his face makes me believe he really does feel guilty for what he did to me, but fuck that.

"I think, after what I did, I owe you the truth, if you're willing to hear it?" I consider that for a minute. Do I want to hear the truth? Yes, but will they expect me to get over whatever happened?

"I'll hear you out, but after that I won't speak to you again." Sadness enters Bronx's eyes for a fraction of a second before he masks it. He nods his head and makes his way over to one of the logs and sits down, and the three of us follow his lead and wait for him to tell his tale. Moments tick by, and the silence is becoming awkward as hell. I can feel the tension in the air. Something happened between the three of them when I passed out. Boston and Memphis avoid looking at Bronx, I can feel Bronx's gaze on me but refuse to acknowledge it.

As the silence continues, I start to get annoyed. I'm not going to sit here all night on this log. "Are you going to tell me or not?" I snap. Bronx releases a long exhale then runs a hand through his dark hair.

"Randall Cane took our sister. We have been trying to find

her for years." What the fuck is it with Randall and taking people's sisters? First my Aunt Soph then my Aunt Stevie and now their sister.

"We had no idea she was taken by Randall until recently. Believe me when I tell you, Raya, that we searched the whole fucking world for her. She isn't some weak magic user—she was nicknamed Storm for a reason."

"What does this have to do with me and Kai?" I don't understand how Randall taking her would warrant their hate for the whole vampire race. I get them wanting to kill Randall, but I don't get why they would want to hurt Kai.

"Randall won't give up her location. He says he doesn't even remember her. Randall doesn't value much in life, but he does care about the vampire race. If the only way we can get him to talk is by linking Kai to all vampires, then we'll do it and kill them all while he watches."

"Wait, what?" I am so fucking confused. I thought they wanted to link Kai and Randall so by killing one you killed them all, or had Kai and my dad got their information wrong? From the cunning smirk on Bronx's face, he knew Kai had figured some of it out. Fuck.

"Your lover has it wrong; you shouldn't believe everything he says."

"You know you sound fucking psychotic, right? You would damn a whole race because of one person?"

Bronx narrows his eyes at me. "I would damn the whole fucking world if it meant getting our sister back. We are not the bad guys here, Raya, all we want is our sister and then we will leave you all be. We never wanted this to happen or to get you involved, but we had no choice. We needed Randall, and you were the only one willing to give him to us."

"Leverage for what, Bronx?" I am so out of my depth here. My mind is reeling, and my head is beginning to hurt from all this new information. I feel like I'm in the movie Now You See Me, and we're at the part where everything gets explained to Morgan Freeman.

"You see, we have watched your family for years. They are a resourceful group of people, if given the right motivation. And let me tell you, Raya, you are the right motivation." I sit there and piece together everything I have learned since I left Uncle Jax's. Pieces start to fall into place. This was all a fucking game. I look at Bronx, really look at him, and see it in his eyes. Holy fucking shit.

"You're hoping my family will help you find your sister? You were never going to kill me; is there even a potion?"

"Yes and no." My mouth drops open in shock. What the fuck! I jump to my feet and begin to pace. Memphis and Boston still won't look at me or say a word. Bronx is looking at me like he is proud of me for figuring this shit out. I have been going insane, thinking Kai is going to die because of these assholes, and now I find out it's all bullshit!

"Why me? Why did you lie to me and not just tell me the truth?"

"Because we needed access to the files Melakai has at the mansion. We're not bad people, Raya. Kai would not have simply handed over the history of his people, so we needed him to access it himself and hope that they figured it all out." Okay, this is too much. I drop back down into my seat and clasp my head between my hands.

"We're sorry." I don't even acknowledge Boston's apology. What's the fucking point. These three brothers are master manipulators, and they have played me like a fucking piano.

"What does the blood moon have to do with anything?" Silence descends, and I drop my hands and look to the three of them to see that they are exchanging uneasy looks between themselves. So the blood moon does mean something to them.

"Nothing," Bronx answers. I call bullshit! Bronx is lying to me, and I fucking know it, and he knows I know it. I don't push him, though. I need to figure a way out of this. A thought hits me then.

"I can help you get the information out of Randall." All three of them snap their gazes at me.

"How?"

"Melakai can manipulate his emotions and get him to talk."

Memphis shakes his head. "If that was the case, he would have done it years ago and been free of Randall."

"He couldn't do it then."

"Why?"

I look Memphis in the eyes and speak the truth. "It's not my story to tell, and I won't betray Kai's trust like that." Before they can answer, a sly smirk graces Bronx's face, and he looks to his brothers and then back to me.

"I guess we are about to find out because he is calling me." What the fuck? "You're coming with us to see your boyfriend." Before I can protest, Bronx says some words in a strange language and then I'm falling backward.

I come to the middle of some strange forest. I look around me and see Boston, Bronx, and Memphis standing on either side of me. We stand in the center of some type of clearing. I look down and see I'm in a pair of sneakers, ripped jeans, and a camisole. Each of the brothers are dressed in a pair of Jordan 1s, jeans, and plain black shirts. Their black hair is slicked back and their faces are clear of stubble. Where the fuck are we and what the hell is going on? I tuck my hair behind my ears and look to Bronx.

"*Where the hell are we?*" A mischievous glint enters his blue eyes as he looks down at me.

"*What you just learned you need to keep to yourself. We're about to meet your boyfriend, and I need you to remain quiet so we can all get what we want, okay?*" He has to be joking, right? The look he gives me tells me he is dead serious.

"*Please, Ray, all we want is our sister, and then you get to go home. We are asking you to help us even though you don't owe us shit. If you do this, we will explain everything, I swear*" Meeting Memphis's gaze, my resolve to hate them starts to crack. I don't know what it is, but even after all the shit with Bronx, I still want to help them. I nod my head subtly, and Memphis releases a loud exhale and relaxes his shoulders a smidge.

Hearing a branch snap at the other end of the clearing has me turning my gaze that way. My breath hitches in my throat when I see Kai break through the dense bushes in a pair of low slung jeans and a tight blue polo shirt. He's barefoot. Fuck, just the look of him has my throat dry and my panties....well...not dry. His blond hair is a mess, like he has run his hands through it a dozen times, he has a small amount of stubble on his face, and his eyes! Oh God, his eyes are looking at me with such an intensity that I shiver. He runs his gaze over me looking for any sign of injury, and when his gaze meets mine, a look of determination crosses his face. I reluctantly pull my gaze from him to see my Uncle Dom and Uncle Jax coming out of the forest behind Kai. Uncle Dom looks like a badass in dark denim jeans, a crisp white button up, and leather jacket, his silver hair slicked back. His violet eyes land on me and he smiles reassuringly. I look at Uncle Jax, who looks like the total opposite—board shorts, sleeveless muscle tee and slides. His brown hair is messy as shit and his brown eyes hold a look of annoyance. Uncle Jax looks like a surfer boy, which he is not. Uncle Jax couldn't surf to save his life.

The three of them stop about twenty feet away from us, and

we all stand there looking at each other. Well the six guys stand there sizing the other up—my attention is snagged once again when I see two figures emerging from the woods. A sob breaks free when I see my mom and dad. Their eyes land on me straight away, and I nearly cry at how good she looks. She's rocking her signature ripped jeans like mine, a hoodie, and chucks. I look to my dad and see he is checking me over for injury. Dads dressed similar to the brothers— jeans and plain white shirt—and his eyes are full of anger, and for once it's not directed at me. They join Kai and my uncles, Dad wraps his arm around mom's waist to keep her from coming to me. It takes everything inside me not to run to my parents—I have missed them so much!

I turn my gaze to Bronx, whose stare is already on me. With a subtle nod of his head, he urges me to go and I smile my thanks and then run to my parents. They meet me halfway and we all wrap our arms around each other in the weirdest three-way hug. Mom peppers kisses all over my face while Dad strokes my hair and asks me a million questions all at once. Tears of happiness are flowing down our faces. I pull back and look at both of them, then quickly wrap my arms around them again.

"I've missed you guys so much," I hiccup.

"Oh, baby girl, we have missed you too, are you okay?" I pull back and look at my parents' and try to smile reassuringly.

"Yeah, I'm okay." Dad darts his gaze over my head and narrows his eyes at the three brothers. "Please don't." He drops his gaze back to me, and so many different questions swirl in his eyes, but he doesn't get a chance to ask any of them because Uncle Dom shoves him out of the way. He stands in front of me, smiling smugly, and I shrug my shoulders and grin up at my jokester of an uncle.

"I knew you would be fine. You're a resilient little cupcake, just like your mom." My grin widens.

"What can I say, I get my sass from my momma." Uncle

Dom and I both chuckle, and he clucks me on the chin with his knuckles then steps aside so Uncle Jax can join us. He doesn't say a word as he wraps me in a bear hug. Uncle Jax is such a sweetheart. He pulls back and looks down at me, nods his head once he is satisfied with his appraisal, and then moves aside. Kai moves to stand in front of me, and we stare at each other, our eyes saying the words our mouths can't. A minute ticks by and I release a long sigh, then I head back toward the brothers so we can get this over with. I can't stand to be near Kai and not be able to touch him because of my dad.

I don't even get a step away before he grips my wrist and pulls me back. I look up at him in shock. He cups my face then leans down and kisses me, and dear God, this kiss is like he is fucking my mouth. A throat clearing has us pulling apart, but Kai rests his forehead against mine, and looks me straight in the eyes.

"I will bring you home, vixen." Before I can answer, an invisible force wraps around me and drags me back to the brothers. I huff and glare at a grinning Bronx. My family and Kai all glare daggers at the brothers, but their glares do nothing to deter them.

"Now that the pleasantries are out of the way, I think we should discuss some business."

Kai ignores Boston's question and asks, "Why the hell couldn't I get to her? What did the three of you do to block me?" Huh, what is he on about? I look at my three travel buddies and find Boston and Memphis looking at Bronx.

"She was...deterred...but I assure you she is fine." Oh good grief, this conversation is going nowhere. I am not interested in these guys standing here and measuring whose dick is bigger. I move to stand in the middle of the brothers and my family, keeping a good distance between each side. I ignore the brothers murmuring behind me and meet the gaze of my family and then Kai's questioning look.

"Bronx, Memphis, and Boston haven't treated me badly—well Bronx is an asshole, but the other two are okay." I don't miss the snickers and grunts from behind me. "We need you to help us."

"Us?" my dad questions.

"Yes, Dad, us."

"Why the fuck should we help them, cupcake?" I sigh. I'm not going to stand here and go back and forth, so I look to Kai.

"Kai, will you help me, please?"

He doesn't hesitate. "Yes. What do you need me to do?"

"I need you to use your abilities on Randall to get him to talk."

"Talk about what, vixen?"

Bronx answers. "We need information from him, and Raya tells us you're the man for the job. If you can get this information from him, Raya will go free."

"What's stopping me from taking my daughter right here, right now?" My dad's voice is dripping such hatred that I flinch.

"You're welcome to take her, king, but when she awakens she will be back with us. After all, this place isn't reality." My dad gives Memphis a murderous look.

CHAPTER 37

Malakai

Raya isn't telling us everything, I can see it in her eyes and in her body language. She is far too at ease for someone who should be scared and wanting nothing more to escape her captors. Something else is going on, and I need to figure it out.

"If you want my help, I need something from you three first." I feel every single pair of eyes on me but ignore all of them as I meet Bronx's stare. The cocky fucker grins at me.

"What is it that you want?"

"The truth, then I will help you."

"Raya told you the truth, vampire king." I narrow my eyes at the smart fuck. I can smell his bullshit from a mile away.

"Dude, wipe your chin cause you're dribbling shit!" I fight the smirk that wants to break free at Dom's comment. The three brothers scowl at Dom, and Raya raises her hand to hide her smile. Jax moves so he is standing slightly in front of us and looks to the three brothers.

"I have a nifty little gift that allows me to detect lies, and I can tell from the information my niece has provided us with that there is truth but also lies. So why don't we get to it and tell us what you all really want, because I miss my fucking daughter *and I want her home! If it is help that you need, then ask. If it is war that you want, then we are ready.*

"We have fought two armies and have come out on top, and I assure you my family and I are happy to make it a hat trick and win three." The three brothers look at Jackson in surprise. I guess they didn't see that bombshell coming. Dom pats Jax on the back like he's a proud father, but Jax shrugs his hand away and maintains his stare with the brothers. Raya moves back toward the brothers and has her back to us. A green mist begins to surround the four of them, and I immediately stalk toward them but stop when Raya turns and raises her hand. What the fuck is she doing? We can't hear shit thanks to the mist. I look to Jax to see if his shifter hearing can catch anything, but he shakes his head.

"What has our daughter gotten herself mixed up in, big guy?" Nico tightens his hold on his wife as he looks down at her.

"I have no idea, little one, I just hope she knows what she is doing."

"If they want a fucking war, well give them one!" The conviction in Dom's voice is awe inspiring, and I know my brothers would do anything for their loved ones. When this is all over, I need to work on my relationship with them. I won't run again. I have missed so much. I want to meet Jax's daughter and Dom's twins. I want to be a part of this family again and not be the outcast.

"I hope it doesn't come to that; we have lived in peace and harmony for two decades. I don't want anyone to fight."

"That's all well and good, Jax, but if I need to fight to save my daughter I will."

"I know, Nico, and it goes without saying that the packs will fight with you, but I just hope it doesn't come to that."

"I say cupcake needs to be punished for the stunt she has pulled when she gets home." The four of us turn to Dom, who just shrugs and says, "What?"

"No one is harming my daughter!"

"A little beating never hurt anyone."

My temper flares at Dom's stupid remark. "Anyone lays a single fucking finger on her and I'll be the one fucking hunting you. You feel me?" Four sets of eyes turn to me, but I don't shrink under their stares. They need to know where I stand when it comes to her. I know I promised Nico I would go, but I don't think I can. The green mist retracting has us all looking to Raya and the brothers.

"Trust me, please." All three of them look down at her; I can see so much mistrust in their gazes but I can also see that they are out of options.

"If this doesn't work, you know what will happen, right?" Raya waves her hand in the air.

"Yeah, yeah, I know, Memphis. You will kill me, blah blah blah." She turns toward us and her gaze locks on mine. "Kai, do you trust me?"

"Yes."

"Good, because you're coming to us."

"The fuck he is! You're coming home, baby girl, you're not staying with them!" Raya shifts her gaze to her father and her eyes soften.

"Daddy, I need you to trust me."

Nico scoffs. "I do trust you, Ray, but I don't trust them!" She rolls her eyes and tries again.

"Then trust me when I tell you that they aren't bad."

Dom growls low in his throat. "They want to fucking kill you and Kai. How the fuck are they not bad, cupcake?" Raya sighs then turns to look over her shoulder at the brothers.

"Please, they won't stop searching unless they know." I start to feel the dream land shudder—fuck. I look at Dom and see he is looking at Ryan; Ryan is looking slightly pale—we need to go now.

"We have to go." Raya turns back to us, panic in her eyes.
"Why?"

"It's Lucian, he's grounding us and channeling from me and Uncle Dom. My magic isn't refueling here, and I can feel myself weakening."

Ryan shifts her gaze from her daughter to look at the brothers. "I am asking you as a mother; please give me my daughter back. If it is help that you need, come to us and I will personally guarantee your safety. No harm will come to any of you. You can keep Randall as long as you don't set him free, but please, I am begging you, bring my daughter home to her family." Raya has tears falling down her cheeks. Bronx steps forward beside Raya and lays a hand on her shoulder, which has a growl tearing out of me, both their gazes cut to me, Raya looks shocked but he just looks smug.

"We will discuss this and send word within a day." Every-thing goes black.

I startle awake. How the fuck was I pushed out of my own dreamland? That has never happened to me before. I look to the others in the room and find Lucian is hunched over with his hands on his knees, panting. Dom and Ryan are checking him over to make sure he is okay. Jax, Nico, and I exchange a look, and their expressions resemble how I'm feeling inside. What the hell just happened? That did not go how I thought it would.

"Why do I feel like Raya is playing double agent?" I grunt my agreement. Jax is damn right. That little vixen is hiding something and I want to know what the hell it is.

After Ryan and Dom helped Lucian to stand, the guys and I

decided to keep digging into Mya to keep our minds occupied until we got word from the brothers. Ryan and Dom joined us, and I could tell something was up with Dom from the tension in his shoulders and by the way he kept sighing every fucking two minutes.

"Spit it out, Dominic, or stop fucking sighing."

"I'm angry as fuck at my wife, as well, but you guys have to know Soph would never hurt Raya. She loves that girl like she is her own." Nico shakes his head, and Ryan smiles at Dom, which confused the fuck out of him and me. Jax even looked slightly put out.

"We know, Dom, but Nico and I have suspected for a couple of days that she and Aurora were hiding something from us."

I throw my hands up in exasperation. "What the fuck is it with everyone and keeping secrets and shit? You all are such a mind fuck!" I grit out.

"And you're in love with their daughter, who just played the biggest mind game of all." I glare at Dom but I don't refute his comment, instead I choose to ignore he spoke at all and ask Ryan to elaborate more. Ryan and Nico turn on the couches to face the three of us. Jax is a tense mess, and Dom just looks like he wants to get this done so he can have all of the pieces to this puzzle.

"I know my daughter and she is no meek female. She is playing the role of damsel in distress for a reason, and that alerted me that there is more going on than what she is saying. That little meeting today confirmed it; Raya isn't trying to escape because she is trying to help the brothers. Our daughter can be very...persuasive when she needs to." I didn't like the insinuation, but I kept quiet.

"We need to figure out why Raya is helping them. I don't believe for a second they want to kill her or you, Kai."

"Why do you say that?" I ask, and Ryan cuts a quick glance to Nico then looks at me. She squares her shoulders and lifts her chin.

"Because after I saw the way she was with you earlier, I know there is no way in hell my daughter would be helping them if they wanted to kill you." Nico curses under his breath, which just causes the rest of us to smile. He really does hate the idea of his daughter having feelings for me.

"What do you suggest, love?"

"I think we need to bring Soph and Aurora in on this, Dom. I don't like the idea of going behind my cousin's back, but it is what it is, and they are too close to Mya."

Dom grins slyly at Ryan. "Don't be coy, love, we all know they have been fucking for years. I'm not judging—a thruple is all good with me." Ryan scrubs a hand down her face and groans. As old as Dominic is he still has no fucking filter!

"All right then, let me go get the girls." Dom leaves to retrieve the girls, and the four of us begin to clean up the newspaper clippings and sort the books out into piles that we have gone through. One of the record books that was open and lying face down on the table I hadn't noticed before; I pick it up and went to close it but stop. Inside the record book was the initials SM. I scan over the page and holy shit—why in the name of God would the three of them want this fucking psycho back? The massacre and the lives she fucking took...what in the hell is wrong with this fucking woman? She slaughtered everyone.

"KAI!" I snap my gaze up and see Dom standing by the closed door with the girls. I shake away my shock and dog-ear the book then close it. I needed some time to process what the fuck I just read before I tell the others. If what I read was true, I don't think finding this woman was a good idea.

"You with us now, you bloody giant?" I cock my brow at the arrogant son of a bitch, who smirks at me before nodding to

Nico. Both the girls look as though they haven't slept–they look just as bad as us. Neither of them will meet our gazes. I know the girls meant well, they just went the wrong way about it. I'm pissed at Soph; after everything we have been through, she could have come to me and told me about Raya, but she chose to play fucking Cupid. I put a lid on my annoyance and watch as Nico moves to stand in front of the girls.

"So-So, when in God's good name have you ever not made eye contact?" Sophia snaps her gaze up to meet her brother's intense stare, and her eyes hold a mischievous glint to them.

"Never, brother, I just didn't want to poke the beast. I know I fucked up, but in my defence, I can sense what they both feel, and I didn't want you to ruin it for her." Nico starts nodding his head like he was okay with what she said, but the tightness in his shoulders gave him away. Before more could be said, Aurora groaned and then began to shake. Everyone knew the deal. You couldn't touch her while she was having a vision; one of us trying to help her could cause her harm, and that is the last thing we ever wanted. The look on Jax's face was pure agony. He hated watching her have visions and fall to the ground while he stood there and did nothing. Aurora's shaking intensified and then she dropped to all fours. Jax released a loud as fuck growl.

"I fucking hate this!" he gritted out. I couldn't blame him; I would hate to watch the woman I loved go through this and not be able to do a goddamn thing as well. The vibe in the room was bleak, we all felt useless but there isn't a fucking thing we could do to help Aurora. A couple more minutes went by before she stopped shaking, and Jax was beside her in seconds and stroking her back, whispering sweet words into her ear. It took her a moment to get herself under control, then she sat back on her haunches and reached out to clasp her mate's hand in her own.

"I'm okay, I swear." Jax grunted but said nothing. Aurora's pale blue eyes swung to Nico and Ryan. "I am sorry for my part in keeping this hidden from you, but you all know I cannot interfere with my visions. If I thought for a second that she was in any danger, you know I would have said something and the consequences could get fucked!" Gasps rung out around the room. Hearing Aurora cuss was as common as seeing an Eclipse.

"What did you see, love?" Dom asks, and Aurora's gaze turns to me, sadness shining in her eyes.

"Raya isn't your real cure, Kai; her blood won't change you, but she will change your heart. Her blood calls to you, doesn't it?" I stiffen but nod my head. "That's because she is your beloved." I stumble back. No fucking way in hell! There is no goddamn way that is true. No one in the world is that fucking lucky, everyone in this room has found their mate or hugacko; there is no way fate would grant all of us this small mercy and give us all our other halves, our soulmates.

"What the hell is a beloved?" Nico asks. I open my mouth but words won't come out. Aurora smiles kindly at me then looks at Nico.

"For fae, their soulmate is a hugacko, for wolves they are called mates, and for vampires, their soulmates are called their beloved." Nico reels back, shocked. I stand here and wait for him to lash out; I know this is the last thing he would have ever wanted for his daughter.

"Hang on then—so if Raya's blood can't cure Kai then why do the brothers need her?" It all clicks into place for me, and everything begins to make sense.

"Because they used her to get us to help them. We don't have time for that; the brothers and Raya are on their way here, now!" Aurora is just full of good news today, isn't she?

CHAPTER 38

Once we get back from the strange dreamland, I lift myself off the ground and then park my ass on the log again and glare at the three smug bastards. They all ignore my glare like it meant nothing. My mind is reeling with all the new information I've learnt. The brothers want their sister but don't want anyone to know why? I run my gaze over each of them. They don't look any older than their mid-twenties, but their attitudes give away their ancientness. I'm pissed that I'm being led astray by these brothers; I don't understand why I even feel the need to help them. If I'm honest, I'm helping them because my heart hurts for each of them. I'm not sure if it's because I remind them of their sister or not, but when they look at me, their gazes are filled with nothing but sadness and heartache. I feel compelled to wipe that look from their eyes.

"So, what now?" I ask the three of them.

"Well, now we decide whether or not we trust you." I narrow my eyes at Bronx.

"I have done nothing but try to help the three of you from the start. What I don't get is why the need for all this secrecy and plotting? You three are strong, really fucking strong. Why hide behind lies and not just come out with the truth? My family and I would have helped you from the start if you had just been honest with us."

"You have no idea the trials we have faced and what we had to do to become what we are now. We weren't always like this; having this power is what made us noticeable enough to even get the smallest scrap of information in regard to our sister. We weren't born with silver spoons in our mouths like you; shit didn't just fall into our laps. We had to work hard to become what we are." The bitterness that coats each of Bronx's words is astounding; these three are like an onion, with so many layers.

"I am so sorry that you have had to go through what you have. I want to help you three, and if you let me I will help you find your sister so your family can be reunited." All three of their faces harden. "Why do I get the feeling you don't want to be a family again?"

"That is none of your concern. Pack your stuff—we leave here in fifteen minutes." I look at Memphis and try to decipher his meaning but come up blank. I choose not to waste any more time on trying to figure these three out.

I pack the clothes I brought with me and dismantle my tent in record time, and I must say I'm proud of myself until I turn around and see the three brothers have packed up everything else, and I mean everything. Their tent is packed, the food station is away, and the fire pit is doused and covered. I huff as I sling my bag over my shoulder and make my way over to them. I notice they have put Randall back in his box.

"What are you going to do with him?" The guys exchange a look before they meet my gaze. Boston reaches out and lifts my hand then turns it over and places a key in my palm. I look up at him in confusion.

"This is the key to his cage. This is us showing you that we trust you to help us."

"Wait, so you're giving us Randall back?" Memphis and Bronx nod while Boston smiles down at me.

"We are taking a huge risk here, Ray; we are giving you back Randall and we're going back to your family so they can help. Don't fuck us, Raya—as much as I like you, I won't hesitate to take you out if any of your family fuck me or my brothers over." I gulp and nod my head. The look in his eyes tells me he is dead serious.

We emerge from the woods at the back of Uncle Jax's where I first left with the brothers. Memphis has his magic wrapped around Randall's box so it floats behind us as we walk. Once we break through the dense brush, the side of the compound comes into view, I release a breath I didn't know I was holding and pick up my pace. We're halfway to the building when wolves in their beast form start to surround us, I turn back to the brothers and see they each have their magic out, Randall's crate is down on the ground in the middle of them.

"Stop!" I shout, the last thing I need is for a wolf to attack and then a fight breaks out. "I am Raya Stone princess of Far—" One of the wolves shifts back and stands before me naked as the day he was born. I make sure to keep my gaze locked on his so I don't see his dangly bit.

"We know who you are but we don't know them."

"They're with me." The naked man scoffs and rolls his eyes.

"Cause that counts for something." I grit my teeth and take a deep breath. I feel two of the brothers come to stand on either side of me. A quick glance each way and I see it's Bronx and Memphis.

"Stand down, pup, or we'll make you!" I snap my gaze to Memphis, shocked to hear such authority come from him. He's using the tone Bronx normally would.

"Go fuck yourself!" The man shifts back to his wolf form and growls low in his throat. I release my magic, hoping that I can form a cage around him so he won't attack and cause a fucking bloodbath. He scrapes the ground with his paw and growls, and the rest of the wolves around us do the same. Oh, shit. A loud howl sounds and the wolves freeze.

"Stand the fuck down now!" I turn back toward the compound and see Uncle Jax running toward us. I take off and run to him, and when I'm close enough I jump and he catches me. Fuck it feels so good to be back!

"Ahhhhhhh, it's so good to have you back, kid." I cringe at the stupid nickname but don't comment. I'm passed from Uncle Jax to Uncle Dom and then to my aunts. I go to Lucian next and God it is so good to see him! I shed a tear when I see my parents. I pull back from them and try to peek around my dad, who groans and mutters shit under his breath that I can't hear, but he steps aside and then I see him.

Standing there at the back of the group, with his hands in his pockets and his blond hair falling onto his forehead, is the most amazingly handsome man I have ever fucking seen. I move toward him but my dad latches onto my wrist. I glare up at him but he shakes his head and then flicks his chin toward the brothers. I sigh then shoot Kai a sad smile; he nods his head.

I make my way over to the brothers. The three of them all stand around Randall's crate, looking like they're ready to go to war at any minute. I stop when I am a couple of feet away, and a look passes between Bronx and me. I'm trying to assure him without words that I won't let anything happen to them, and I'll help them. The look he gives me isn't as reassuring; the welcoming party they just received doesn't make my claims of them being welcomed here hold much merit.

"I'm sorry." Bronx cocks a brow at me, and I grit my teeth and try again. "That won't happen again, Bronx. I know you don't trust me, but I am asking you to give me a chance here." He eyes me skeptically for a moment then nods his head stiffly. I release the breath I didn't know I was holding and turn to face my family. I feel uneasy having all these other wolves around us, and I sure as shit didn't want to have this conversation in front of them.

"Uncle Jax, is there any way that we could talk without an audience?" He smiles then orders his wolves away. I hate the distance between me and my family. I feel like I'm in the middle, and I hate it; if this is to work, the brothers need to trust me and my family.

"Mom?" I motion for her to come to me, and I do the same to my aunts, and they follow my mom without question. When they are on either side of me, I face the guys and each of them look confused as fuck—good.

"Bronx, Bos, Memph—I would like for you to meet my mom Ryan, my Aunt Sophia and my Aunt Aurora. I know you three think the problems lay with the males, but you couldn't be more wrong, around here it's the women that run the show." I can hear the guys behind us snickering, but I ignore them.

"If you can convince these three that you all can be trusted, then I promise they will have the three alphaholes behind us falling into line." Mom and my aunts are trying to conceal their laughter. Memphis moves to stand by Bronx and then catches my eye.

"And what about blond vamp?" I release a whoosh of air, and I can feel every pair of eyes on me and I hate it. I try to think of a good response, or anything really, but no words come. I jump when I feel a body behind me. I look over my shoulder and I'm gobsmacked to see it's Kai. His body heat is burning my back in the most delicious way. It takes more control than I would like to admit not to lean back into him.

"Got something to say, Melakai?" Memphis sounds like a condescending prick, and it pisses me off! Kai reaches out and brushes my hair back over my shoulder and then leans down so his chin is resting there. He wraps one of his huge arms around my waist, which causes me to gasp. The three brothers look like they are ready to strike, and Kai chuckles, places a kiss on my cheek then stands again, but doesn't drop his hand from around my waist.

"I think I just said all I have to say." Oh. My. God! Did Kai just have a dick measuring contest with Bronx, Boston, and Memphis?

"What the fuck am I, chopped liver?" A chuckle bursts out at me at Lucian's outburst, and I wave my hand in the air to shut him up.

"My cousin won't cause any problems. If he does, Mom and Aunt Soph will sort him out." Mom and Aunt Soph nod in agreement. I can feel mom's gaze on me but I can't look at her. I'm such a coward.

"Would you like to come inside?" The three brothers look at Aunt Aurora like she has sprouted a second head, and she chuckles at their perplexed looks. "I promise my mate will be on his best behaviour and so will his brothers." The brothers still don't move or say a word. Sighing, I reluctantly pull away from Kai and go to Boston. I can see he wants to come inside but won't go against his brothers. I turn back to face Kai then reach into my pocket and pull out the key that Bronx gave me and chuck it to him. He catches it with ease.

"Can you, Dad and the others put Randall back where he belongs, please?" Kai looks at me like I'm crazy but when he turns his gaze to Bronx, his face changes to understanding. He moves toward him and stops when there is a foot of space between them and offers Bronx his hand.

"Thank you. I know it must not have been easy to hand over your bargaining chip." Bronx nods but doesn't shake Kai's hand.

"Dick," I mutter under my breath. Bronx turns indignant eyes my way. "What? You know that was a dick move, don't even try to deny it."

Raya and the girls lead the three brothers inside while I and the four guys stay outside. We all stand here staring down at this crate that holds Randall. I was glad to see that the bastard still looks like shit; it gave me great pleasure to see him suffering.

"We have to take him out." I snap my gaze to Dom.

"We can't fit that crate in the shack; we have to take him out then take him to the cells." Fuck. Dom was right, there is no way the five of us and the crate would fit in the elevator. He may be weak and at death's door, but I would never underestimate him. This motherfucker is resourceful. Dom and Nico release their magic while Jax and Lucian stand at either end of the crate. Once the four of them give me a nod, I undo the padlock and open the lid of the crate. Randall didn't even stir. I reach down and grip his bony arm and haul him straight out of the crate. Jax moves quickly and grips his other side, Lucian runs ahead to the shack door and holds it open for us. Once we're all inside, Nico places his hand against the scanner. Only Dom, Jax, Nico, me, and two of Jax's most trusted guys can get to the cells. The scanner works off magic signatures, and we were yet to figure out how the fuck Raya managed to get down to the cells and free Randall in the first place.

Once we reach the cell floor we drag Randall to his cell at the end, Lucian opens the door. Randall lifts his head and then begins to struggle against our hold, his attempts are futile, he is too fucking weak to even be a problem. Jax and I throw him into his cell then Lucian slams the door shut. The five of us watch as Randall struggles to his feet.

"K-kill me." This is the first time I have heard him speak in twenty years. His voice sounded so brittle and raspy from years of not using it.

"I wouldn't give you the fucking satisfaction of dying after what you did to my wife and son, you lowlife bastard!" With that said, Dom spun around and left, and the others followed. I remained behind, just staring at the man that changed my whole fucking life. I used to fear him but now I just want to bask in his misery. I won't let this fucker have any more sway over me. I hate what I had become because of him. I despised all vampires for a long time because I associated them with him, but over the years I have learnt that not all vampires are bad.

"P-please." I snarl at the bastard and glare down at him, and he flinches and stumbles back a step.

"You dare to ask me for a favor?" I laugh but there is no humor to it. "I will never end your suffering. You will live a long fucking life and I will bask in every minute of your misery, you piece of shit. I will never let my people fall victim to your crimes." I turn and stalk back toward the others who are waiting at the end of the hall.

Nico claps me on the back and says, "I'm proud of you, I always knew you would be a fucking awesome king."

Once we exited the cells, we made our way to Jax's office, where the girls and the brothers are. We made sure to remove all the books and newspapers from the office to my new room; we are not at the point where we would be sharing any info with them yet. Jax pushes his office door open and strolls in, the rest of us following his lead. The three brothers sit on the couch that faces the door, and I smirk. They want to have a full view of the room and not be left with a blind spot. The three girls sit on the couch to the left of them, Nico, Dom, and Jax take the couch on the right, which only leaves me and Lucian to sit next to Raya on the other couch directly facing the brothers.

Lucian sits down one end and Raya remains in the middle. I take the vacant seat next to her. She stiffens the moment I sit down, and I narrow my eyes at the side of her head.

"Okay, this is awkward." Groans break out around the room. "You're all thinking it, you fuckers, so don't moan!" I will be the first to admit it; I have to fight to keep the smirk off my face. I see the girls trying to do the same, Nico and Lucian don't even attempt to hide their laughter.

"You're not wrong, though." I'm surprised to hear humor in Boston's tone; I expected them to be pissed. Dom leans over and puts his fist out to Boston, who doesn't hesitate to fist bump Dom. What the hell is going on here?

"My man. Now the tension is broken, let's get down to business so I can bang my wife." Nico clips Dom across the back off the head. "The fuck was that for?"

"That's my fucking sister, you asshole!" Fucking hell, here we go again.

"Dude, get the fuck over it! She has been my wife for how long now? We have kids together, so get the fuck over it man. I may be banging your sister, but Kai is banging your daughter!" I glare at the fucking cockroach, who doesn't even look guilty that he threw me under the bus. Raya groans and covers her face with her hands.

"Are they always like this?" Memphis asks no one in particular.

"All the fucking time!" Sophia snaps while glaring at her husband and brother.

"Babe, he started it—"

"Shut it, Dominic! The pair of you need to grow the fuck up. We're supposed to be a united front and look the part in front of these three, and you two just fucking ruined it! Now the both of you sit there and shut the fuck up so the grownups can talk." Dom and Nico both glare at Soph then cross their arms over their chests and lean back into the couch.

"I apologize for my husband and brother-in-law acting like idiots." Ryan tries to smooth over the situation with the brothers, but they don't even seem bothered.

"Don't be sorry, it's amusing to watch." Boston smiles kindly at Ryan and then turns his gaze to Raya. I instinctively lean toward her. "What now, Ray?" Raya releases a breath and then sits up straight.

"Do you trust me, Bos?" Raya and Boston sit there for a minute, staring at each other, before Bronx answers for his brother.

"Yes!" Raya looks to Bronx, and a wide smile spreads across her face. Bronx has a ghost of a smile on his lips. "Get to it, Ray." Raya bites her bottom lip to stop her smile from breaking free.

"Okay, so we need your guys' help to find someone."

"Who?" Lucian asks.

"We need you guys to help us find their sister. I made a deal with them. I need you all to honor it."

"What deal did you make?" I ask, and she refuses to meet my gaze as she answers.

"They gave you Randall back as a show of goodwill."

"Lie!" All eyes turn to Jax, and Raya cringes and then looks to the brothers.

"We did give you Randall as a show of goodwill, but we are also not stupid enough to give up our only bargaining chip." Raya stiffens beside me, and I reach out and turn her face so she is looking at me.

"What did you do, vixen?" She takes a deep breath then answers me.

"I let them cast a spell on me, if we don't come up with answers in two days when the blood moon is at its peak, I will die." I sit there, stunned, as chaos breaks out around the room. She is out of her fucking mind! After everything we have done to get her back and ensure she is safe, she just throws her fucking life away like that? There has to be more to this situation than she is saying; no one is that stupid to put their own life on the line for some idiots.

"Why did you do it?" The room grows silent as we all wait with bated breath for Raya's answer. Her troubled eyes meet mine, and I implore her with my gaze to tell the truth.

"Honestly, I have no idea. A part of me feels so drawn to them—"

"Sexually?" I grit out, and Dom and Lucian chuckle.

"No, Zilla, like...spiritually. I feel like I need to help them. I can't explain it. I just feel like I have to do this. I knew if I didn't let them cast the spell, Dad and you would go all G.I Joe on their asses and they wouldn't get the help I promised them."

She is either the smartest person I know or the stupidest, I just can't quite decide which one. She has known them a month and has pledged her life for their stupid cause! I want to wrap my hands around her tiny throat and squeeze until I can strangle some sense into her pretty little head.

"Stop looking at me like you want to kill me! We both know you won't, so stop, we have more pressing shit to deal with." She reaches over and interlaces her fingers with mine, turns to the brothers and says, "Shall we break for an hour then reconvene and start this search? I think the big guy next to me needs to rip me a new one, and I would rather do that without an audience." I glare at the side of her head but Nico throws his hands in the air and shakes his head.

"You are not leaving my sight! Kai can fucking deal with it. No breaks, no time outs, no nothing. We start this fucking search thing now so they can undo the spell and fuck off for good." Raya flinches next to me at her father's harsh words, but I tune out the ensuing argument and just observe the three of them. They watch Raya with such an intensity. Boston looks at her like she is his light in the darkness, Memphis looks to her like she can save him, but Bronx—Bronx looks at her like she is everything. Their bodies are coiled tight and ready to strike; they're not going to fight for themselves but for her—why? What the hell kind of a hold does Raya Stone have over these three?

I see the way she looks at them, but she doesn't see them the way they see her, and she looks at them like friends–brothers, even. I grin when everything clicks into place, how the fuck could we have all been so blind? How the hell could I have missed it? I cut Nico and Raya's bickering off when I clasp her face between my hands and pull her to me so I can kiss her.

3...2...1...

"Get the fuck off her now!" I release her and smile widely at Bronx as I feel Nico burning a hole in my head with his eyes.

"Why?" Bronx and I sit there and stare at each other, neither one of us willing to back down and let the other win.

"Cupcake, why do I feel like your harem of men are about to shed blood?" Both Bronx and I turn to glare at Dom. "Well it's true!"

"Shut up, Dominic!" Nico snaps. "Someone better start explaining what the hell is going on and it better explain why the fuck you just lip-locked my daughter, asshole!" I don't need to explain shit to the entitled fucker, and I have a feeling Bronx and his brothers won't disclose shit in front of the others, so I choose to brush it off and ignore Nico all together.

CHAPTER 40

Raya

After finally getting my dad to agree to a break, he and the others reluctantly left the room. As soon as the door shut behind my mom, the tension in the room spiked. Between Kai and the three Masters brothers, I have no idea who is going to cave first and get this little chat over with. The tension rolling off Kai is suffocating, and the fact that the giant doesn't voice his feelings is making this whole situation worse! I look to the brothers, hoping they will be the ones to say something. One look at them and I know I'm shit out of luck.

"Right, so can we break this tension already?"

Bronx ignores my question and addresses Kai. "Say what it is you need to say and then leave." Kai scoffs, and I stiffen in my seat.

"How about the four of you start telling the truth!" Kai turns and peers down at me, and the look in his eyes has me shrinking back. "Lie to the others but do not lie to me, vixen."

"I...What do you mean?" Kai rolls his eyes then points an accusing finger at the brothers.

"They are never going to harm you!" My eyes widen, and I dart my gaze to the guys and see the three of them staring at Kai.

"Tell me the truth now or I walk out that door, Raya. I will not be played for a fool." The sound of betrayal in his tone has my resolve crumbling. I can't lose Kai, but I made a promise to the guys.

"Kai, please—" Kai shakes his head and stands. Oh my God, he's going to leave, and I don't think he will come back if he walks out. Disappointment shines in his eyes as he looks down at me. I drop my gaze to the floor so he doesn't see the tears gathering in my eyes. I hear him walk away and my chest constricts.

"There is no spell!" I snap my gaze to Boston, shocked that he caved.

"Why lie?"

"Because we knew her family wouldn't help if they thought we didn't have a solemn threat over her. We did cast a spell, but it was only to transport her here; it was the only way to pass Jackson's lie detector."

"Who gave you that idea?" I can hear the accusation in Kai's voice and brace myself for the fallout when Boston tells him.

"Don't blame her, she owes us nothing and wants to help us."

"I still don't get why she wants to help the three of you. The only reason I can deduce that she is even still trying is because there was never a potion, you never planned to kill me or her did you?" The three guys share a look, this time it isn't Boston that answers its Memphis.

"No. We never planned to kill you per se, there is a potion that can link you and Randall and all living vampires together. All we needed to complete the potion was a few drops of Ray's blood, and that was all it would take to end your whole race." Kai is quiet for a moment as he digests what he just learnt.

"Why did you stop? Why not continue with your plans and use Raya to get to me so you could end the vampire race? The three of you know very well I would have taken the potion to save her."

"Don't gloat, Melakai, it doesn't suit you! Thank Raya for your survival and my brothers—I still want to link you to all your subjects and rid your kind from the world." Bronx's harsh words stings but I know he is only saying it out of anger.

"Why the change of heart?" Kai ask's Memphis and Bos.

"Because she reminds us of someone we used to know. She also assures us that you're nothing like Randall and will not cause any problems like that gutless cunt did." Kai nods and murmurs his agreement.

"His blood may have created me, but I am nothing like him. If his death is what you seek, then do it! I never wanted him to survive; I wanted him skinned alive and then burned to death." I recoil at the venom in Kai's tone, the brothers on the other hand all grin and nod their heads. What the fuck is wrong with them?

"You would allow us to kill him without the consent of the others?"

Kai cocks a brow at Bos.

"You really want me to stand here and act dumb? I know you three were the ones to grant Raya access to the cells. If you really wanted to, the three of you could get down there now couldn't you?" Each of the brothers have a cocky smirk plastered across their faces, the smug bastards. Why the hell did they get me to do it then?

"Touché, Kai. What else have you figured out?" Kai returns to the couch and drops down beside me. He rests his arm across my shoulders and then begins to stroke my arm with his thumb.

"That you only wanted Randall for information on your sister."

"You're smarter than we gave you credit for."

Kai scoffs and pulls me closer to his side. "Your sister went missing in the 80s and you're still searching for her now. The part I don't get is if you three are really as strong as I have been led to believe, then why can't you find her yourselves? Why the hell do you need us to help you?"

The three guys sit there quietly, and I straighten up and wait for their reply. I am dying to know the answer to this question; I have learned more about the brothers in the past five minutes than the few days I was with them. I can tell from the looks on their faces they are struggling with whether or not they should tell us or keep their secret guarded and strong arm us into doing their dirty work.

"We thought our sister was dead, and then we learned she was kidnapped by Randall. We searched for her for years, and finally, when we found her, she wasn't the same person we knew anymore." The tone of Bronx's voice has my heart hurting for him; I can see the anguish in his eyes. What the hell did Storm Masters do to her brothers?

"Why am I sensing that this search isn't going to end well for your sister?" I turn to Kai, surprised.

"You're very perceptive, Melakai."

"I haven't gotten where I am today by being a fool."

"What happens between us and our sister is none of your concern. All you need to know is when we have her back, we will vanish, and you will never see us again." A feeling of hurt settles inside me. Is that it? They reel me in and then when they get what they want, they just leave?

"What was the point of getting me to trust you guys then? All you planned to do was use me for my family to get your sister back and then you're going to leave?" I don't care that they look put off by my harsh tone; they fucking sucked me in and used me. "Why the hell would you go through all of this when all you had to do was ask and we would have helped you?" Memphis shakes his head.

"No, you wouldn't have. None of you would have helped us; we needed you to get Randall so we could question him. He held no answers for us, so we had to go with plan B." Anger swirls inside me.

"I'm plan B? You three fed me some sad fucking story and I fell for it. Shame on me!" I stand and leave the room. I'm hurt, embarrassed, and so fucking ashamed of myself. I left with them and broke Randall fucking Cane out of his cell, all for them to just use me. I thought we had developed some kind of friendship, but how fucking wrong was I? I keep going until I exit the compound and storm off toward the woods around the back. I ignore all the looks the shifters are giving me and choose to hold my head high like I haven't just royally fucked up.

My dad is right. I am too rash, and I don't stop to think things through. I am such a fucking idiot! My head is hurting from over thinking; I try to take a few deep breaths as I maneuver my way through the dense underbrush. I'm so lost in my own thoughts I don't see her until I nearly walk into her. I stumble back a step and gasp. I smile and then launch forward so I can wrap my arms around her. She is such a sight for sore eyes and I'm thankful she is here to distract me.

"What are you doing out here?" I ask as I move back.

"I was looking for you, actually." I furrow my brow in confusion.

"Is everything okay? Has something happened to Chase and Alex?" She smiles sadly and then shakes her head.

"No, but Ray—I need your help."

"What do you need?" When the look in her eyes changes to anger, I start to worry.

"I need you to come with me, are you able to portal us somewhere?" A tiny voice in the back of my mind is telling me not to do this but that same tiny voice is the one that told me to trust those stupid brothers, so I choose to ignore it. I do as she asks and open a portal, she clasp's my hand in hers, and we make our way through the portal.

We emerge in front of an old cabin. I look around and find we are surrounded by nothing but trees. The only sounds that can be heard are the wildlife. I follow Mya to the cabin, and she whispers a spell under her breath and then the door opens. Cool.

I follow her inside and look around to see the cabin isn't dusty; someone has been using this hunting cabin. From the outside, it looks old and rundown, but inside it is clean and smells fresh. I follow Mya over to the couches. I drop down into one of the seats and watch as she begins to fill the open fire with logs and kindling. She uses the matches to start the fire and then claims the single seat. I wait for her to explain why the hell I am here. There is furniture, but aside from that, there are no personal touches. No pictures adorn the walls and everything is bare to the bones. Something doesn't feel right, but who am I to judge? I took off with three strange brothers all because I felt the need to help them!

"I need you to hear me out before you say anything." I look at Mya but find her gaze is focused on the flames in the open fire.

"Okay?"

"I have lived a really long life. I don't age like other witches." Witches and warlocks are the only supernaturals that age at a human rate; the rest of us do age, but at a slower rate. Mya is an oddity among her people.

"I know."

"Do you want to know the reason why?" A sense of dread washes over me; something really isn't right.

"Mya, what is going on?" Her eyes meet mine, her brown eyes are haunted. A sad smile graces her beautiful face.

"Maybe we should start with you calling me by my real name." I gulp but nod my head anyway. "My name is Nevada, but I was given a nickname by my brothers that I have gone by since I was sixteen." I know what her name is now, but I need her to say it.

"What's your nickname, Nevada?" Her eyes take on a hard edge.

"I'm known as Storm Masters."

"Why did you three use her?" I don't even attempt to mask the anger in my voice; they hurt Raya and I won't let that go.

"It's not what you think."

"Then paint me a different picture, Memphis, cause all I have heard is what she did for you, not what you did for her."

Bronx scoffs. "Why the hell should we tell you?"

"Because now that I know her life isn't in any danger, we don't owe you shit." Bronx narrows his eyes to slits.

"Enough!" I turn to stare at Boston; I can tell he is torn about telling me the truth. "We never meant to use her. We did plan to use her blood to make the linking potion to take out the vampire race, but then she changed our minds about you and your race. She was the one who offered to help us find Storm. We only have until the blood moon to locate her; after that we are fucked."

"What happens on the blood moon?"

"In order for us to get what we want back, we need to make a trade. A life for a life." What the fuck? "Storm took the life of someone we cared for, and in order to get that life back, you need to sacrifice the one who did it."

"What the fuck are you on about? I have never heard of such a thing."

"Storm killed someone we loved. We need Storm to die in order for that person to come back." You have got to be kidding me! This is some twisted shit, and I don't think we need to be getting involved.

"All of this, because she killed someone? How long ago did she do this?"

"Decades ago," Memphis grits out. I throw my hands into the air, this has to be a joke, right?

"You three have lost your ever loving minds!"

Bronx jumps to his feet, I do the same and glare at the asshole. "She killed my wife and unborn child!" The anger flees my body in a rush. Memphis and Boston sit there with their gazes on the floor. Bronx is vibrating with rage, and his eyes are glowing with anger. Guilt gnaws at me.

"She reminds you of your wife, doesn't she?" The anger flees Bronx's gaze.

"Yes, she looks exactly like her." I feel for him; what a burden to bear.

"You didn't really need her, did you? You could have taken her blood and then made the potion?" Bronx nods again. "She isn't your wife, Bronx."

His gaze snaps to mine and he glares.

"I am well aware she isn't my wife! All I wanted was Randall to give up my sister's location, but the old slimy cunt doesn't know shit! She spelled him to forget her. Raya offered to help, and we took her up on that offer. If you help us, I will spell Raya so her blood won't call to you!"

"I don't need your spell; I know why her blood calls to me now. She isn't my cure for vampirism; she is my cure for life." The three of them look at me, confused, but I refuse to answer any more questions. "We will help you find your sister, I just hope you know that bringing your wife back isn't something I would recommend."

"What if it was Raya and your child?" Memphis's question is a fair one. Would I do the same thing? Could I risk her coming back and not being the same person I knew before?

"I don't know—" The office door slams open, cutting off my reply, Nico, Ryan, Jax, Aurora, Dom, Sophia and Lucian enter with looks of worry and fear on their faces.

"Chase called. Mya fled and left a note saying she is sorry for everything." Ryan's eyes dart to the brothers, and I see Nico looking around the room before his gaze finally lands on me.

"Where's Raya?"

"She got upset and left about twenty minutes ago," Boston answers, Nico narrows his eyes at me.

"A few of the pack saw her heading toward the woods on the east side of the compound. One of them saw her talking to a lady with grayish hair." Oh dear God.

"Holy fuck, cupcake is with Mya." Thank you Dominic, I think we all got that from Jax's comment.

"So, if Mya fled and Ray is with her then that means—"

I finish the sentence for Lucian. "Mya is Storm Masters, and she is a cold-blooded killer." Dread settles in the pit of my gut, chaos erupts, and everyone is shouting and cursing. I can't think straight with all the noise. A heavy hand lands on my shoulder and I turn to see it's Memphis.

"Can you take me to where she was last seen?" The room goes silent as everyone stares at Memphis.

"Why?" Nico snaps, and Memphis turns to look at the brooding king of the fae.

"Because I can see things, and I might be able to track her." Nico quirks a brow but doesn't say anything else.

We all stand back and watch as Memphis circles the area where he said Raya stood. Bronx and Boston stand near their brother but give him enough room so he can do his thing. Memphis crouches down and lays his palm flat against the ground. He closes his eyes and black magic begins to cover the ground where his hand touches.

"Show me what she saw." I look to the others and see them staring at Memphis with looks of apprehension and wonder. Bronx and Boston look tense. Memphis's eyes snap open and the girls gasp. His eyes are all black, and his magic begins to grow and starts to cover him. It moves at a steady pace, but when it begins to get closer to his chest, Bronx and Boston step forward and each of them place a hand on their brother's shoulder and release their own green and red magic, which begins to push the black magic around Memphis back down until there is nothing left. Memphis drops down to his ass, panting, and none of us move as we stare at the three brothers.

They are more powerful than we could have ever imagined. How did they get this strong? There is no way in hell they were born with this power; they wouldn't have been able to fly under the radar for all these years with that amount of power between them. Bronx helps Memphis to his feet, and Memphis looks to each of his brothers and nods his head. Bronx and Boston both start cursing under their breath. Ryan moves toward the brothers and stops a few feet away.

"Thank you for what you just did." Memphis looks taken aback by Ryan's gratitude.

"It was nothing."

"It wasn't nothing to me. Were you able to find my daughter?" Memphis nods his head.

"She went with our sister. It seems we didn't need to search for her after all; she came to us." Nico starts screaming and yelling, accusing the brothers of putting Raya in harm's way. Jax and Dom try to calm him, but are unsuccessful.

"Shut the fuck up and stop!" Everyone stops and looks to Lucian, who is staring at Aurora. Jax growls low in his throat. Her eyes are pure white and she is shaking like a leaf. Memphis moves toward the seer but is stopped when Jax slams his hand against his chest and growls.

"Don't fucking touch her." Memphis doesn't get angry or even try to remove Jackson's hand.

"I can help her, alpha; I can guide her through this vision so she isn't met with any harm." Jax looks at Memphis with wary hope.

"Trust him, he taught our sister how to control her visions." Boston is imploring Jax with a look when Aurora drops to her knees and cries out. Jax drops his hand.

"Help her, please." Memphis nods and moves past Jackson to kneel in front of Aurora. He releases his magic so a black mist is circling his hand, and then he lays it on the seer's shoulder.

"Where are you?" he asks.

"The woods." Aurora sounds so breathless.

"Deep breaths, darling." She does as she is told. "Slow the vision." She begins to shake her head. "You control them, they don't control you. Slow your breathing and calm yourself. Your fear feeds into the manic. Let the fear go, do not be afraid of your visions."

"She isn't—"

Bronx cuts Jax off. "Shut up and let him do his thing. Your mate is petrified of her visions, that's why she cannot control them." Jax snaps his gaze back to Aurora, shock clear on his face.

"I can't, so much bad—"

"Shhhhh, the good outweighs the bad, darling." Aurora's shaking eases some, and her breathing evens out. "Where are you?"

"In a clearing...near a cabin."

"Describe it to me." Memphis sounds so calm and collected.

"Wooden pillars, two windows, either side of the green front door. Two rocking chairs out front, three steps, and a green roof—it looks like an old hunting cabin."

"Is it warm?"

"No, I'm so cold. I can see smoke coming from the chimney."

"Let the vision play out." Silence, we all stand by with bated breath as Aurora goes quiet. A few minutes later her eyes return to their normal pale blue, and her gaze lands on Memphis. She reaches out and cups his cheek, tears gathering in her eyes.

"Thank you, I have never been in control before." Memphis removes her hand from his face and gives it a gentle squeeze before he helps her to her feet.

"You're a powerful seer. I will help guide you through these visions. Fear is the reason you cannot control them. How long have you feared your visions?" Aurora drops her gaze to the ground and stiffens.

"Since I saw my parents'...deaths." Jax rushes forward and breaks the moment, wrapping his arms around his mate and holds her close. His eyes meet Memphis's.

"Thank you. Whatever you need, my pack will help you. Just please help her. I can't watch her get hurt anymore." The vulnerability in Jax's voice hurts to hear.

"I will help her with or without your pack's aid." Jax nods his head and mouths a thank you. "Can you tell us what you saw inside the cabin, darling?"

"Raya is bound to a chair...and she is hurt. Mya has her." A sob breaks free from Ryan, and Nico wraps his arm around her and pulls her to him. Worry begins to gnaw at me. Why after all these years is Mya now starting to hurt Raya?

"I'll fucking kill her!" Nico grounds out.

"You can't! What else did you see, darling? Did you see anything that will allow us to find this cabin?" Aurora shakes her head against Jax's chest.

"Why now?" All eyes turn to me.

"What the fuck does that mean?" Nico snaps.

"Brother, this isn't Kai's fault!" I appreciate Sophia's need to defend me, but she doesn't need to do that.

"What do you mean, Melakai?" I look to Boston as I answer him.

"Why now, after all these years, is Mya doing this? She loves Raya; she wouldn't hurt her."

"Our sister is unstable, Kai; her knowing that we have finally caught up to her will cause her to snap. Storm isn't someone to underestimate, she is cunning and ruthless." I smile wickedly.

"Raya is cunning, and I am fucking ruthless. I will show her that she fucked with the wrong man's woman." I ignore Nico's growl and make my way toward the compound. We need to search for cabins and try a locator spell to find Raya.

CHAPTER 42

Raya

Stunned doesn't begin to describe how I am feeling. How the fuck could Mya be Storm Masters? I have known her my whole life!

"I don't want to hurt you, Raya."

"Then don't. You have no need to hurt me. Bronx, Boston, and Memphis are searching for you—" Mya's scoff cuts me off.

"They are looking for me so they can sacrifice me at the blood moon. I will not allow them to bring that vile bitch back. They hate me because of what I did."

"What did you do, Mya?"

"I killed Bronx's wife and her unborn child." I gasp and jump to my feet. I try to make a break for it and head for the door. I rip the door open and try to exit, but I end up thrown back on my ass. I look up to see shimmering waves around the doorway. Holy shit, she spelled us inside the cabin! Mya looms over me, and I see anger and regret in her eyes.

"I wish it didn't have to be this way, you left me no other choice. Once the blood moon passes, you will be set free." Anger courses inside me.

"Fuck you!" I shout, and Mya's eyes harden.

"So be it." I'm too slow to react when her foot comes down on my face, and everything goes dark.

I come to with a splitting headache. I try to reach up and rub my head, but my arms won't move. I peel my eyes open slowly and see my hands are bound to the arms of a chair. I try to move my feet but they are taped to the legs of the chair. I start to panic and dart my eyes around the room, but I see nothing. The only light is the fire Mya lit earlier. I try to pull against my restraints, but nothing, I call on my magic, but nothing happens! What the fuck is the point of having powers if you can never access them? The front door opens, and Mya strolls in with her arms full of firewood. She ignores me and kicks the door shut behind herself.

"They're going to come for me, and when they do, they will fucking end you!"

Mya laughs a hollow laugh, drops the logs near the fire, and turns to face me. "You are in no position to make threats!"

"Why the hell are you doing this?" A cruel smile graces her face.

"I like games, always have. Playing the part of Mya has been fun. I enjoyed it and thought I could even see myself living as her for many more years. But then you had to fuck it up when you went to my brother's vault! You brought all this on yourself. I was free of them until your stupid ass ruined everything! I made sure to keep Kai away from you—"

"Why?"

"Because my vision showed me that Kai meeting you would bring my brothers out of hiding. I have no idea what fucking link or hold you have over them, but it needs to end. All I want is to be free and not be hunted and used by them anymore." Mya sounds so unhinged. I have no hold over her brothers or over Kai.

"You know, you look exactly like her, maybe you could be her doppelganger. That might be the reason why they are linked to you. I tried to stop this from happening. But then Aurora and Sophia had to have a vision and see your life and meddled and made sure you met Kai. I had no choice but to go along with it so they didn't suspect anything. You ruined everything! I was finally free and I fell in love for the first time in my life." Oh my God, she was talking about Chase and Alex.

"Then don't do this, Mya–Storm, or whatever the hell your name is. Chase and Alex love you—anyone with eyes can see that—but they won't forgive you if you do this."

"You fool, it's already done! My brothers are coming for me, and the only way for them to get their stupid love back is for me to die." I gasp.

"They want to bring her back from the dead?"

"Yes!" This is more fucked up than I thought; they should know better than to fuck around with that stuff.

"What do you need from me, Mya?" My question seems to throw her off guard.

"I need them to search for you, so I have a chance to disappear."

I shake my head. "If what you have just told me is true, they won't stop. Chase and Alex won't stop searching for you either. Don't do that to them, please."

"They will eventually grow old and die, and their suffering will end, but mine won't." I can hear the yearning in her voice; she isn't scared to die.

"You're not scared of dying. You're scared of watching the two men you love die while you live on."

She narrows her eyes to slits. "I have to be honest, your

whole fucking family is nuts, and y'all are the worst at mind-fucking people, honestly. I want this to be over so my mind can stop reeling and my family and I can go back to being normal." A tiny smile splits her face.

"We weren't always like this, you know. My brothers and I were once really close." Her eyes have a faraway look in them.

"What changed?"

"They met Mackenzie McGregor, and everything went downhill. They were so focused on getting her attention that they forgot about me. Memphis and Boston were supposed to come into town with me one day but blew me off because Mackenzie was there. They chose her over me, and that was the day Randall Cane took me."

"I'm so sorry."

"Don't be, my brothers tried to rescue me, years later. So, I did what I had to do—I killed Mackenzie and her bastard child so they would leave me alone! Bronx should never have married that slut!"

"You killed his wife and child, Mya!"

"It wasn't his kid! Mackenzie's pussy was like a fucking drive-thru, it was open 24/7 to anyone! My brothers were too dumb to see that. The only reason she married Bronx is because she found out she was pregnant and didn't know who the father was, so she passed it off as Bronx's baby." Wow, this Mackenzie sounds like a real charmer, but that still doesn't mean she deserved to be killed. Her baby sure as shit didn't deserve to die!

"What are you not telling me, Mya? There must be more. I have known you my whole life and there is no way you would kill someone in cold blood. Being angry and being taken by Randall I can understand—"

"Don't try to psychoanalyze me, Raya, it won't work. I am far too damaged to be fixed. I have done things in my life that I am not proud of, and I deserve to die for those things—"

"You don't want to die, though, because you finally found two reasons to live?" She releases a whoosh of air and nods her head. "What if your brothers had found you before you met Chase and Alex?"

"I would have gladly let them end my suffering." I'm trying to think of a way out of this for her, but I keep coming up blank. Bronx, Memphis, and Boston won't forgive her. They want her dead so they can bring back this Mackenzie. "If she was as kind and sweet as you, I would never have killed her."

"What did she do to you, Mya?"

"Mackenzie McGregor told Randall Cane about me. She knew he wanted a seer and offered me up on a silver platter. If my brothers had listened to me from the start, I would never have been taken." Oh my God, now it all makes sense. My family and I are stuck in the middle of their war.

"Let me go, I can try talking to them for you." Mya shakes her head.

"They won't listen. I made my bed and now I must fight to sleep in it." She flicks her wrist and the tape binding me to the chair disappears. A moment later I feel my magic surge inside me. I dart my eyes to hers and she shrugs. "I spelled the tape so you wouldn't be able to access your magic."

I rub my wrists and then begin to flex my legs so I can get some blood flowing through them again. I stand then turn and face Mya. Her back is to me as she gazes into the fire. I move and stand beside her, wrapping my arm around her waist and pulling her into me.

"I'm sorry I stomped on your face."

I chuckle and shake my head. "Don't worry about it, it will heal." We both stand there in a comfortable silence, just gazing at the fire.

"Go home, Raya, go be with your family." I pull away from her, shocked. "Don't look at me like that. I told you living as

Mya has changed me and taught me a better way to live. Go back to Wonder Lake and tell my brothers I will meet them at the summit at the peak of the blood moon."

"Mya, no! You can't do that, what about Chase and Alex?" Her tear-filled gaze meets mine.

"If I don't go, they will hunt them down and do what I did to them. I am doing this because I love Chase and Alex enough to die for them. I'll find them in the next life, Raya, maybe then we can finally be together, and I won't have to lie about who I really am."

"Please don't do this, I will talk to them and explain—" Mya cups my face between her hands and smiles sadly at me.

"Don't worry about me. Go get that man of yours and don't let him push you away. He was prepared to die for you, and now that you have changed my brother's plans, you need to live for Kai." Tears are trailing down my cheeks. These past two weeks have done nothing but fuck with my head. Standing here in front of Mya and knowing the whole truth, it breaks my heart. All these secrets and lies for nothing! Their whole family was torn apart because of lies. I wrap my arms around Mya and weep into her shoulder. I can feel it in my heart—this is the last time I will ever see her again.

She rubs my back and whispers how proud she is of me. "I wish you nothing but happiness, Raya, you deserve it. I am sorry for today and what I did to you."

"It's okay, I forgive you." We hug each other tighter; Mya pulls away and holds me at arm's length. A sad smile graces her lips.

"Have they told you what you are to him?" I shake my head, confused. "Go now, child, time will show you what you are to him. I am sorry for trying to keep you apart; I was selfish." I turn toward the door, tears clouding my vision. I turn back to her one more time before I step outside.

"I love you, Mya."

A stray tear falls from her eye. "And I you, Raya."

I close the door behind myself and take some time to process what the hell just happened. Mya is Nevada 'Storm' Masters; she has been living under our noses for years. Mya lost her family because of lies, and I don't want that for my family. I need to be honest with Kai, as well, and tell him how I really feel before it's too late.

"Portaly openinga wundera awa." I move toward the portal, and just before I step through, I turn back and see Mya staring at me through the window. I take a mental picture of her in my mind. I can't do this. I quickly change my chant and then open a portal to a new location. I really hope this works!

CHAPTER 43
Malakai

We have spent hours scouring maps and trying to perform locator spells. Ryan has tried to get in touch with Alex and Chase, but they won't return her calls. She and Lucian even portaled to the Knox coven and found they weren't there. They have gone off grid and we all know why that is—they're searching for Mya.

"Guys, it's getting late—"

"I'm not sleeping, Jackson, my daughter is hurt and needs me," Nico snaps.

"My sister can manipulate visions." All eyes turn to Memphis. "If what Kai said is true, that she really does care about Raya, then I think she manipulated Aurora's vision."

"Stop! All your family's shit has done is caused us all trouble. Once we get Raya back, I want the three of you, and Mya or Storm or whatever the fuck her name is, gone! Your family shit has done nothing but cause Raya pain. Do I have your word?" The three brothers stare at me like they want to argue, but I have had enough of their shit. They are nothing but professional mind-fuckers, and I, for one, cannot do it anymore.

The three of them reluctantly agree; they have no reason to

stick around after that. I am only helping them because of Raya. These fuckers tried to link me to Randall and kill me to find Mya; I really don't owe them anything!

We spend another few hours watching Ryan and Lucian try different spells. Hell, even Soph tried to help. I know it, and they know it too. We won't be able to locate her that way without Chase and Alex to help us. I just don't have the heart to say anything to them, but after another twenty minutes, Nico stands and pulls Ryan away from the table.

"Nico, stop!"

"No, love, you have sliced your palm three times and still nothing. You're dead on your feet and need to rest." Ryan has been using her own blood to try and locate Raya that way.

"No! She needs me."

"She needs you to be strong, love, not a total wreck. Rest for a couple hours and then we'll try again, little one. I will bring our little girl home!"

By the time I shower and get into bed, it's after one in the morning. My body is aching, and my mind is tired as fuck, but I still can't fall asleep. My mind keeps wandering if Raya is okay. I have tried countless times to reach her in her dreams, but I can't feel her. I know she is alive because I can feel the tether, but she isn't sleeping, so I can't pull her to me. I'm so fucking frustrated. I close my eyes and try again to get some sleep. We're meeting back at Jackson's office at five to spend the day searching. I have tasked Eric and the other vamps to search for her, and Jax has done the same with some of his wolves around the world. Nico has sent some of his fae out to search. Dom, Soph, and Aurora returned to New York and will come back in the morning. They needed to go check on the twins and Lily. I sigh and roll over, hoping sleep will claim me soon.

I wake to the sound of my bedroom door clicking shut. I remain still. Whoever the fuck it is will get the surprise of their lives if they think they can take me out! I lay there and keep my breathing even, so I don't alert them to me being awake. I feel the bed dip on the other side and feel them moving closer to me. As soon as I feel they are close enough, I strike. I move at vamp speed and pin the asshole beneath me and wrap my hand around their throat and growl.

"Zilla." I release my grip on her throat and pull back, shocked.

"Vixen?" She sits up and wraps her arms around me. I shake myself out of my stupor and return her embrace. A moment later she pulls back and pushes me down till I'm flat on my back and straddles me. I notice then she is only in her bra and panties. Am I dreaming? I reach out and pinch her side. She yelps then swats me on my naked chest.

"What the hell was that for?" she growls.

"I thought I might be dreaming." She rolls her eyes. "How are you here?"

She releases a long sigh. "Can we talk about it later? Right now, I just want to be here with you and enjoy this moment. I know when we face my parents and the others tomorrow, shit between us will change, and I don't want to think about that right now." I deflate beneath her.

"Just answer me one thing?"

"Okay."

"Is Mya a threat?" Her eyes soften, and she shakes her head.

"Not to us she isn't." I don't get a chance to reply before she captures my lips in a searing kiss. Kissing her feels like home, and now that I know what she is to me, I won't let her go. I'm not scared of hurting her anymore. Her blood still sings to me, but for an entirely different reason now. If I were to bite her, I wouldn't lose control; it would just mark her as mine for all eternity. Her tongue probes my mouth and I open for her. I let her explore my mouth for a minute before I take control.

I reach up and unclasp her bra, and she pulls back so I can peel it from her body. I chuck it to the side and then capture her nipple in my mouth, and she moans. I switch sides and pay homage to her other nipple. She grinds her hips against my cock, and I release her nipple with a pop. I grip the back of her neck and spin us, so she is beneath me. I grind my cock against her pussy, and she moans.

"I want you inside me, Kai." I wish I could draw this out and savour this moment, but the truth is I can't. I want to be sheathed inside her so bad. I don't bother to pull her panties off; I tear them from her instead, and her shocked gasp turns me the fuck on. I slide down the bed and spread her legs further apart. The sight of her glistening pussy has my mouth watering.

"Your cunt is dripping, vixen." She releases a small whimper. "You want me to eat your wet pussy?"

"I want you to make me come on your tongue and then fuck me, like it's the last time you will ever have my pussy." Her words nearly make me cum on the spot. I don't hesitate; I dive in and lap at her, and she cries out when I swirl my tongue around her clit. I insert two fingers inside her tight cunt and pump. She cries out my name, but I don't ease my pace. I suck her clit into my mouth and finger fuck her at a brutal pace until she comes all over my hand and screams my name as she climaxes. I'm too fucking horny to go slow. I pull out of her and sit between her legs before lining my cock up. I reach forward and grip the back of her neck so I can pull her up toward me. I hold the two fingers out on my other hand that has her come all over them and hold them in front of her mouth.

"Suck them clean, now!" She opens her mouth and indulges on my fingers. When she moans at the taste of herself, I release my hold on her and push her down. When her eyes meet mine, I slam inside of her. We both moan at the feeling of being joined together. Fuck, being inside her is my favorite place in the world.

"Fuck me, Kai." I move inside her at a slow pace, teasing her. "Fuck, Kai, please! I need more." I stop moving and capture her lips in a heated kiss. I pull out of her and then climb off the bed, and before she can protest, I pull her over to me. I flip her so she is lying on her stomach, kicking her legs apart and lining my cock up to her pussy. I grip her hair with one hand while I use the other to guide my cock inside her. She moans loud enough to wake the compound.

"Keep quiet, vixen, or I won't fuck you!" I grit out, and she releases a small whimper.

"I can't help it!" I slam the rest of the way inside her, and use my free hand to cover her mouth while I fuck her hard. She screams against my hand, and I can feel her pussy clenching my dick, trying to milk me of my cum. Not yet, baby.

She screams into my hand as an orgasm tears through her body, but I don't give her a chance to come down. I pull out of her and then flip her over. I pick her up once more and she wraps her arms and legs around me. I slam her against the wall and thrust my cock back inside her. Her eyes roll back and a moan escapes her.

"I fucking love your pussy." She moans in agreement. "Who does this cunt belong to, vixen?" I slow my pace so she can catch her breath and answer me. She leans forward and kisses me like I'm the air she needs to live.

"My wet cunt belongs to you. Only you, Kai." I growl my approval and then slam my hips into her. "Oh God...please." I grip the back of her neck and pull her face to mine so I can kiss her to keep her quiet. She moans and screams into my mouth as another orgasm hits her, and I roar my release into her mouth and cum inside her tight pussy.

I release her lips and drop my head into the crook of her shoulder, holding most of my weight off her. We're both panting and sweaty. I feel her pussy start to quiver and it makes me smirk. I pull back then gently ease my cock out of her, and she unwraps her arms and legs and tries to stand but ends up flopping against the wall. I lean over and turn on the lamp, looking at her just-fucked hair, rosy cheeks, and glassy eyes. I look down and see my cum dripping down her legs and grin. I love seeing my cum on her. She reaches down and runs her finger down her thigh and through my cum. I follow her hand as she lifts it to her face, and her eyes meet mine as she puts that finger inside her mouth and moans. I groan. Raya Stone is going to be the death of me if she keeps that shit up.

"Wanna suck the rest off my cock?" I meant to only tease her, but when she drops to her knees in front of me and sucks my cock straight into her hot, greedy mouth, I lose all train of thought. Holy fuck, her mouth feels like heaven.

After sucking Kai's cock clean, he ushers me into his adjoining bathroom and tells me that we have to shower so we can wash away the scent of sex, or Uncle Dom and Uncle Jax will know we just fucked. Not wanting to draw any more attention to myself, I do as Kai says. Kai is a complete gentleman and leaves me to wash my hair and body, but when I turn around and see him standing there with water droplets running down his chest and his hands lathering his body, I begin to get fucking turned on again.

"Stop looking at my cock like that, vixen." I snap my gaze to his and smile sweetly.

"Like what?" I close the space between us and then grip his cock. He hisses but doesn't stop me from pumping him. He moans and I push him till his back is against the wall. He looks down at me with so much lust in his eyes. I hold his gaze as I drop to my knees, but Kai reaches out and hauls me back up before I can suck him. I growl my frustration. Kai reaches down and cups my pussy, and I whimper when he runs one of his fingers through my folds.

"You're already fucking wet for me again."

"I'm always wet when you're around." Kai hums his approval then pushes a finger inside me. "Oh my God, Kai." He withdraws his finger then puts it in his mouth and sucks, liquid pools between my thighs at the sight of him sucking my wetness from his finger.

"You taste so fucking good."

"You taste even better with my come on your cock." His eyes darken, then with lightning fast movement, he has me against the shower wall with my legs wrapped around him and his hard cock pushing against my tight hole.

"You want my cock inside you again vixen?"

"God, yes!"

"Then tell me who this pussy belongs to."

I meet his gaze. "You." He slams inside me, and I cry out.

"Will another man ever touch what is mine?"

"No." He thrusts inside me again.

"Will you ever suck another man's cock?"

"No." Thrust.

"Will you ever let another man see you come?"

I narrow my eyes at him. "No! I will only let you touch me, fuck me, eat me and cum on me. Now for the love of fucking Christ, fuck me so I can come all over your cock." That's all he needed to hear; Kai fucks me hard and fast and I climax so hard screaming his name like it's a prayer. Once I'm done he pulls out of me and pushes me to my knees and he pumps his cock in my face. I dart my tongue out and lick the head of his dick while he continues to pump and moan my name.

"I'm gonna come all over that pretty fucking face, vixen." I hum my approval. I reach down between my thighs and start to rub my clit; it's so sensitive from just orgasming, so I know I won't last long. I moan and Kai's eyes trail down my body to see me playing with my pussy.

"Kai, I'm gonna come again soon, and I want you to come with me."

"Fuck yes! Get there, vixen, 'cause I'm about to cum." I rub my clit faster and start to feel my body coil in anticipation of my next orgasm, and just as it hits, Kai roars my name and his hot cum spurts out and lands all over my face and tits. I follow a second later, screaming his name as I come all over my hand.

After washing ourselves again in the shower, we dried off and then both climbed into bed naked. I can see the sun peeking through the gap in the curtains and know it must be still early. If we're lucky, we might get an hour or two of sleep. I rest my head on Kai's arm and he pulls me against him. Lying here in his embrace, I feel content and happy. My eyes begin to droop, and I'm losing the fight against sleep. Just before I'm pulled under, I hear Kai whisper.

"You are mon salut, mon espoir, mon eternal."

I fall into a deep sleep, and I don't dream of a single thing. I haven't slept this heavy in so long.

"THE FUCK IS THIS?" Kai and I both bolt upright, and I clutch the blanket to my chest to hide my nakedness. My eyes double in size when I see the people standing in the doorway. Uncle Dom, Uncle Jax, and Lucian are wrestling my dad out of the room while Kai and I sit here, stunned silent. My mom, Aunt Soph, and Aunt Aurora all wear looks of relief.

"I would hug you, sweetie, but I feel like that might be inappropriate given the state of both of you." Kai rubs the back of his neck and chuckles. Me, on the other hand, I turn a shade of red and want to die.

"How about we save the hug for when we get dressed and meet you in Uncle Jax's office?" My mom and my aunt's eyes shine with mischief, and Aunt Soph flicks her brows at me as they all exit, chuckling. As soon as they close the door, I drop back down and pull the covers over my face. "I wish the floor would open up and eat me."

"I thought we already established that I am the only one who is allowed to eat you?" I groan and Kai chuckles at his own stupid joke. I throw the blankets back and hop off the bed. After a short search, I locate my torn panties next to my jeans. I eighty-six the panties and pull my jeans on commando. I feel Kai's eyes on me the whole time. I find my bra and slip that on, and then I spot Kai's plain white shirt slung over the back of one of the couches and pull it on. I turn to face him and see he is smirking at me.

"What?" He flings his legs over the side of the bed and lazily strolls toward me, leans down, kisses me, then turns toward the closet.

"There's a spare toothbrush in the top drawer, vixen." I shake myself out of it and head to the bathroom to take care of business.

Kai and I walk side by side the whole way to meet the others, worry and dread settle inside my stomach the closer we get. As we round the corner that will lead us to Uncle Jax's office, Kai grips my hand and pulls me to a stop. We stand there gazing into each other's eyes. Kai's mask is firmly back in place, and I cannot get a read on his emotions. I hate when he does that; it makes me feel uneasy.

"I'll be beside you the whole time." I wish I could say I feel reassured by his words, but I don't. I mean, I still don't even know what the fuck Kai and I are! The question blurts out before I can stop it.

"What are we?" I cringe internally and try to pry my hand from his, but he won't let me. He stands there staring down at me for the longest time but still says nothing. "Can we just get this over with, please?" Kai nods his head robotically and then leads the way with my hand still clasped in his. He opens the door, and I take a deep breath as we enter. Everyone stops talking and turns to face us. Dad, Uncle Dom, Lucian, and Uncle Jax stand by the bookshelves behind the desk. My father's eyes zoom in on Kai holding my hand and his eyes narrow. I look to the side and see the three brothers sitting on one of the couches, with my mom and aunts sitting on the couch opposite them. Mom lifts her coffee cup to her mouth to hide her smile, and I roll my eyes and then face the brothers. They all look on edge.

"So, how about we get the awkward birds and the bees talk out of the way." I cringe again for the like tenth time this morning at Uncle Dom's comment.

"Shut up, Dominic!"

"Well don't blame me when you become a grandfather to your best friend's kid." My eyes double in size and I gulp. Dad smacks Uncle Dom on the back of the head. "The fuck was that for?"

"You need to be fucking muzzled!" Dad turns his angry eyes to Kai and me and opens his mouth to speak, but I cut him off.

"Can we get this shit with Mya over with first before you tear me a new one, please?" Dad grinds his teeth together and nods his head stiffly. We move over to the couches and sit down. Kai still won't release my hand. Bronx, Boston, and Memphis look at me expectantly. Kai gives my hand a reassuring squeeze, and I take a few deep breaths and then begin.

"Mya is one hundred percent Storm aka Nevada—"

"Wait, you are all seriously named after places?" The three brothers turn and glare at Lucian. Uncle Dom is the only one to find what his son said amusing.

"Anyway, she is your sister."

"That's it?" I meet Bronx's frosty gaze, and this time I pull free from Kai's grasp. I stand and move toward the brothers. I sit down on the coffee table in front of Bronx and reach out to clasp both his hands in mine.

"I am so sorry for your loss." Tormented blue eyes meet my gaze.

"She told you?" I nod. "What else did she have to say?" His voice holds an edge to it.

"She told me about Mackenzie and how I look like her. She also told me about how she was kidnapped by Randall—"

"She left with him willingly!" Boston snaps, and I see so much hurt in their eyes. Guilt eats at me for what I have done.

"No, Bos, your sister was...sold, I guess you could call it, to Randall." Gasps ring out around the room, and the three Masters brothers look baffled. "Mackenzie was the one who told Randall about Storm and her seer abilities. Randall used her, and when you three found her, she took her revenge out on your wife, Bronx."

"She killed my child, Raya!" So much hatred coats his tone.

"The baby wasn't yours, Bronx," I whisper, and he tears his hands from mine and stands, towering over me.

"You're lying! Mack would never do that to me!"

"Sit down or I will fucking make you. You will watch your goddamn tone when you speak to her, feel me?" I stiffen at Kai's words. He is such a mind fuck! He won't answer my question but he'll defend me? Get fucked, Zilla.

"Why do you say that, Ray?" I turn to Boston, he yanks Bronx back down into his seat.

"Mya told me she hated her for years. She never wanted this. I don't know what she went through at the hands of Randall Cane, but it was enough for her to commit murder."

"Where is she?" Bronx grits out. I'm too much of a coward to meet his gaze.

"She's gone."

"Gone where?" I take a deep breath and meet Bronx's ice cold eyes.

"Give her till the blood moon, please. Let her say goodbye to them first."

"Goodbye to who, sweetie?" I turn and meet my mom's knowing gaze; she already knows the answer but wants me to say it.

"When Mya let me go last night, I went to Alex and Chase and took them to her." Tears cloud my mom's eyes.

"Thank you, baby girl." I nod and then turn back to the brothers.

"She said she will meet you at the summit at the peak of the blood moon. I don't know what that means, though, I'm sorry."

"When the moon is at its peak, that is when the sacrifice will be made." Memphis's ominous tone fills me with dread.

"Please don't do this. Mya isn't a bad person. I have known her my whole—"

"We will keep our word." Bronx focuses his gaze above my head, looking directly at Kai. "We will conclude our business with Storm and then we will vanish." Bronx stands and stares down at same, an unreadable expression on his face. "I'm sorry for what we put you through." With that said, Bronx exits the room, and I climb to my feet as does Memph and Bos.

"Remember what I told you?"

I nod my head at Memphis. "If I hurt your brothers you'll

kill me?" Growls sound out around the room, and Memphis chuckles and shakes his head.

"No. Never let your guard down, Ray. Be strong and fearless, but most of all, be happy." Memphis shocks the hell out of me when he pulls me into a hug. He lets me go then follows after Bronx. Boston now stands in front of me.

"I wish we met under different circumstances." I smile sadly and nod my head. "Do you want to know why you feel so obligated to help us?" I reel back, shocked.

"Yes," I stammer out.

"Because you have a good heart, Ray. You see the good in people, and that is not a trait that many people have today. As a courtesy to you and your family, for all the help and for what we have done, I will make sure my brothers hear what Storm has to say before we...you know." I nod my head.

"I have a favor to ask."

"Name it."

"If Alex and Chase are with her, promise me no harm will come to them." Boston doesn't hesitate.

"On my honor, no harm will befall them, Ray. Thank you for everything." Boss and I hug, and before he leaves the room, he turns back to Kai and says, "Look after her. If you hurt her in any way, we will come back, and you don't want that, Melakai." Kai nods his head.

A feeling of sorrow fills me when Bos leaves the room. What will happen to Mya? I want to believe that they could talk it out and be a family again, but the blood moon is tomorrow, and somehow I don't see them working it out in time. My mom rushes over to me and grips my face between her hands. She looks me over for any injuries, and when she can't find any, she wraps me in a hug. Lucky for me, Kai gave me some of his blood to heal the cut on my nose from Mya's boot last night.

"No more, baby girl. The amount of times Luce had to help

me get control back isn't funny. I'm getting a tracker implanted on you or something." I grip my mom tighter and just hold her.

"Thank you for being the most amazing mother. I'm so sorry for the dumb shit I have pulled the past couple weeks. I promise I won't do it again. My head still hurts from all the lies and secrets." Mom chuckles.

"I think all our heads are going to be reeling for a while, love. Those three boys definitely know how to weave a tale and stretch the truth." She sounds like such a mom right now. I pull away from her and hug Aunt Aurora and then Aunt Soph. Aunt Soph demands that I debrief her on what happened with Kai later, I quickly rush away from her so I don't have to answer. Luce and I hug for ages. We're finally free of the shit we started.

"All things aside, we still saved your mom, Ray." I nod my head against his chest. I would do it all again for her. Uncle Dom and Uncle Jax don't say much as I hug them, and the tension in the room skyrockets when I stand in front of my dad. He looks down at me with so much disappointment in his eyes that it hurts to maintain eye contact.

"Nico–" I don't lift my head at the sound of my mom's voice; she can't save me from Dad's wrath.

"Stay out of this one, love." I flinch at the harshness in my dad's tone. "You will return to Farrarie and continue your training, without any arguments." I die a little inside. He has no idea how much the idea of going back there and living my life like a robot kills me inside! "You will not leave Farrarie without my consent, do I make myself clear?" I lift my gaze to my father's, tears gathering behind my eyes, but I refuse to let them fall.

"Crystal, your majesty." Dad narrows his eyes to slits.

"Don't sass me, Raya, not after...what I saw," he grits out, and my anger surges forward.

"So you're grounding me because you caught me sleeping in a bed with Kai? If you had been there two hours earlier, you would have found me on my knees in his shower!" Gasps ring out, and Dad stumbles back until he smacks into the bookshelf.

"Fuck me, cupcake, I think you just gave us all a mental picture we don't need!" I ignore Uncle Dom as I glare at my dad. He looks shocked and horrified. Well, I have the nerve, I need to tell him or I never will.

"I love you, Dad, but I won't go back—not yet, anyway. I'm nineteen, I wanna live a little and make friends. The girls back home only want to know me because they can say they're friends with the princess."

"Exactly, you're nineteen! You shouldn't be doing what you're doing with him! You're too young and you need to explore the world before doing...that stuff." I hide my smile; Dad is a jumbling mess right now.

"If I recall, Smurf was eighteen when she met you." Dad turns and glares at Lucian. "Right, shutting my mouth now." He turns back to me, and all the fight drains from his eyes. He closes the space between us and pulls me to him. I wrap my arms around him and hold him tight.

"I love you, Daddy." I hear the whoosh of air leave him.

"I love you too, baby girl. I hate to admit it, but I am proud of how you handled yourself." We stand there, lost in each other's embrace for a moment, before he asks, "What do you want to do then, Ray?"

I pull back and look up at him, shocked, and he scoffs and rolls his eyes. "What? I'm known to be reasonable sometimes." I hear mom snort behind us and I chuckle. "Ignore your mother, she's just pissed I won't let her get another dog."

"It's a fucking Chihuahua, Nico, not a horse."

"You already have six of the fucking ankle biters!"

I sit here quietly watching Raya and Nico. I know Nico is avoiding looking at me at all costs, especially after Raya's outburst. I must say I am proud of him for asking her what she wants; she deserves to choose her future. I just hope that her future includes me. I know I don't deserve it, but I want to be with her. I just haven't found the right time to tell her that she is my beloved. Fate has chosen her for me, and I don't want to put that kind of pressure on her, yet.

"I want to take dance classes and cut down on combat training. I also only want to deal with the political bullshit of our realm once a fortnight. I want you to let me live, Dad. I'll always be your little girl no matter what, but you need to let me have some freedom." I smile, so proud of her for telling him what she wants. I know that can't be easy for her.

"So...that's it?"

"Yeah."

"Deal! Everyone heard her demands, right?" I look around the room, confused, and the three girls are glaring at Nico. The guys look irritated. Then it hits me—Raya never asked about me.

"Dad?" Nico's gaze flicks to me briefly before looking back at his daughter. His shoulders droop in defeat.

"There are so many other good guys, millions of others, why him?" That hurt.

"Why not him?"

"Because he's Kai, and I've known him my whole life, and he's ugly." I scoff, Dom and Jax both chuckle, so I glare at them. "Plus, he's really fucking old!"

"Oh my God! You're like a hundred years older than mom!" Nico reels back like she slapped him.

"That is different; I'm your father, so you need to do as I say not as I do!" He's fucking having a laugh, right? That made no fucking sense whatsoever.

"How about you let me work my own shit out, and I won't tell mom you secretly leave the gate open so her dogs will run away." Nico looks down at Raya in horror, his gaze quickly cutting to an angry looking Ryan.

"Whoops!" He snaps his gaze back to Raya and glares at her. She starts to back up and he follows her movements, and she turns and runs toward me. I jump to my feet just in time to catch her when she launches herself at me. She wraps her arms and legs around me and smiles down at me. I ignore Nico's groans and cursing and focus on the beauty in my arms.

"I think I'm gonna be sick!"

"Oh, you're gonna be more than fucking sick!"

"Little one, please!" I tune out Nico and Ryan's bickering and get lost in my vixen's eyes. She wiggles out of my hold, and I set her on her feet. She reaches out and offers me her hand to shake. I look at it and snap my gaze to hers. She quirks a brow at me, so I place my larger hand in hers.

"Hi, I'm Raya, and I think you're pretty cute. Wanna get a drink with me sometime? I know a really great club in Colorado called Salut." I burst out laughing, like a proper belly laugh!

I shake her hand and say, "Any chance you have I.D.?" The both of us burst out laughing.

"Soph, I wanna do some role play," Dom whines.

"Eww, Dad, that is fucking gross!"

"Shut up, Lucian, the night you were conceived your mother was pretending to be a cowgirl." Lucian and Nico both glare at Dom. Soph shakes her head and motions for Dom to come sit beside her. I don't think he will ever grow up.

I decide to take a walk to the stream in the woods. Raya is having dinner with her parents. She offered for me to join them, but I declined. I need time to think about how I'm going to tell her what she is to me. She told Nico she wants to live her life and go to dance classes and all that, but where? A strange feeling settles inside me at the thought that she might not want to come back with me to Colorado. Could I let her go and not follow her? Rustling behind me pulls me from my thoughts, and I don't need to turn to know it's them. They sit down either side of me and pass me a bottle of Johnny Walker, red label.

"I thought you were having a family dinner?" I ask Nico, and he shudders and shakes his head.

"I ran out as soon as they started talking about safe sex." I laugh at the horrified look on his face. "I swear on my life, if you get my daughter pregnant, I will cut your fucking dick off!" Dom, Jax and I all laugh. We all settle into comfortable silence and sip on our bottles until Jackson breaks the silence.

"Do you guys wanna know something funny?"

"Yeah," we answer in unison.

"Kai has seen both your wives and now your daughter's

vagina, but he hasn't seen my mates, so I'll take that as a win!" The three of us all glare at him, and Dom smacks him up the back of the head.

"The fuck?"

"It's not nice, is it?" The four of us burst out laughing at Dom's reply; normally it's always him getting slapped. After our laughter dies off, we all sit there in silence again for a while until Nico breaks it.

"Don't break her heart, Melakai. Despite my dislike of this thing between you and my daughter, I know you will care for her. I may not like it, but if there was ever a man that I thought would be good enough for her, it would be you." I turn and look at him in shock; I never thought he would say something like that.

"Thank you?" he scoffs and rolls his eyes.

"That doesn't mean I like it, though! I don't ever want to see you kissing, touching or making fuck-me eyes in front of me, and I swear to God if I ever catch you naked with her again..." The three of us laugh, but I agree to his terms. "Will you tell her what she is to you?"

"No."

"Why?" Dom asks.

"Because, I want her to choose me because she wants to, not because she has to. If she chooses to travel and explore the world, I won't hinder that for her. I just want her to be happy." Nico claps me on the shoulder.

"Thank you, Kai." We spend the next hour catching up and discussing future plans. I tell them about my build in Arizona, and Dom tells us that Soph wants to open another shelter. Nico admits he wants to take a break from all his king duties and take Ryan to the places she has always wanted to visit. Jax tells us he and Aurora are going to take Lily to Disneyland in the summer.

It feels like old times, being here with my best friends—my

brothers. I didn't realize how much I've missed this. The guys and I agree to meet up once a month at the pub we had met all those years ago when we were just children. I think it will be good for us to catch up monthly.

"A boys' night once a month sounds fucking epic! Trust me, I need a night off, because the twins are killing me. They answer back and always mumble shit as they walk away, and they constantly embarrass me in public. I love them to death but their fucking demons!"

"You do realize they get that from you?"

"Nico's right, you literally just described yourself."

"Hate to say it, brother, but Jax and Nico are right."

"You all can go fuck a duck, seriously!"

CHAPTER 46

Raya

Should I knock?

Should I just walk in?

I have been standing outside Kai's bedroom for five minutes, deciding whether or not I should knock or just walk in. My nerves are frayed after talking to my mom. I cringed the whole way through her birds and the bees talk, and it was so fucking awkward! It was so good to talk with her and catch up on things, she and I are both still so worried about what will happen tomorrow for the blood moon. She still hasn't heard a word from Alex or Chase, which is making her anxious, but I trust Boston, he won't go against his word. I'm pulled from my thoughts when the door opens, and a shirtless Kai stands in front of me. I trail my gaze down his naked chest and stop at the waistband of his low-slung sweats.

"My eyes are up here, vixen." I snap my eyes back to his handsome face. "Are you gonna stand out here all night or come in?"

"I was just…"

"Standing out here for the past five minutes? I know. I'm a supernatural, vixen, and a vampire. I could scent your blood the moment you stopped outside my door." I scowl at him as I brush past and make way inside. I stop at the foot of the bed and turn to face him. He kicks the door shut then crosses his arms over his naked chest.

"What do you want, Kai?"

"This isn't about me, vixen." I throw my hands in the air.

"You're so fucking frustrating! Just give me a straight answer."

"Then ask me, Raya, ask me what you really want to know." I steel my spine and hold his gaze.

"Do you want me?" There, I said it.

"Since the first moment I saw you sitting in that metal chair in the holding room." I'm shocked.

"Why did you push me away?" He runs a hand through his hair.

"Because I'm fucked up, and I thought I didn't deserve someone as pure as you. I want you, Raya, in every way possible, but I also won't hold you back. If you want to travel and see the world, then do it, I'll still be here. I'll wait for you. I have waited my whole life to find my other half, and now that I have you here in front of me, I want to be selfish. I want you to stay and choose me. I'm in love with you, vixen, and I want you forever, so if you want to experience life and travel, do it. I'll wait—"

I raise my hand to stop him, tears pooling behind my eyes.

"You love me?"

"Yeah, vixen, my heart is yours." I launch myself at him, and he catches me, of course. I wrap around him like a snake and pour all my love into my kiss. He spins us so my back is against the door, then he pulls back and looks up at me. "I love you, Raya." I melt in his hold.

"And I love you, Melakai. I have for a while now." Kai kisses me until I'm breathless then carries me over to the bed. I drop to my feet and shimmy out of my jeans and chuck Kai's borrowed-slash-stolen shirt next to my jeans then crawl onto the bed and slip beneath the covers. Kai joins me a moment later, wrapping his arms around me and holding me close.

"Would you really let me go if I wanted to travel?"

"I wouldn't let you go, vixen, I'll never let you go—but I would let you leave for a short amount of time." I chuckle, what an ass.

"Zilla?"

"Yeah?"

"What does the writing on your bicep mean?"

"Mon Salut, mon espoir, mon eternal?"

"Yeah, salut is the name of your club and I've heard you say those words to me before." He clasps my face between his hands and lifts my head till I'm looking at him.

"Before I tell you, I want to know what you have decided." I hide my grin and make sure to keep my emotions hidden. Kai's eyes search my face, but he can't get a read on me.

"I'm going to take some dance classes and I'd like to study, but the college is so far from here, and I don't have anywhere to stay."

"Where is it?" he grits out, and I smile.

"Colorado." Kai's eyes blaze then in one swift move he's on top of me and I'm pinned to the mattress.

"You're coming to Colorado?" I smile up at him and nod. "Then you stay with me."

"But your house is so far—"

"I'll buy another fucking house, right next door to your school then." I laugh. God he is so freaking cute.

"No, your house is fine where it is. Do I have to stay in the spare room?" Kai growls and narrows his eyes at me.

"All your shit will be moved into my room. I'll get you your own car and whatever else you need." I reach up and cup his cheek.

"I just need you, Zilla. Now tell me what that means and why you named your club that."

"It means, my salvation, my hope, my ever after. I named my club Salut because it was my salvation after leaving my brothers—"

"Wait, you called me mon salut before we even slept together." Kai smiles down at me.

"Because, Raya Stone, you are my salvation, my hope for a better future, and you made me believe in ever after. I'd like to be your ever after. When you left with Dom and Soph, I knew then what you meant to me. I knew that night that I had lost my heart to you, and I wasn't mad about it. So, I got those words tattooed in that place so you would always be close to my heart." Tears leak from my eyes at his words, and he looks so vulnerable right now.

"You have always been my ever after since the first moment I met you. I am unconditionally yours, as is my heart," I choke out.

6 MONTHS LATER!

"Hurry up, vixen, or we're gonna be late!"

"I'm coming, hold the hell on." I can hear him muttering under his breath, but I ignore him and finish applying my lip gloss before I exit the bathroom. He's sitting on the end of the bed in one of his signature suits. Don't get me wrong, I love him in jeans and shirt, but seeing him in a suit does things to my pussy.

"Don't you dare give me fuck-me eyes when we're already late!" I groan and stomp my foot, and he smirks as he stands and makes his way over to me. "You look fucking stunning." His compliment warms me, and I stand on tiptoe so I can place a chaste kiss on his lips.

"Can't we skip this and stay home? I promise to be a naughty girl." Kai closes his eyes and pinches the bridge of his nose.

"Fucking hell, Raya!" He only calls me Raya when I piss him off or I'm in trouble. "I want nothing more than to tear that scrap of material from your body and fuck your tight pussy, but Dom and your father will kill me if we miss the twins sweet sixteen party." I pout and look down at my outfit. I'm wearing a peach-colored one shoulder dress that hugs my curves in all the right places. It's open on the side of my hip, so it shows off some skin. The dress stops just above my knees and I paired it with some nude stilettos. Kai loves it when I wear heels, outside and inside the bedroom—who am I to deny my man, right?

"Let's go, Zilla. The quicker we get there the quicker we get home, and you can fuck me in my heels." I exit our room with his cursing following me out.

We exit the portal I opened at the back of their Uncle Dom and Aunt Soph's house in New York. I still think it is so cute that they live in the same house with Uncle Dom's dad. Kai clasps my hand in his and leads me toward the growing crowd. These heels and walking on grass aren't a great fucking idea!

"Want me to carry you over?" I smirk up at my handsome as fuck boyfriend-slash- beloved. Kai told me a couple months after

I moved in with him about me being his beloved. I was shocked, but I won't lie—I was over the fucking moon knowing that he would be mine forever! Kai has changed so much in the past six months; he doesn't close his emotions off from me, and he is so fucking supportive. He helps me with all my assignments and loves the fact that I take dance classes three times a week. Every day after school, Cam picks me up and then I go back to Salut to do my schoolwork while Kai does all his stuff for the club. I still train with my dad and Cyrus on the weekends, but Dad has backed off so much with all my training and is allowing me to live freely and make my own choices. I know it's still awkward for him, with me being with Kai but he is slowly getting there. Mom loves the idea of me being with Kai; she says she couldn't have chosen a better man for me herself.

"If you carry me Dad is going to lose his shit." Kai has a devilish smirk on his face as he bends down and carries me bride-style across the back lawn. As we near the picnic tables, I see my aunts and uncles grinning at us. Lucian has a shit-eating grin on his face and Kailyn and Avery start laughing. Even Lily has a smile on her face. Everyone knows as soon as my dad sees me being carried, he's going to explode. I spot mom out of the corner of my eye and send her a wink. She shakes her head and taps my dad next to her to get his attention. When his eyes land on me and he sees Kai carrying me, the smile vanishes from his face. Kai stops a few feet away from them.

"Nicky boy, how are you?" Dad growls and narrows his eyes.

"Put my daughter down so I can punch you in the face!" Dad casts his gaze to me, and I smile sheepishly. "You are grounded and have a lot of explaining to do!"

"Me? What the hell did I do?" Kai places me on my feet but keeps an arm wrapped around my waist. Dad points an accusing finger at me then at Kai.

"This is your entire fault!"

"The fuck did I do?" I can hear the shock in Kai's voice.

"Nico, calm down."

"No love, our daughter is all over the fucking internet because of him." I look at Kai and see he is just as confused as I am. Uncle Dom, Uncle Jax, Lucian, and my aunts join us. Uncle Dom slings an arm around my dad's shoulders and then smirks at us.

"Who knew my niece would become famous for giving lap dances?" Dad shucks out of Uncle Dom's hold and glares at him. The penny drops, and Kai and I both break out into fits of laughter. Kai has been salty as fuck about me giving Cam a lap dance all those months ago, so I got Cam and David to help me set Kai up. Long story short, Kai was sitting on a chair in the middle of the dance floor at the club, and I gave him the show of his life. It ended with me being fucked over his desk at Salut, so all in all I think he has finally forgiven me.

"This is not funny! I saw you carry her upstairs and...fuck!" A shudder rips through my dad. People recorded my little show for Kai and posted it online, and the video ends with Kai carrying me up the stairs to his office in just the same manner that he did now.

"Nico, they live together, of course other...things...happen."

"Doesn't mean I need to see it on the internet!" Dad snaps at Mom.

"Well, I for one loved your moves. Maybe you could teach me sometime?"

"Sophia! No, that is not going to happen. The fucking pair of you need to go to a nunnery and take a vowel of celibacy." Everyone laughs at my dad, and mom tries to soothe his ego and calm him down, but it's not working.

"One, your sister is married and has three kids. Two, Raya is twenty years old and isn't a child." Dad glares at Kai, and then a devilish smirk crosses his face.

"How about you don't touch my daughter again until you're married or engaged at the least." Kai doesn't miss a beat.

"Of course, Nico, I would hate to upset my future father-in-law." I glare up at Kai and ignore my father's triumphant smile.

"The fuck, Zilla?" Kai turns to face me, and I can see he is trying to mask his emotions, but I can tell he is nervous. He begins to unbutton his suit jacket.

"The first moment I saw you, I felt this unexplainable pull toward you." He chucks his jacket to my mom, and she catches it, much to my dad's dismay. Kai begins to unbutton his white dress shirt. "We have been through so much in such a short amount of time, and I would do it all again if it meant I still get to be with you." He removes his shirt and stands there in front of everyone, shirtless. Kai has everyone's eyes on him, but he is only focused on me. I can't help it, my eyes trail across his naked torso and my mouth waters at the sight of my tattooed god. He cups my face between his hands, and when he looks into my eyes, I see nothing but love in them.

"Raya Stone, you are my everything. You are my sunshine on my darkest days and the light at the end of a really long, dark tunnel. Will you make me the happiest and luckiest man in the world and become mon salut, mon espoir, mon eternal?" He lifts his arm so I can see his tattoo he got for me. Right there beneath the words he just spoke it says "will you marry me?" Tears trail down my cheeks as he fishes a small box out of his pocket and drops to one knee in front of my family. He opens the lid and I gasp. Sitting there nestled in velvet is the most beautiful ruby ring. It is huge, and the stone on it will no doubt weigh my hand down. "Marry me and become my wife, Raya. Become Mrs. Cane."

My dad clears his throat. "You can always say no and come

home." I turn and give my dad the best shut the hell up look I can muster through my tears. I drop to my knees in front of Kai and kiss him. He pulls back and smiles at me.

"So, is that a yes?"

"That's a fuck yes, Zilla." Everyone around us cheers and applauds. Melakai Cane has just made me the happiest woman alive. How many people can say they got their happily ever after?

Epilogue

MALEKAI

I exit the portal my beautiful wife opened for me and make my way toward Finley's pub to meet my brothers. We still meet here once a month to catch up and talk shit. I always look forward to it, I know Dom does as well. Lucian and the twins have moved out and have their own lives now. He and Soph have opened eleven shelters for women across the globe, and I couldn't be prouder of them. Jax and Aurora welcomed another baby girl into the world four years ago, and they couldn't be more smitten with their new born. Lily is helping Jax run the pack, and I tell you what, that girl is like an army sergeant. Lily loves to train, but she also loves the political side of things. Aurora is training, as well. We all know that she is still getting help from Memphis Masters, but won't admit it. We don't know what happened to Mya. Chase and Alex haven't returned to the Knox coven since the night Raya took them to Mya. We searched for them but couldn't find a single trace. Ryan has taken over the coven until her cousins return. None of us have the heart to tell her we think it's a forever thing.

Nico tried to track the brothers down, but he can't locate them; it's just like they promised they really did vanish. Nico and Ryan still search for the Knox brothers, but if you ask me, they will never find them. I have a feeling deep inside that Mya and the Knox boys are together and the master's brothers let her go. I think Raya's speech all those years ago gave them a change of heart.

"You coming or what?" I shake myself out of my thoughts and look up to see Jax standing in the doorway. I nod and follow him in. We head toward the back where Nico and Dom occupy our usual table. The waiter takes our order when we sit down. I smile at my brothers; they haven't aged a day, and all still look the same.

"Why are you smiling like that? It's weird. I'm still not used to you smiling so much." I laugh and shake my head at Dom.

"Honestly, I'm a happy man." Dom reels back and slaps his hand over his heart.

"Blink twice if you're okay, are you under duress?" I glare at the fucker.

"Ha-ha, I'm serious. I never thought I would ever have this feeling, and man I fucking love it. Look at us, we have come so fucking far from the four misfits who met at this pub decades ago. We all have amazing women in our lives, and you guys have beautiful kids. Although I have to say, I think Nico has the best-looking kid out of the three of you." Nico and I laugh while Jax and Dom throw some peanuts at us.

"Fuck you, dick, my sons and my daughter are stunning."

"You can stay the fuck away from my girls, they are way too young for you, bro." Dom and Jax laugh this time while Nico and I shake our heads. The waiter returns with our four beers, and we all hold our glasses up to cheers each other.

"You know, I never thought we would be where we are today, but man I have to say I am fucking glad. I have the most amazing wife, the most beautiful daughter—"

"And the greatest fucking son in law!" Nico cuts his gaze to me and glowers.

"You may be married to my daughter, but don't ever refer to yourself as my son in law."

"Yes, Dad." We all break out into laughter, we spend the rest of the night catching up and celebrating life. I for one am so grateful to have my brothers back with me and to have the girls in our lives, as well as all their kids. Above all else, though, I am beyond grateful for the amazing, talented wife I have at home, mon salut, mon espoir, mon eternal.

Acknowledgments

Where do I even begin?
Writing this book was so much fun and such a rush. I loved hiding away and writing this one, it blew my mind once the creative juices started flowing.
I hope you all enjoyed Kai's HEA because we all know that he bloody well deserved it after everything he has been through.
Willie, girl where do I even begin with you? You are magic, these books wouldn't be what they are without you, thank you for joining me on this crazy ass ride. Thank you for taking a chance on me.
My love and my babies, thank you! Thank you for entertaining the kids while I wrote these books and for your support. My babies, these are for you. Chase your dreams and never give up, mummy didn't and now look.
To my amazing readers, thank you!
Your support and recognition to these characters is the reason that drives me to follow my dreams.
Sam. Xxx

Also by Samantha Barrett

Mafia Romance

<u>Murdoch Mafia Series</u>

Played By The Bishop

Tormented By The King

Tortured By The Knight

Tempted By The Queen

Turned By The Pawn

Ruined By The Rook

<u>Murdoch Mafia Novella</u>

Stalemate

<u>Memento Mori Series</u>

Reign Of Royal

Broken By Sin

In Havoc Lays Chaos

<u>Godfathers of the night</u>

London has Fallen

Damned By His Angel

<u>Re Della Strada</u>

Shattered Soul

Fractured Heart

Tainted Essence

<u>Fairytales With A Twist</u>

Condemned Beast

Secret Society/ Bully

Filthy Few

Forever Filthy

Filthiest Of Them All

Masked Men Novella (Pure Smut)

Dirty Priest

Dirty Daddy

Sports Romance

Playing For Keeps

Offside

Touchdown

End Game

Hail Mary

Blindside

RH Sports

Hate Us Like You Mean It

MM

Love Me Like You Mean It

Paranormal Romance

The Veil Of Obsidian

Of Time And Carnage

Curse Of Fate

Dream

Fate

Nightmare

Redemption

Anarchy

Brutal Savages

Savage Lies

Brutal Truth

Savage Beast

Brutal Beauty

About the Author

Samantha Barrett is originally from Auckland, New Zealand but living in Brisbane, Australia.

Sam writes all things dirty dark and delicious with a side of twisted mind fuck.

She is a lover of all things red flags and an anti-hero is a must.

9 780645 116540